PROTECTING HAWK (SPECIAL FORCES: OPERATION ALPHA)

PREY SECURITY #5

JANE BLYTHE

Cover designed by Q Designs

Dear Readers,

Welcome to the Special Forces: Operation Alpha Fan-Fiction world!

If you are new to this amazing world, in a nutshell the author wrote a story using one or more of my characters in it. Sometimes that character has a major role in the story, and other times they are only mentioned briefly. This is perfectly legal and allowable because they are going through Aces Press to publish the story.

This book is entirely the work of the author who wrote it. While I might have assisted with brainstorming and other ideas about which of my characters to use, I didn't have any part in the process or writing or editing the story.

I'm proud and excited that so many authors loved my characters enough that they wanted to write them into their own story. Thank you for supporting them, and me!

READ ON!

Xoxo

Susan Stoker

I'd like to thank everyone who played a part in bringing this story to life. Particularly my mom who is always there to share her thoughts and opinions with me. The wonderful Amy Queau of Q Designs who made the stunning cover. And my lovely editor Lisa Edwards for all her encouragement and for all the hard work she puts into polishing my work.

CHAPTER ONE

February 1st

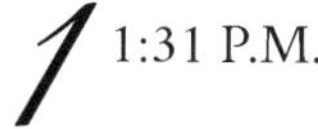1:31 P.M.

THIS WASN'T the first time Hawk Oswald had brought a woman back to a hotel room with the intention of having hot, no strings, no expectations, no attachment sex, and yet it was the first time that he felt kind of … weird about it.

He really liked Maddy No-last-name.

They'd agreed when they'd met at a bar earlier tonight that they wouldn't exchange their full names because this was a one-time thing. He knew her only as Maddy, and she knew him only as Hawk. While that was in fact his real name, she had assumed it was a nickname, and he hadn't corrected her. It was better if they didn't have a way to find each other afterward because he suspected that he might actually be tempted to track Maddy down.

"You sure about this?" he asked as he kept hold of her hand with one of his while his other went searching for the key card in his back pocket. Part of him hoped Maddy might say no. Although he'd only just returned from a long deployment this morning, and he had needs that he wanted to attend to, Maddy felt too special to have for just one night.

Returning to the news his sister Sparrow had managed to avoid death three times in the previous two weeks was not a good way to come home. He'd needed to unwind, chill, and yeah, meet a woman he could take to bed for the night. What he hadn't been expecting when he hit a bar on the beautiful Santa Monica beach was to meet a woman he'd spent the last few hours talking and laughing with.

There was a connection there, he felt it, was sure Maddy did too, but he wasn't ready to fall in love and settle down. This meant he either enjoyed her for just one night or cut her free now because she had the power to break right through his wanting to remain single wall.

Maddy hesitated for a moment, and he could see a flicker of doubt in her pretty hazel eyes, but then he saw her steel herself. "I'm sure. Positive in fact."

Hawk nodded, nervous anticipation swirling inside him as he opened the door to his hotel room. Most of the guys on his team had already booked flights to go home, but he'd intended to hang out and go home in the morning. If he'd known what had gone down with Sparrow though, he would have headed straight to New York.

If he had though, he would have missed out on meeting Maddy.

He couldn't even put his finger on what exactly had him so enamored with her. From the second he'd laid eyes on her he'd gotten this weird feeling in the pit of his stomach. It was like ... he couldn't even describe it, but the slightly nervous-looking woman had immediately snagged his attention, and he'd found he wanted to know why she looked uncomfortable.

So, he'd sauntered over, and they'd hit it off right away. They'd laughed, talked, shared dinner, and when it was time to say goodnight, he hadn't wanted to let her go, so he'd blurted out that he'd love to take her back to his room to continue their evening.

Maddy had chewed on her bottom lip, looking torn and clearly having some sort of internal conflict, but she'd agreed and here they were.

Hawk was torn between knowing he was about to have the best sex of his life and not wanting to hurt Maddy because while he was no stranger to one-night stands, he had a feeling this was her first.

"It's okay to say no, caramel," he said after he closed the door behind them.

A smile curled her lips up. "Caramel?"

"All these golden-brown locks, they remind me of caramel." Hawk stepped toward her and ran his fingers through Maddy's silky soft hair. Twirling a lock around his finger, he leaned in close until his lips were right above her ear. "All night I've been wondering if all the hair on your body is the same gorgeous color."

A soft gasp fell from her plump, pink lips when he put a hand between her legs and lightly swept his fingers across her denim-clad center.

He thought she'd pull away, tell him that she couldn't do sex with a stranger, but her lips parted, and her tongue peeked out and ran along it. The move was sexy although he didn't think Maddy had meant it that way. She seemed far too sweet and innocent to do anything even remotely provocative. It was that very sweet innocence that had caught his attention in the first place.

"There's one way to find out," she whispered. Her voice was breathy, her hazel eyes shining with the same heavy dose of desire he felt coursing through his veins.

Hawk groaned, he wanted to rip her clothes off and slide into her right now, but he also wanted to take it slow and make it count because he was only getting one go at this. There would be no forever for him and Maddy, no second chance to touch or taste her. He had to make the most of tonight.

"I'm going to kiss you now, caramel," he said as he gripped her hips and pulled her into his body.

Her gaze met his, then dipped to his lips before returning to meet his. "I can't wait any longer."

That first touch felt like heaven, and Hawk felt a moan ripple through him. The kiss was perfection. Maddy's lips immediately opened for him, and their tongues met in a dance of passion that had him growing harder and Maddy shifting restlessly against him.

They were both wearing jeans, his a dark blue, hers white, he had on a simple black button-down shirt, and Maddy a jade green sweater that hugged her slim curves. With her white pumps, she was still several inches shorter than his six-foot-one. Hooking an arm around her waist, he lifted her so their bodies aligned and ground his length against her.

Maddy hummed her appreciation, her movements becoming almost desperate as she clutched at his shoulders, bringing him closer.

He carried her to the bed and laid her down, breaking the kiss only long enough to remove his clothes while Maddy shimmied out of hers. He would have liked to remove that sexy lacy red matching bra and panties, but he felt a pull to get inside her that he'd never experienced before.

It wasn't that Hawk slept around all the time, but when he returned from a long deployment with his Rangers unit, he usually went to a bar, picked up a woman, and spent the night with her. It was always just about sex, he never usually spent hours talking with them before, and he never stayed the night. But Maddy was different. He kept feeling torn between the all-consuming need to bury himself inside her tight, wet heat, and wanting to draw this out, make it last as long as he could.

In the end, it was Maddy who decided how this would go when she reached out and took his length in her hands. Her fingers were slender and nimble, and she traced him with an almost reverent quality that implied she wasn't quite as experienced as he was.

Catching her hand, he pulled it away. "Keep that up, caramel, and I'm going to embarrass myself."

She giggled softly. "I don't think so. I've never seen someone so ... well endowed."

At least she wasn't a virgin, so that pressure was off his chest, but still he didn't think she'd been with a lot of men, and he wanted to make this good for her. "Trust me, babe, if you don't come first, I've embarrassed myself."

Her skin was silky soft just like her hair, and he kissed his way from her lips, down her neck, pausing to touch the softest of kisses to both of her nipples, then down her flat stomach.

"Caramel curls," he murmured when he settled between her legs.

"I've never ... I don't know ..." Maddy said, trying to close her legs.

Hawk placed a hand on her stomach to calm her. "You don't like it, babe, then I'll stop. Promise."

When Maddy studied him before giving a slow nod, he

closed his lips around her little bundle of nerves and suckled hard.

Maddy's hips flew off the mattress. "Oh my." She gasped.

"You like that, caramel?" he asked with a grin.

"It's … it's … yeah, I like it."

He returned his mouth to her sensitive flesh, licking, sucking, dragging moan after moan from Maddy as she squirmed beneath him. Her fingers reached down to tangle in his black locks, and he watched her as he continued to taste her sweetness.

"Hawk … I … more," she begged.

Happy to oblige, Hawk worked a finger into her slowly. She was so tight, confirming his suspicions she wasn't experienced and hadn't been with many men, and likely no one in a long time. She was going to feel like bliss when he finally got inside her, but not before he got her ready to take him. The last thing he wanted was to hurt her.

Maddy's fingers tightened in his hair when he began to slide his finger in and out of her channel, and he wasn't sure if she was urging him on or trying to stop him as he could feel her orgasm rushing toward her.

She came with a whimpered scream as her internal muscles clamped around his finger, his length quivering as it practically begged to get inside her.

As Maddy drifted down from her high, he grabbed a condom from his discarded jeans and sheathed himself. "Last chance to back out, caramel," he warned as he stretched out above her. Even though he had made her come, she didn't owe him anything and if she wanted to stop here, he would.

In answer, she reached for him, guiding him toward her entrance, and he sunk inside her slowly.

When she gasped he stilled. "You okay, caramel?"

"Fine, just tight, it's been a while."

Hawk slowed his pace even further, pressing his lips to

hers and balancing his weight on one hand so his other could attend to her. Taking his time, enjoying the feel of her, savoring every second he got with this sweet woman.

If things were different, if he wasn't in the Rangers, if he was ready for commitment, if they lived closer to each other, he could see himself holding onto Maddy and not letting go. But things weren't different, and this was all he was going to get with her.

Maddy's legs lifted to grip his hips, and Hawk began to thrust harder and faster, chasing pleasure that was circling around him, but he wanted Maddy to come again first. He could feel her getting closer. Her body was trembling, her breathing fast and ragged, there was desperation in their kisses, and she clutched at his shoulders again, holding onto him like she felt the same connection between them he did.

When she came, she screamed her pleasure into his mouth, and the feel of her internal muscles clenching around him snapped the last thread of his control, and he found his own release.

It hit him like a tornado, barreling through him, tossing around everything he thought he knew about himself and what he wanted out of his life.

"That was nice," Maddy murmured.

"Hey! Only nice?" he teased as he almost reluctantly pulled out of her.

She giggled. "Okay, more than nice. It was really good, the best sex I've ever had. I didn't even know it could be that good."

"You're good for my ego, caramel," he said as he disposed of the condom and went to the bathroom to grab a washcloth so he could clean her up.

As he returned to the room and touched the warm cloth between her legs, Maddy watched him with an expression he couldn’t read. He was pretty sure that she didn't regret what they’d done. Was she feeling the same sense of loss he was?

It was crazy, they’d only known each other a few hours and that wasn’t long enough to get attached. Yet Hawk thought he would miss her once she walked away.

“Should I go?” she asked uncertainly when he stood and tossed the face washer onto the bathroom counter.

He should say yes. It was better for both of them if they didn't share anything more, and spending the night in each other’s arms was too intimate. Yet he wasn’t ready to let her go just yet.

Just a little more time.

He could hold her for a few hours, and then in the morning they could say their goodbyes.

Moving Maddy so he could pull back the covers, he slid into the bed beside her and covered them both up, spooning her against him. “Stay.”

CHAPTER TWO

February 2nd

6:41 A.M.

MADELINE MONTGOMERY WOKE with a smile on her lips, and a heavy arm draped across her middle.

The smile had everything to do with the sexy stranger currently curled around her back, right where he'd been when she fell asleep. For the first time in a long time, she'd slept straight through the night, and from the looks of things she had slept so well and so deeply that she hadn't even rolled over or moved a muscle.

Again, that was all thanks to the stranger from the bar.

Hawk, no first or last name, didn't feel like a stranger though. It felt like she'd known him forever, not just a measly twelve hours.

Twelve hours?

Was that all it had been?

When she'd walked into the bar last night, determined that she give herself a night off from her somewhat obsessive work schedule, the last thing she'd expected was to meet a man she'd really liked. She'd thought she'd just chill out, have something to eat, maybe a drink or two, perhaps even kiss a guy. But coming back to a hotel room with a man she didn't know and having sex with him and then sleeping in his arms had not been on her to-do list.

Wanting to spend more time with him shouldn't be on her list either.

One night.

That was what they had agreed to.

No strings, no expectations, no attachments.

That was the deal.

Yet Maddy wanted strings, she definitely had expectations building, and she had already started to get attached.

This was totally why this had been a bad idea, and yet she didn't—couldn't—regret it.

It was about time she took a little time for herself. That was what her few friends were always telling her. Her work as a victimologist who specialized in studying the relationship between victims and their assailants took up all of her time, and often required that she travel extensively. Plus, she could be a little obsessive, and once she started a case, she couldn't let it go until she found answers. A personal life was pretty low on her list—and she did love her lists—so it had taken some persuasion to get her to let go for one night.

Score one for her because she'd say that her first night off in a couple of years had turned out amazing.

Too bad one night was all it would be.

She didn't know Hawk, and yet she felt like she *knew* him. Not his real name, not what his job was—although she suspected military—not where he lived, or if he had family, and yet she knew this man intimately. She knew he was funny, knew he was sweet, knew he was thoughtful, kind, and respectful. And she knew that she wanted to get to know him better.

But that wasn't what they had agreed to.

This was all she was going to get with Hawk.

Maddy shifted slightly in the bed. She had no idea what the protocol was for the morning after a one-night stand. Was she supposed to get up, shower, get dressed, and sneak quietly away? Was she supposed to wake him up and have an awkward goodbye? Was she supposed to ask for more, see if he would be willing to exchange real names and phone numbers or email addresses so they could get to know one another?

Even though she knew it was stupid to keep hoping for more, she couldn't seem to stop.

Which was exactly why the whole one-night stand thing was a mistake. She just wasn't built that way.

Still, when a large hand lifted to smooth her hair, and her heart did a funny little flip flop, Maddy knew that she would never regret what she'd shared with Hawk and would relive these precious few hours for a long time to come.

"Morning, caramel."

The warm, sexy voice washed over her and made her insides gooey. What were the chances he'd say yes if she asked for his name and number?

Better not to get her hopes up. The last thing she wanted to do was ruin her memories of what they'd shared by embarrassing herself.

But that nickname … it was so sweet, and she hadn't had anyone call her anything but Madeline or Maddy in a really long time. Not since she was a little girl before her father had been murdered. The endearment was the thing that had tipped the scales from thinking Hawk was a fun guy, one she was definitely attracted to, to one who was sweet and made her long for more.

“Morning,” she returned, wriggling around so she was facing Hawk. His black hair was a little long, sometimes falling over his eyes, which were the prettiest shade of blue she’d ever seen. His body was something out of a woman’s fantasy, all hard lines and muscle, and she had to wonder what it was this man who could be a model would see in someone like her. She was five-four, with golden brown hair, hazel eyes, and a few too many freckles for her liking. It wasn’t that Maddy thought she was bad-looking, Hawk was just way out of her league. He should be dating supermodels or actresses, not slightly geeky, over-the-top organized women who spent their days surrounded by death like her.

Hawk’s hand moved to palm her cheek. His fingers were calloused but gentle as they softly caressed her skin. “You're even more beautiful than I remember.”

She huffed out a laugh at the line. Since she’d just woken up her hair was no doubt a mess, she hadn't washed off her makeup last night, so it was probably smeared on her face, and she had a habit of sleeping with her hands folded beneath her cheeks which meant she often woke up with red handprint marks on her face. “Yeah, sure.”

“Hey,” Hawk said, his gaze growing serious. “You are without a doubt the most beautiful woman I have ever met.”

Then why don’t you give me your name so we can stay in touch?

The question was one she couldn’t ask aloud. It didn't mean she didn't want to, though.

Instead, she smiled at Hawk. “You’re so sweet.”

He made a face that said sweet was the last thing he wanted to be called, then leaned in as though he were going to kiss her but hesitated at the last minute and pulled back.

Just like that, the spell that had kept the two of them in a magical little bubble broke and reality came crashing back in.

"You should go grab a shower, get dressed, and then I'll take you back to the bar so you can get your car," Hawk said, already climbing out of bed and searching for his clothes.

She wanted to get out of there as quickly as she could before she embarrassed herself and said something stupid like, please don't let things end like this. Didn't he feel it? Their connection, she had been so sure when she said yes last night that he felt it too, but maybe she'd been projecting. Maybe his interest in her in the bar, talking to her, asking questions, making her laugh, maybe it had all been just his way of ensuring she would say yes when he asked her back to her hotel.

Maybe the whole night had been her just projecting her loneliness on the first man to show her a little attention.

Mortified when tears began to burn the backs of her eyes, she quickly scrambled out of bed and began to gather up her clothes. "Thanks for the offer, but I think I'll just get dressed and then take a cab."

"I'd rather drive you," Hawk said with a firmness to his voice that said he was prepared to argue the point because he didn't want to not be a gentleman, but Maddy had already made up her mind.

She had to get away from him as quickly as she could.

She wanted him too badly, and the longer she stayed, the higher the chances she'd make a fool out of herself and ruin the whole experience.

One night.

That was all he had promised her and obviously all he intended to offer.

While she'd been floating in that magical little bubble it had been so easy to believe that she wouldn't regret last tonight, that she could do a one-night stand, that she was capable of no strings and no attachments.

But in the cold light of day, it was much harder to delude herself.

She didn't know how to do this, didn't know how to just walk away from the first man who had ever made her feel this way. She wanted so badly to spend more time with Hawk, get to know him better, and see if something real could be brewing between them, but it was clear they were on completely different pages here.

Not just different pages they were in different books.

It took everything she had not to run into the bathroom, but she managed it. She washed her face, used the toilet, then threw her clothes back on. Running her fingers through her hair, she examined her reflection, and when she was convinced she could go out there without crying, she breezed back into the room.

"Goodbye, Hawk. Thank you for last night," she said as she grabbed her purse, looking in Hawk's direction but not directly at him. Because much like the sun, if she looked directly at him, she'd wind up burned.

"Goodbye, Maddy."

Somehow, she managed to make it all the way through the hotel, through the cab ride back to the bar until she was safely tucked away inside her car before the tears came. She had just walked away from a man she would never forget, and it hurt. It shouldn't, but it did.

CHAPTER THREE

October 11th

11:37 A.M.

HOW COULD ONE RED, lacy bra have become his obsession?

Hawk fingered the thin material before slipping it back into the furthest corner of his nightstand, feeling like some sort of creepy stalker.

Not that he'd actually done any stalking of his pretty caramel, he still only knew the same amount of information about Maddy as he had when they'd parted way over eight months ago.

The temptation was never far away though, and it often took actual energy not to ask someone from Prey Security—the company he owned with his siblings, although he was the only one who wasn't actively engaged in running it—to try to find her for him. If anyone could, it was his oldest sister Raven or his sister-in-law Olivia, but fear of rejection had held him back.

At first, he'd flown back to New York and spent time with his siblings, including older sister Sparrow who had been recovering from hypothermia after being kidnapped and left for dead in the Appalachian Mountains. Back then, he had been sure the feelings he had for Maddy would pass quickly once there was an entire country separating them. His leave had flown by, and then he was deployed again, and when he continued to find himself thinking about his pretty caramel, he had finally accepted that he wasn't going to forget her so easily.

Only by then months had gone by, and it was too late.

No doubt Maddy had moved on, forgotten all about him, and if she did still think of him, it was no doubt with a cringe because they hadn't left things on the best of terms.

That was his fault. He'd wanted to kiss her when she'd woken up all sleep tousled and adorable, but he'd known prolonging things was only going to make it worse for both of them. It was presumptuous to think Maddy would want more than they'd agreed to, so he'd pulled back. It wasn't until he'd seen the hurt in her hazel eyes that he realized he should have kissed her.

By then it was too late, their connection had snapped, and it was obvious Maddy couldn't get away from him fast enough.

Did she regret their night together?

He didn't.

In fact, he was still so enamored with his caramel that he hadn't been with another woman since. Which he admitted to himself was stupid because he and Maddy weren't together and weren't going to be. As much as he liked her, as much as he couldn't stop thinking about her—and pulled out the bra she'd left behind that morning almost every day—he still wasn't ready to offer her a commitment, that was if she even wanted one.

When had a supposedly simple no strings attached one-night stand gotten so complicated?

Right, when the woman was as incredible as Maddy was.

The lift to his penthouse dinged, signaling he had guests, and a moment later a voice called out, "Baby squad is here."

Hawk smiled despite the heaviness that had blanketed him ever since he let the perfect woman walk away. He was on leave again, back home in Manhattan, and this time there had been two new additions to the family to meet.

Oldest Oswald sibling, Eagle, had married Olivia Wakefield at Easter and Olivia had given birth to their first child, a little girl they'd named Luna, four months ago. The oldest girl in the family, Raven, had remarried Max Hathaway her ex-husband and father of her almost fourteen-year-old daughter Cleo on the Fourth of July, and two months ago had given birth to their son Roman. Middle brother Falcon had married Hope Delancey last month, and middle sister Sparrow had recently become engaged to Ethan Zimmerman, an old friend she'd reconnected with early in the year when he saved her after a helicopter crash.

Everyone in his family seemed to be moving on except him, and he kept missing everything.

He hadn't been able to get leave to make it home for any of his siblings' weddings, and he'd missed the birth of his little niece and nephew. Although he had been convinced he wanted to remain in the Rangers until he retired, which was why he hadn't wanted a serious relationship or to drag a woman into that lifestyle, he was tired of missing out on family moments. Sparrow was the only other one of his siblings who was still active military, and she was retiring in

February and would be setting up Prey Search and Rescue with her soon-to-be husband, Ethan.

Maybe it was time he considered moving on. He had a job at Prey if he wanted it, although he wasn't sure what his role in the family company would be. If he wasn't a Ranger anymore, then there would be nothing standing between him and Maddy.

"Everything okay?"

He looked up as Olivia popped her head through his bedroom doorway. She had a wriggling Luna in her arms and a concerned look on her face.

"Everything is fine," Hawk assured her as he closed the nightstand drawer and went to relieve his sister-in-law of her adorable bundle. It wasn't like he had to figure out his entire future today. "Give me this cute little munchkin." As he took Luna from her mother's arms, the baby stared up at him with huge blue eyes and smiled.

"Ga-ga-ga-ga-ga," Luna began to babble.

"Almost, honey. Ha, ha, ha, Hawk," Olivia said, kissing her daughter's cheek before turning and heading down the hall toward the kitchen.

"Let me guess," Hawk said as he carried Luna into the kitchen and saw Roman fast asleep in his stroller, "the king of sleep is asleep?"

Raven grinned at him from the table. "Yep."

"I've never seen a baby, no let me correct myself; I've never seen a *person* who sleeps as much as that boy of yours. I don't think I've ever actually seen him awake," Hawk said.

"Yes, you have." Raven swatted at him and then reached over to run a hand over the soft, fuzzy hair on Roman's little head. "And trust me, when you have kids, you'll pray for a baby who sleeps as much as Roman does. Do you know how nice it is to sleep through the night? You take it for granted now, but one day it's going to seem like a dream. I remember when Cleo was born, she woke up every two hours for the first year of her life. I swear I thought I would be sleep-deprived for the rest of my life. So, you mock, but you're going to be jealous one day when your babies wake you up all night."

Babies had never been on his life plan.

Not after he'd watched Raven's pain when her then three-year-old daughter Cleo had been abducted and sold on the black market. He'd been seventeen at the time and clearly remembered those horrific months when his sister struggled to function after losing her little girl. Then after becoming a Ranger, he'd seen too many guys have their marriages turn into disasters. Affairs, divorces, bitter custody battles; there was no way he was voluntarily signing up to endure that.

But if he left and joined Prey, maybe kids could be in his future.

"What're you thinking about so hard?" Olivia asked as she set out rolls and fillings on the table.

Hawk sat down, sitting Luna in his lap, and absently picked up a toy octopus and jiggled it in front of the baby, who gurgled and grabbed at it. "Just thinking about the future."

"You finally ready to come work at Prey?" Raven asked, her eyes lighting up.

When Eagle first started the company, Raven immediately came on board to run the tech division, and Dove was the chief financial officer. But he, Falcon, and Sparrow had been silent investors. They'd contributed money, but that was it. He'd never had any plans to work there. But then Falcon had left Delta due to injuries, and Sparrow had fallen in love, and now he felt like maybe he wanted to be more involved too.

"Maybe," he answered slowly.

"Eagle will be thrilled," Olivia said as she set three plates down, one in front of each of them then took the seat beside his. "He's always wanted all six of you to work together at Prey. And now I work there, and Ethan does, I bet he'll be trying to figure out how to get Max and Hope to join the team too. He wants the whole family together."

Family.

He'd never really thought that he was missing out when it came to family. After all, he had five siblings and was close with all of them. But these last few months, ever since Maddy, he felt like something was missing in his life. At first, he hadn't wanted to admit that it was a wife and kids of his own, but it was getting harder and harder to convince himself that he didn't want exactly that.

He was going to have to do some serious thinking about what his future looked like and maybe say a prayer that Maddy hadn't moved on in the last eight months. Still, he had time, it wasn't like taking a few more days, weeks, or even months to figure out what he wanted was going to make any difference.

* * *

10:58 P.M.

Maddy cowered in a corner of the bathroom as someone hammered on the door.

How had they found her here?

She'd been so careful. She'd traded in her car for a new one and taken out a bunch of cash which she'd used to buy a burner phone and a whole new wardrobe just in case anything she owned had been bugged. Then she'd started driving across the country, paying cash for tiny motels well off the beaten path.

She'd done everything she could think of to try to stay safe, but it still hadn't worked.

Now she was so close to where she'd been heading only to be found.

Her gaze skimmed the tiny and not particularly clean bathroom. Maddy had debated on whether to pull in to get a little sleep or just push through and make it to New York City a few hours earlier, but in her condition, sleep was important, and so she'd opted to take a break.

That decision might wind up getting her killed.

Seeing nothing she could use against whoever was hammering on the door of her motel room, she had to figure out a different plan. There had been other cars in the parking lot, so she knew for sure that meant there were other guests. Sooner or later one of them would call the cops.

While Maddy would love to be able to have the cops help with her situation, that just wasn't possible.

They couldn't be trusted.

Not with this.

Which was why she had been driving to New York. She needed help, and since the police were out, there was only one place she could go with the resources she needed to stay safe.

But first, she needed to get there in one piece.

The knocking on the door changed to thumping, and she knew they were trying to break their way inside. She'd pushed the room's heavy dresser over to block the door. Not a wise move for someone in her condition, and not an easy feat, but she'd needed the extra security it offered in the tiny room. There was a window, but it had metal bars on the outside, a clear fire danger but something that would work in her favor. If whoever was out there wanted in, they'd have to go through the door which should buy her just enough time to escape.

Using the vanity to help her get to her feet, she hurried back into the bedroom to grab her bag. She needed it. Not only did it have cash and clothes in it, but it also had all her notes on this case. If she was going to get help tracking down the serial killer after her, she needed everything she had spent the last few months painstakingly compiling.

Just as she slung the strap over her shoulder, the door began to crack.

Tamping down a scream that came out as a whimper instead, she grabbed the chair from the desk in the back corner of the room and hurried into the bathroom. Setting the chair in front of the vanity, she somehow managed to climb up on it and then onto the counter so she could reach the window.

It was going to be a tight fit. Looking down at her huge belly she rested her hand on her swollen stomach, praying she would be able to make it through the window.

As though sensing she needed a little reassurance, Maddy felt her baby kick against her hand, and she couldn't help but smile.

Finding out you were pregnant from a one-night stand wasn't the best way to bring a child into the world. When you did everything you could to find that man, who you only knew by his nickname, but came up short time and time again, it definitely made the whole experience harder. But Maddy was determined to raise her baby on her own and was excited about it.

Well, serial killer hunting her aside, she was excited.

Although running for her life certainly put a dampener on what should be one of the best times of her life.

Another thump in the other room had her shivering in fear, they were so close. Another few hits and they'd be inside.

With no more time to waste, Maddy carefully turned the lock and shoved against the glass.

Nothing.

"No, no, no," she murmured. The window couldn't be stuck. If she broke it, she would tip her hand. The man after her would abandon his quest to get through the door and come around the back of the room to the window.

It had to open.

It had to.

If it didn't, she was as good as dead, and unfortunately, she knew all about how this particular killer ended his victims' lives.

Using both hands, Maddy shoved against the window-pane with everything she had, not an easy thing to do with her pregnant stomach in the way, but when the glass began to shift, she let out a huge sigh of relief.

Opening the window as far as she could, she dropped the bag out first and then maneuvered herself through as best as she could. It was a *really* tight fit, but she managed it, and her feet hit the ground just as she heard the sound of splintering wood and knew that her assailant had managed to make it through the door and into the room.

Snagging her bag, she took off running. She'd parked her car down the end of the parking lot where it was quieter, hoping it wouldn't be spotted.

Obviously, that hadn't worked, and she had to wonder how this person kept finding her.

She hadn't taken *anything* with her when she left.

Nothing.

Not a single thing.

So how were they tracking her?

As she slid the key into the lock and opened the car door, tossing her bag inside and clambering into the driver's seat,

Maddy supposed the how wasn't the most important thing right now. Right now, the most important thing was getting to the city and then to the offices of the world-renowned Prey Security. If anyone could keep her alive while they tracked down this killer, it was the Oswald family and their employees.

Her hands shook so badly she almost couldn't get the key into the ignition, but after several failed attempts she managed it, and her car sprung to life.

Just as she was driving off, she saw a shadowy figure come bursting out of her motel room. He'd found out she was gone, and he wasn't happy about it.

The figure waved its arms at her as she roared past and then aimed a weapon.

Maddy let out a shriek as he fired at her, but somehow the bullet missed, and she stomped her foot on the gas and kept her eyes glued to the rearview mirror where she saw her would-be assailant running toward a vehicle.

What should she do?

The other car wouldn't be far behind hers. It would easily catch up to her, there weren't many roads in and out of this tiny town, and he could see which direction she went. For all she knew, he knew she was on her way to Prey Security and would try to get ahead of her and take her out that way.

If she couldn't outrun them, she'd have to outsmart them.

Stamping on the gas, she let the tires screech as she took the next turn, wanting to let him know where she was going. Then as soon as she was safely away from the corner, she quickly shut off her headlights and turned off the road, maneuvering her car between the tall trees lining the street.

Now all she could do was wait and pray.

A minute later she saw a car take the turn way too fast, tires skidded, but the driver kept control of their vehicle and went rocketing down the street right past where she was hiding.

Maddy let out a sigh of relief and rested her forehead against the steering wheel.

She was safe.

For now.

But he'd found her here, clear across the country and he wouldn't be giving up. He would keep coming to her until he got his hands on her and silenced her for good. It was the only way he could keep doing what he loved, and self-preservation was a powerful motivator.

Which made Prey her only hope.

If they couldn't—or wouldn't—help her, then she was out of options, and she'd be out of money. She was using the trust fund from her stepfather that she'd vowed she'd never touch to pay Prey's fees, and as long as she was being tailed by a serial killer she couldn't work, which meant she would be jobless, and then homeless, and then penniless.

Going to Prey was her only chance at survival, and she prayed with everything she had that they were as good as their reputation implied because if not, she and her baby would soon be dead.

CHAPTER FOUR

October 12th

 :06 A.M.

"I'M SUPPOSED to be on leave you know," Hawk grumbled. "That means vacation in case you didn't know. Which means I shouldn't be here working."

"Stop complaining," Eagle said, not even bothering to spare him a glance, his gaze fixed on the computer file he was reading. "This is your company too, and it's not like you've been doing anything other than moping around your place for the last week anyway. If I hadn't dragged you down here to help with this new case, then you'd still be there moping. You may as well just call the woman and get it over with. Haven't you learned anything from the rest of us in the last eighteen months? When it happens, it happens. No use fighting the inevitable."

Hawk had no idea why his family kept assuming that he was hung up on a woman because he hadn't mentioned anything about Maddy, yet Eagle was bringing her up—albeit not by name—and yesterday, Raven and Olivia had grilled him over lunch. Was it really that obvious that he'd met someone he couldn't stop thinking about?

"I never mentioned a woman," he said, aiming for nonchalance. He didn't know what his future held yet. Hawk had been convinced he was in for the long haul when he'd joined the Army. He'd never even considered doing anything else with his life. And that life hadn't included a woman or a family. How could he ask someone to be with him but actually spend more time alone than with him? How could he ask someone to basically raise their children as a single parent and spend most holidays alone? He had been convinced that any relationship he might start would wind up in divorce, so it hadn't seemed worth the trouble. It was why he'd walked away from Maddy even though his entire being had screamed at him not to.

"You didn't have to. Was written all over your face the moment you came back on your last leave," Eagle said, this time lifting his eyes from the computer to throw a quick smirk his way. "I'm sure you have your reasons for not pursuing things with her, but if she's really the one then you're fighting a losing battle, little brother."

Was he fighting a losing battle?

It was hard to believe he was. He'd spent one night with Maddy, around twelve hours total. Sure, he'd had fun. They'd talked, laughed, and had amazing sex. Yes, holding her in his arms while she slept gave him a level of peace he hadn't known existed. But maybe he'd blown the whole thing up in his head, made it out to be more than it was.

"There's only one way to know," Eagle said with a knowing smile. "It's to call her, ask her out and get to know her, in case you were wondering."

Hawk just nodded, he wasn't ready to make a decision yet. Either about Prey or Maddy, but maybe helping out with a case was the way to get the answers he needed. What he did about Maddy depended on his career choices, and the only way to find out if he would like working at Prey was to try it out. He had another three weeks to go before his leave ended. He could spend some of that time here, see how it went, then decide what his future looked like.

"Okay, tell me about this case," he said as he straightened his chair on the other side of Eagle's desk.

"We don't know a lot," Eagle replied. "Got a call about an hour ago from a woman named Madeline Montgomery. She said she was on her way in and believes a serial killer she's been tracking is after her."

"She a cop?"

"No. She said she's a victimologist. She studies victims to profile their assailants. She said she can't go to the cops and hopes we can help her."

Hawk arched a brow. "Can't go to the cops? We think she's on the run because she did something illegal?"

"According to the background check we ran on her, she doesn't have a criminal record or any criminal connections we could find. We'll run something deeper and dig into every crevice of her life before deciding whether to take on her case. She wouldn't go into details on why exactly it was there was a serial killer after her or why she couldn't go to the cops. She said she had to keep moving, that she'd already been found once, and that she would explain once she got here."

"What did she mean when she said she'd already been found once?"

"Said the killer hunting her tracked her to a motel last night, shot at her, but she was able to get away."

"So, what exactly does she want from us?" Hawk asked. Prey mostly did black ops missions for the government, hostage rescue, and sometimes personal security for wealthy clients. What they didn't do was track serial killers.

"Protection and help."

Before Hawk could ask anything else the phone on Eagle's desk rang, and his brother picked it up. From what he could hear of Eagle's side of the conversation Madeline Montgomery had just arrived.

"That her?" he asked when Eagle hung up.

"Yep. She's waiting for us in the lobby. You ready to work your first case for Prey?"

"You don't know yet if you're taking it on," he reminded Eagle as they both headed for the lift.

"If she's telling the truth no way we'll turn her away. If we can't provide what she needs then I'll find someone who can," Eagle said. As they stepped into the elevator Eagle eyed him curiously. "So, what's her name?"

"I thought you said it was Madeline Montgomery."

"Smart alec." Eagle playfully punched his shoulder. "You know I mean the woman who has you all tied up in knots."

"I only know her as Maddy. We met in a bar. It was supposed to be just one night, that's what we agreed, no strings, no commitment."

"But you can't stop thinking about her."

It wasn't a question, but Hawk answered anyway. "I think about her, I dream about her, I wonder if she would have said yes if I asked for her number. I wonder if she's forgotten about me or if I blew the whole thing up in my head and made it bigger and better than it was. And I wonder what it would be like to see her again."

The lift doors opened onto the Prey foyer, and Hawk's

gaze immediately landed on a nervous-looking woman standing beside the reception desk.

Petite.

Golden brown hair.

Large hazel eyes.

And a large pregnant belly.

Hawk's stomach plummeted.

"Maddy," he said as he stalked across the distance between them.

Her eyes grew wide when the vacant stare morphed into shock. "Hawk? My Hawk? I thought ... nickname ... I didn't ... you're Hawk Oswald?"

"The very one." The punch in the gut knowing that Maddy was either pregnant with his baby and hadn't told him or she'd slept with someone else right around the time she'd slept with him had him feeling like the world had opened up beneath him, ready to swallow him whole. "You're pregnant."

It came out as an accusation if the way she flinched was any indication. "I tried to find you when I found out, but all I knew was that your nickname was Hawk. At least that's what I thought, and you never corrected me."

"So, it *is* my baby?" he demanded. What she'd said made sense. How could she have known who he really was, and how could she have found him when she didn't even know his name? Still, talk about a shock. The woman he'd obsessed over for eight and a half months had just turned up at Prey, pregnant and claiming she was being hunted by a serial killer.

Fire sparked in her hazel eyes, wiping away some—but not all—of the fear. "I don't sleep around. You were the first man I'd had sex with in over a year, and I haven't been with anyone else since." She rested a hand on her swollen stomach, a softness on her face now. "It's your baby, and I really did try to find you. I went back to the bar and asked around about you, but no one knew who you were, or if they did, they weren't talking. I even went to the hotel to try to get your name, but they don't give out that information. I looked everywhere for you, but when I couldn't find you, I decided to raise this baby on my own. I already love it, and no one is going to hurt it, which is why I'm here. Someone wants me dead, and I don't have anywhere else to turn. If I ever meant anything to you at all, then please help me."

The desperation in her voice cut him deep, and he glanced at Eagle who nodded. "Of course we'll help you," he said soothingly as he took a step toward her and almost tentatively wrapped his arms around her. Hawk wasn't sure if he was more worried that she would shove him away, refuse his comfort, or if touching her again after dreaming about it for eight long months wouldn't be as good as he remembered.

He shouldn't have worried.

About either.

Maddy wrapped her arms around him and clung to him and holding her wasn't just as good as he remembered it was so much better.

Whoever was after his woman and his baby now had the entire might of Prey Security and the Oswald family to go up against.

* * *

9:19 A.M.

For a moment, Maddy allowed herself to forget everything except the fact she was in Hawk's arms again.

She'd missed him.

So many times over the last eight and a half months she had dreamed of this moment. Of the two of them being reunited, only this time they would find a way to make it work. The only difference between this moment and the ones in her imagination was that in her dreams she wasn't on the run for her life.

Her momentary indignation at Hawk's suggestion that she slept around and her baby wasn't his had faded. It had been a shock for him to see her like this when he probably never expected to—maybe even never wanted to—see her again. Now he knew he had a baby coming, and whether he wanted to be a part of her child's life or not, nothing could change the facts that he would soon be a father.

Maddy had no idea that her Hawk was actually none other than Hawk Oswald of the world-renowned Prey Security. She'd never even considered the possibility because, well, why would she?

Now that she knew she was starting to second-guess that this was in fact a good plan. It was one thing to come here for help when she had just thought they were the best in the business, but now that she knew this was Hawk's family's company everything was a lot more complicated.

Maybe it would be better if she left.

As much as part of her wanted to do anything to get out of this awkward situation, Maddy knew she didn't have any other options.

She needed Prey.

This meant for the time being, she was stuck here with the man she wanted so badly it hurt. She wanted to give her baby everything. A mommy and daddy, the perfect family, siblings, and a happy home, all the things she had lost as a child. But it was pretty clear Hawk wouldn't be in that picture. She'd thought he hadn't found her because all he knew about her was her first name, but now knowing that he owned Prey, Maddy knew he could have found her if he wanted to.

He just hadn't wanted to.

A voice clearing broke the spell and Hawk released her and stepped back.

"This is my brother Eagle," Hawk said, indicating the voice clearer. There was no mistaking the similarities between the two men. They were both tall, both were solid walls of muscles, both had black hair and blue eyes, and both exuded a calm confidence that went some ways toward soothing her battered nerves.

"Hi," she said, holding out a trembling hand to shake his.

"Nice to meet you, Madeline," Eagle said as he shook her hand, his grip firm but not crushing.

"I usually go by Maddy," she said, casting a quick glance at Hawk who was looking at her with something like wonder in his eyes., Her heart leaped. Did that mean he'd thought about her too? Regretted the way they'd left things? Did it mean that maybe he wanted her as much as she wanted him?

With a somewhat amused look on his face, Eagle pointed to a door just off to their right. "Why don't we all sit down, and you can tell us what's happened that brought you here," he suggested.

Maddy nodded and followed the oldest Oswald sibling into a large conference room. There was a huge oak table taking up most of the room, with a whiteboard on the far wall, a small table with glass jugs of water and a coffee maker, and a couple of tablets and a laptop on another table beside it.

Eagle snagged one of the tablets and took a seat at the head of the table. Hawk pulled out a chair next to Eagle and she sunk into the soft black leather, finding herself pleased when he took the seat beside her.

"You hungry?" Hawk asked.

Her stomach had been in knots for days with the stress of trying to dodge a killer's attacks, and she'd been too desperate to get here to stop much for meal breaks, but now that she was here, and she wasn't fighting this battle alone anymore, Maddy found she was a little hungry. "I could eat."

"What do you want?" Hawk asked.

"Waffles?" she asked. They were her favorite thing to eat, but she had no idea what the options were.

"Waffles it is," Eagle said, picking up his phone to presumably order some waffles.

"Have you been … taking care of yourself?" Hawk asked hesitantly, reaching out to touch the pad of his thumb to the dark circles she knew were under her eyes.

"Best as I can."

"And the baby? Is it healthy?" His hand hovered above her stomach, the same look of wonder in his eyes as she'd had when she first realized she was pregnant and got over the initial shock. It was clear he didn't want to touch her without permission, but she was okay with the baby's father feeling his child move inside her.

Taking his hand, she pressed it to her stomach. "The baby is healthy."

"Do you know if it's a boy or a girl?"

"No, I was waiting to be surprised when it was born." She had gone back and forth on her decision, but in the end, decided since she was doing this alone it would be nice to have that surprise when the baby finally came as though that would make up for having to go through labor alone.

"And you're okay?" His hand remained on her stomach, but his gaze lifted to hers, searching almost desperately. "I mean, your morning sickness wasn't too bad? You didn't have any complications?"

Warmed by the fact he obviously cared, Maddy smiled and reached for his other hand, curling her fingers around his. "The pregnancy has gone smoothly. I really did search for you, Hawk. I wasn't trying to keep the baby a secret." The opposite in fact, she would have loved to have his support these last several months even if it had only been as a friend and the baby's father.

"I believe you," he assured her, and something inside her settled. She hadn't known she needed his reassurance until he gave it.

"Waffles will be here soon. You ready to get started?" Eagle asked.

Maddy shuddered, not wanting anything to ruin this moment with Hawk, but she nodded. That was why she was here, after all, to get Prey's help finding the killer who was after her. "Yeah, I'm ready. Where should I start?"

"Start at the beginning," Eagle said.

Drawing in a deep breath, Maddy began her story. "It started a little over a year ago. Young women were being murdered and the police couldn't find a link between them, so they called me. I studied them carefully, looking into every aspect of their lives until I found it. The link. Every single one of them had a parent as a victim of a violent crime while they were a young child. As I continued to profile them closer, I came to the conclusion that they had all been killed by someone in law enforcement. Not necessarily a cop, but someone with access to old case files and current computer systems to be able to track these women down. When I reported this to the detectives working the case, they dismissed me like I was an idiot, like it wasn't my job to study victims and figure out who might have hurt them."

"Is there a chance you might have been wrong about your assumptions?" Eagle asked.

Because he asked it with a simple, factual tone, one without an iota of judgment or condescension, Maddy didn't lose her temper. "There's always a chance I could be wrong. But right after I reported my findings to the detectives, I started feeling I was being watched. From there, things began to progress. There were a few break-ins at my house, then someone tampered with my car, I was almost run off the road, then I was attacked, but I managed to fight my assailant off." As she spoke, Maddy was aware of how tense Hawk was beside her, and she had to hope it was because he cared and not just because he was worried about their baby.

"Did you report everything?" Eagle asked.

"Yes. Everything. The cops agreed I had a stalker just not that it was the serial killer I was hunting. But none of it started happening until I suggested to the detectives that they were looking for someone in law enforcement. I sold my car, took out a bunch of cash, and started driving out here. I've heard of you, of course, and your reputation is unparalleled. I can't trust the cops, and somehow this guy is tracking me because my motel room was broken into last night and I was shot at as I escaped. He's after me, he's been following me, and in a couple of weeks I'm going to have a newborn to care for. I need help," she said softly, fighting back tears. For months she'd been battling this alone, and now help was tantalizingly close, but she didn't know yet whether Prey would take her on as a client. "Please, will you help me?"

* * *

9:38 A.M.

HIS HANDS WERE SHAKING.

Visibly shaking.

To the point where Hawk had to move them under the

table and clench them together in his lap so that nobody saw them.

It was bad enough knowing that he'd left Maddy pregnant and alone. All these months he'd debated tracking her down only to decide she was better off without him, and all that time she had needed him. Needed him to be there through morning sickness, and to help when she got too big to do things. Most of all, she'd needed him there to protect her and their baby while she was being stalked and harassed.

Someone shot at her last night.

Shot at her.

Knowing that made it almost impossible to breathe.

He could have lost her and all because he'd been too pigheaded to allow her room in his life because he had been convinced that any relationship they had would end badly. Lost her and a child he hadn't even known existed.

He had already missed out on so much, hadn't been there for the sonograms, and hadn't got to watch as Maddy's stomach grew. Nor had he been able to prepare for the impending birth. He knew nothing about how to support a woman through labor, or how to take care of a newborn. Playing with his nieces and nephew and then handing them back to their parents for feeding, changing, and when they cried was one thing, but now he was going to be completely responsible for a new little life.

There was no way he was turning her away, and he knew his family wouldn't either. That baby was one of them, and by extension, so was Maddy.

"Hey." He reached out and took one of her hands, squeezing just tightly enough that she knew she was no longer in this alone. "Of course we're going to help you." Hawk just prayed they found this guy before he came after Maddy again.

"Maddy, why don't you start writing down everything

you have on this guy? Organize files if you have them. I just need to talk with Hawk for a moment, and then we'll be right back," Eagle told her.

The look Maddy gave his brother clearly communicated that she knew they were leaving the room to talk about her, but she nodded anyway, took the sheet of paper and pen Eagle offered, and began writing.

Even though he didn't want to leave her alone, not even for a moment, Hawk followed Eagle out a different door than the one they'd brought Maddy through, into a small observation room where Falcon and Raven had been watching their exchange with Maddy.

"So that's her?" Raven asked when she saw him. "The woman you've been obsessing over the last few months. She's pretty."

"Smart, and funny, and sweet too," he added, staring through the one-way glass to watch Maddy fervently writing.

"What's our first step?" Eagle asked. "She going to cause problems for you with the baby, try to keep it from you, do we need to petition the court for a DNA test, bring in the family lawyer? Or should I contact the lawyer about setting up a trust fund for the baby and we'll find someone else to help Ms. Montgomery with her problem? Or ..." Eagle drew out the word dramatically, "is this someone you're serious about in which case we should help her but butt out of your personal life?"

Raven snorted. "As if we're going to butt out of his personal life."

Hawk smiled and relaxed, knowing both he and Maddy had his family's help and support meant a lot. "I really like her. Did from the moment I saw her. I believe that she tried to find me when she learned she was pregnant, but I let her think Hawk was a nickname, so she didn't really have a way to find me. I could have found her and wanted to so many times, now I wish I did. I don't like that he was able to track her." His smile faded, and a worried frown took its place.

"I don't either," Raven said. "I'll check all her stuff for trackers. I'll have to check her too. She could have had something planted on her."

The idea of someone being close enough to Maddy to plant a tracker on her body made him sick, but he nodded his agreement.

"You should have a DNA test done," Falcon said, speaking for the first time as he finally took his eyes off Maddy and turned to face the rest of them.

"You think she's lying?" he demanded. He knew in his gut that baby was his, and Maddy wasn't faking her fear. "She was just as shocked to see me as I was to see her. If she knew who I was she would have come after me as soon as she found out she was pregnant."

"She's not lying about the stalking," Raven spoke up. "I checked while you were talking to her, and she reported everything that happened. She's not lying about the serial killer either, she was working with the cops in San Francisco on a case, and she did report her findings that someone in law enforcement was responsible. If she knew she was in danger, why would she have waited this long to come to Hawk if she knew who he was all along?"

"Maybe she thought if she claimed the baby was Hawk's she'd secure his help," Falcon suggested.

Before Hawk could argue with his older brother, Eagle said, "My gut says she's not lying, but a DNA test is a good idea anyway. How she reacts when you ask her would help us determine if she's telling the truth, and even though you like her you two aren't together. A DNA test also protects your rights as the baby's father."

As much as he didn't like it, Hawk had to agree it sounded

like the sensible thing to do. He wanted to get to know Maddy and be there for her through the final weeks of her pregnancy, and he hoped well past that. But a DNA test meant his name would go on the birth certificate, cementing his place in his child's life regardless of how things worked out with his or her mother.

"Yeah, okay, I'll ask her about it, but regardless of how things turn out with me and Maddy she's still the mother of my child. I know it. I *feel* it. The DNA test will confirm it, which means that baby and Maddy are a part of our family now. We're doing whatever it takes to help her."

"Absolutely," Eagle soothed. "Congratulations, little brother. I hope things work out the way you want."

"So do I." Was Maddy even in the same place he was? Had she thought about him as anyone other than the man who had knocked her up? Did she have any feelings for him? Would she try to fight him on being a part of their child's life? Would she be willing to give them a chance?

"You know there's only one way to get answers to those questions I can see running through your head," Eagle said. "Go talk to her, ask her where her head is at, and then we need to know everything about this case. Every suspicion she had, every detail of the stalking, and every theory she has even if it's just her gut telling her something. I don't think this guy is going to back off."

"Where is she going to stay?" Hawk asked. "If he tracked her to the city, he might know she came here and could be watching the place. If we take her to a hotel, he might find her there."

Eagle didn't even hesitate. "She'll stay here in one of the apartments. If this guy is in law enforcement, he might be able to get her name and room number if he does know she's here even without following her. She's safest with us."

There was nowhere safer for Maddy right now than with

him and his family at their secure office building. And while Maddy was here, it gave him the perfect opportunity to get to know her, convince her if she wasn't already convinced that they could be good together. It also gave him a chance to make up for missing the first eight and a half months of her pregnancy.

He wasn't missing anything else.

It might not have sunk in yet, but he was a father now. In just a few weeks his little one would be making its grand entrance into the world, and from that moment on, his life would forever revolve around someone other than himself.

Seemed like the answer to what his future looked like had answered itself.

Now that he had a baby on the way and a mission to woo the mother of his child, Hawk knew he wouldn't be re-upping when his current contract ran out. He'd be finding his place at Prey and staying with his family.

His family.

As he headed back in to talk to Maddy, he couldn't wipe the smile off his face. This might not be how he thought his life would turn out, a woman and kids weren't what he thought he wanted, but now that he had it, he couldn't be happier.

* * *

10:00 A.M.

HAWK WAS GRINNING as he re-entered the conference room. That had to be a good thing. Right?

She would have sworn it wasn't possible, but he looked even better than she remembered.

How many nights had he filled her dreams?

How many days had she found herself thinking of him rather than her work?

When she found out she was pregnant, Maddy wished and prayed for his support. She knew he was an honorable man. Even if he didn't want to be with her, he would have stepped up for their child, been supportive of her through the pregnancy and a great dad to their baby.

Now she needed his support more than ever, and she hoped she had it. It would be completely plausible if Hawk and his family sent her away. They might not believe her or might think it was easier to pass her on to someone else for help. After all, she and Hawk had agreed to no commitment, and she'd just handed him the mother of all commitments, one that would last for the rest of his life.

If he chose to take it.

Maddy was well prepared for him to decline being part of their child's life, and if that was the case then she was ready to face life as a single mother.

"So?" she asked, almost hesitantly, "did your brother override your offer to help me? That's why he took you out of the room, right? To discuss me and whether or not Prey will help me find this serial killer?"

"Don't be mad," Hawk said as he resumed his seat beside her.

Not good.

Her mind began to whirl in a million different directions as she tried to figure out what her next move would be. She'd been counting on Prey's help, and she didn't really have a backup plan. She was going to have to come up with one quick.

"Hey, it's not what you think." Hawk's hand landed on her shoulder and gently eased her back into her chair. She hadn't even realized she had stood up. "I meant what I said before, of course we'll help you, that's not in question, never was."

He blew out a breath, sending the lock of dark hair hanging over his forehead floating up and then back down. "I'd like to do a DNA test if you don't mind."

Relief hit her hard.

That was all he wanted.

For a moment there, she thought she was back to facing a serial killer alone.

"Oh, that's all." Maddy sunk back into the soft leather. "Of course you can have a DNA test done. I know this must be a huge shock to you, believe me I do. I remember how I felt when I realized I was late and might be pregnant. I mean, we used protection. I know it's not infallible, but still, we agreed to no attachments, and I've now shoved one major attachment on you."

"Hey, it's not your fault." Hawk took her hands and laced their fingers together. "It was my condom anyway, and it came from a brand-new pack. We just got unlucky, or lucky I guess, depending on how you look at it." His blue eyes searched hers, she assumed looking for a clue as to how she felt about the impending birth of their baby.

"I'm excited about the baby, Hawk," she assured him. "I can't say I wasn't in shock at first, and it was scary when I looked for you and couldn't find you and had to accept I'd be doing this on my own, but I'm happy." She took a deep breath, knew this had to be said but dreaded hearing the answer. "If you don't want to be involved it's okay. I'm not going to come at you for child support or try to get my claws into your money. I didn't even know you had money until an hour ago. If you want me to sign something saying that, I will, and we can do the DNA test now or wait until the baby is born. I'm prepared to raise this baby on my own with no help from you. When I couldn't find you, it was what I had planned on doing anyway, so this doesn't have to change anything. It's up to you whether you want to be involved in the baby's life, and how involved. If you want joint legal and physical custody then I'll look at relocating, or you can. If you want visitation, we'll find a way to make it work. And if you don't want to be involved at all then that's okay too."

She waited anxiously for his response, she'd love for him to be involved in the baby's life, but she wouldn't force him to be. Either he would be part of their lives because he wanted to be or he wouldn't be at all. The last thing she needed on top of everything else she was dealing with was her child's father being belligerent because he didn't want a kid.

When Hawk didn't respond, she felt her heart drop.

Why did she have to fall for the one guy who had told her point blank that he was only interested in one night with her?

While she might hope the fact they were having a baby would change things it was obvious it hadn't.

Her stomach cramped painfully as reality sunk in.

She really was in this alone.

These last few months, ever since she'd found out she was pregnant, she'd been harboring secret fantasies of her and Hawk getting together, brought back together by their child. She'd thought if she could ever find him, he'd be thrilled to learn he was going to be a father. He'd drag her into his arms and kiss her like she had given him the most amazing gift, and then he'd whisper in her ear that he hadn't been able to forget her and ask her out on a date, a real date, which would be the beginning of a beautiful love story.

Stupid.

She'd been so very stupid.

"Maddy, I ..." Hawk began.

Before he could begin with his letdown speech—which she was sure he would deliver gently although the impact would still be the same, a swift kick to the heart—something wet suddenly soaked her jeans. "Hawk …"

He gave her an amused smile. "I'm trying to explain, caramel, if you would let me talk," he teased.

"No, I wasn't trying to interrupt. I think my water just broke," she exclaimed. Now whatever he'd been about to say was no longer important. Her baby was about to enter the world four weeks early.

"What?!" he shrieked, shoving away from the table and pulling her chair back with it. "You're going into labor?"

"I've been having stomach cramps. I thought they were from anxiety, I always get a nervous stomach when I'm stressed, but it must have been contractions."

"Get in here now!" Hawk screamed, casting a frantic glance at the door he'd just come through a few moments ago.

The door was flung open, and Eagle and two other people came hurrying into the conference room. Since both had the same black hair and blue eyes as Hawk, they had to be his siblings, older brother Falcon, and she suspected the oldest sister, Raven.

"What's going on?" Eagle asked.

"She's having contractions, and her water just broke," Hawk said. He was still holding her hand and judging from how tightly he was squeezing it, he was struggling not to freak out.

Well so was she.

She wasn't ready yet.

She wasn't at home, didn't have any of the things she had bought in preparation for her baby's birth, she didn't have her music, or …

"Relax," Hawk said, returning his attention to her as he must have sensed her growing distress. "It's going to be okay, I'm here, I'm not going anywhere, everything is going to be all right." He kept his hold on her hand but addressed his siblings again. "We can't take her to a hospital. It's too easy to track her there. We need a doctor upstairs ASAP. I'm going to take her to the apartment she's going to be staying in. She can have the baby in there. We're also going to need a crib, change table, diapers, baby clothes, toys ..."

"Relax, little brother, everything will be fine," Eagle soothed. "You take care of Maddy. I'll make some calls and make sure we get everything you need delivered. Raven will call a doctor, get one here right away."

"Staying here?" Maddy asked as Hawk scooped her into his arms, apparently, that was what her brain had latched onto.

"Want you and the baby somewhere safe, caramel. I want you here with me where I can keep an eye on both of you," he said as he carried her out of the conference room and toward the lift.

His words made her heart soar. Maybe he *did* want a chance for them to see what could be between them. Maybe she wasn't completely alone.

"Hawk?" she whispered as the lift doors dinged and opened.

"Yeah, honey?"

"I'm scared," she admitted softly.

"Me too," he said as the doors closed behind them, leaving them alone together. "An hour ago I had no idea I was going to be a father, and now in a few hours I'm going to meet my baby. It's ..."

"Huge," she finished for him.

Hawk smiled down at her, then ducked his head to touch a kiss to her forehead. "Yeah, it's huge. But you know the best part?"

"What?"

"I get to do this with you. I get to be here to hold your

hand as you bring our baby into the world. When you get scared, just take my hand and remember we're in this together."

No words had ever been spoken to her that touched her as deeply as that one simple promise.

CHAPTER FIVE

October 13th

5:02 A.M.

"I CAN'T DO THIS ANYMORE," Maddy said as she sagged back against the pillows. Her hair was pulled back into a messy ponytail, sweat dotted her forehead, her cheeks were flushed from pain and exertion, her breathing was ragged, and yet to Hawk she had never looked more beautiful.

She was bringing his child into the world.

His *child*.

It still didn't seem real.

Not even twenty-four hours ago he hadn't even known Maddy's full name, and now he was holding her hand while she was giving birth to their baby.

"Yes, you can," he said, leaning down so he could meet her

gaze. "You can do anything. You already did eight and a half months of pregnancy all on your own, and you've done nineteen hours of labor like a champ. Doc says it won't be long now." Hawk had no idea where Eagle had managed to find the doctor, but since the man had passed Prey's security checks, and had obviously been fine with signing a non-disclosure agreement, which they needed since they didn't want to expose Maddy's location if the man hunting her didn't already know where she was, then he had to be good at what he did. Eagle wouldn't have brought anyone he didn't trust to Prey's offices.

"What if the baby's not okay?" Maddy asked, her scared hazel eyes begging him for reassurance. "It's too soon. It should be in there another four weeks. I'm scared, Hawk."

His heart clenched. There *could* be problems with the baby. It wasn't unheard of with a baby born at thirty-six weeks, but he had to believe that their baby was a tough little thing. After all, its mother had rocked pregnancy alone while being stalked and harassed. If there was a problem with the baby and it had to be taken to the hospital, he'd go with it and watch over it while he trusted his family to keep Maddy safe.

"I'm scared too, sweetheart," he said as he gently stroked his knuckles across her temple and held up his other hand. "But remember what I told you earlier."

She gave him a shaky smile as she took his offered hand. "That we're in this together."

"Right. And the way I figure it is with a mom like you, our little one has to be a fighter."

"Its daddy is quite the fighter too. You're in the military, right? That was my guess when we met."

Since he one hundred percent intended to pursue a relationship with Maddy as long as she was willing, and at the very least they would be co-parenting their child, he didn't intend for there to be any secrets between them. Which meant she would get the truth to every question she asked, and once the baby was born and she'd gotten some rest, they'd have a proper talk and clear the air, get things sorted, and make sure they were on the same page going forward.

"Yeah, caramel, you guessed right. I'm an Army Ranger. Actually, all my siblings except for Raven, who you met earlier, and Dove, who's currently in England, were or still are in the military. Eagle was a SEAL, Falcon was Delta Force, and Sparrow is a Nightstalker, although she's retiring in a couple of months."

"What about you?" Maddy asked. "Are you considering ..." she broke off as another contraction obviously hit and squeezed his hand so tightly, he wouldn't have been surprised if she'd broken a bone.

"It's almost time, Ms. Montgomery," the doctor said. He had stepped back to give them some space while they were talking, but now he stepped between Maddy's spread legs and gave them both a smile. "I can see the head. Your little one is crowning, it's time to get pushing again."

"You got this, Mads," Hawk assured her as he wrapped an arm around her shoulders. Her music played in the spare bedroom of the apartment she'd be staying in. Eagle had already organized to have all of the baby's furniture she'd bought flown here and had set up the other spare bedroom as a nursery. After the baby was born, they'd move Maddy to the master bedroom where she could relax properly.

"Don't go," she said, shooting him an anxious stare.

"Told you I wasn't going anywhere," he soothed. "We're in this together." He wished they'd had time to talk before she'd gone into labor, but it was like once their baby had heard his voice, and finally had both his or her parents together, and decided it couldn't wait a second longer to meet them.

"Together," she repeated like she needed to convince herself.

"Together," he echoed. If she needed a little reassurance, he was happy to give it to her. He might not have known about the baby, but still he could have decided to track her down at any time over the last eight months, and he'd chosen not to. Wishing he had wouldn't change things, he was going to give Maddy everything she needed now that they were together again. Fate might have pushed him, but even though he'd spent months trying to talk himself out of it this was still what he wanted.

"Together," she said again, more confidently this time. He didn't know much about Maddy—although he intended to find out everything there was to know about her—but he had a feeling she was used to being alone, and the idea of having someone at her back was a foreign one to her. That was something he would definitely be changing.

Another contraction came, and for the next little while, they were focused only on the fact that Maddy was pushing their child out. He held her hand and supported her shoulders when it looked like exhaustion was catching up with her. He encouraged her as best he could and wished that he could take this pain from her.

By the time the baby was finally born, he was in awe of women in general and his Maddy in particular.

"Congratulations, you have a baby boy," the doctor announced, holding up a red, squirming little bundle.

"A boy?" Maddy exclaimed, looking thrilled. He couldn't have cared less what they had as long as it was healthy.

"He okay?" Hawk asked.

"He's looking good," the doctor assured him. "Dad, you want to cut the cord?"

"Yeah," he said, a little shaky now that the baby was here. A father. He was a father. He had a son. With trembling hands, he cut the cord and stared in shock at his little boy.

As soon as the cord was cut, the baby was laid on Maddy's chest. She'd pulled the hospital gown down so she could rest the baby on her bare skin. Her breasts looked completely different than the last time he'd seen them, but damn, if this didn't look a million times better.

His son on his mother's chest.

Tears blurred his vision, but when Maddy looked up at him with tears coursing down her cheeks his heart felt like it was about to burst open with love, and he allowed his own tears to spill out. How was it possible to love someone this deeply he hadn't even known existed this time yesterday?

What he felt for this tiny little baby was unlike anything he had ever experienced.

The baby chose that moment to let out a huge squawk making both him and Maddy laugh through their tears.

"I can't believe I ... *we* ... have a son," Maddy said, giving him a shy smile. "I love him so much already."

"Me too, honey, me too."

"I've been thinking of names, and if it was a boy, I was going to name him Louie after my father, but if you don't like that name, we can think of something else."

"I like that. I love that you want to name him after someone you love. Louie Montgomery." While he would definitely be a part of his child's life, he and Maddy hadn't talked yet, so he didn't know if she was okay with their son taking his name.

"Louie Montgomery-Oswald," she corrected. "Actually, I'd love to name him after your father as well, if you'd like to."

His heart swelled. He might not be able to say he loved Maddy yet, they didn't know each other well enough to claim that. He did know that he liked her a lot, they shared a child, and he wanted to learn all there was to know about her.

There was nothing he would love more than to have his son take on his father's name. "Louie John Montgomery-Oswald, I like it."

"That's perfect," Maddy breathed.

Louie let out another squawk and blinked open his eyes to take his first look at the world. The baby seemed to look right at him and then right at Maddy before giving another cry, making them both laugh.

"I think Louie approves," Hawk said.

"Yeah, I think he approves," Maddy agreed, but her gaze was on him, not their son, and there was a longing on her face that said she wanted the same things he did. For them to be together. A family. Hawk prayed he was right because he couldn't imagine letting the two people on the bed walk out of his life, not even for a moment.

* * *

3:34 P.M.

"HAWK, LOOK," she exclaimed. "He's eating this time." They'd tried a few times to get Louie to latch onto her breast, but the baby hadn't been interested, preferring instead to look around the room, taking in the world, and sleep. Louie might only be nine hours old, but he seemed to love his sleep. She prayed that stuck.

"Looks like the little guy is hungry," Hawk said as he moved to perch on the bed beside her.

For some reason, Maddy wasn't embarrassed to have Hawk see her bare breasts, after all, she remembered when he'd fondled them and put his mouth on them. Having him watch her feed their son seemed completely natural. Everything with Hawk felt so natural, it was like they had been together for years, even though it had been eight and a half months since they'd last seen each other.

"It feels so weird," she said as the baby suckled on her nipple.

"Weird bad or weird good?" Hawk asked, watching in wonder as their baby ate.

There was just enough of a hint of heat in his blue eyes to make her feel like he still saw her as someone other than the mother of his child. While they shared a bond that would join their lives forever, she wanted more.

She wanted a chance for them to get to know one another and try out being a couple. They were kind of doing things backward, it wasn't ideal, but she was actually excited about her future for the first time in months.

"Definitely good weird," she replied. Kind of like what was happening between her and Hawk. It was weird because months had passed since they spent their night together, yet they'd just had a baby. Although it didn't seem Hawk was upset about it or even shocked, he was surprised of course but it seemed to be in a good way.

"We need to talk," Hawk said. There were no panicky feelings at his words because his face was soft and his eyes warm. Instead, she got nervous butterflies in her stomach. The good kind, the kind that said something exciting was coming.

She glanced down as Louie drifted off to sleep, his lips still on her nipple. "Guess the little guy tired himself out eating. I better put him down to sleep then we can talk."

"Bring him with us, I want to show you something. Are you okay to walk?"

After Louie had been born and whisked away to be checked out by the doctor, she had been moved into this gorgeous master bedroom in the apartment above Prey's offices where she would be staying. She had been to the bathroom earlier, but that was all she'd seen of the apartment other than the spare bedroom where she had given birth and this room.

She'd love to take a look around. Even if she wouldn't be here for long, this was Louie's first home, and she knew it would be a comfortable stay. Especially if the sexy man beside her was going to keep them company.

"I can walk," she replied.

Hawk gently took the baby from her arms, and then helped her to stand up. She'd changed into a loose-fitting nightgown so she didn't have to worry about the back of her gown gaping wide open.

With their baby snuggled in the crook of one arm, Hawk wrapped his other around her shoulders and helped steady her as her legs trembled a little as she climbed out of bed.

She was tired but wired and excited, way too excited for sleep. When she wasn't trying to feed him, all she did was stare at Louie in wonder that he was hers and he was here. Hawk was never far away from them, and she was already getting used to and maybe a little attached to his presence.

He led her out of the bedroom and into a hallway. Down the end she could see it opened up into a living area. To her right was a door to a bathroom. Next to it was the room where she'd had Louie, and on their left was another door. It was closed, but Hawk removed the arm around her shoulders to open it and then ushered her inside.

As she stepped into the room Maddy gasped. "How did you ...? What is all this?"

"It's Louie's room," Hawk replied. His arm went back around her shoulders, and he urged her to lean against him. "I know you guys aren't going to be staying here forever, just until we find this serial killer who's after you, but I want this place to feel like home while you're here. And it's the first place Louie will ever live, so I want it to feel special."

Her heart turned to mush at his words.

This was one of the sweetest most thoughtful things anyone had ever done for her.

"But how did you do all of this?" she asked, looking around the room.

It was painted and decorated exactly as the nursery in her apartment back home in San Francisco had been. The same shade of pale yellow on the walls, the same Noah's Ark motif decorating one wall. There was a big white rocking chair by the window, which was framed by yellow curtains that matched the paint. There was a white crib, a white change table, a white bookcase, and on the floor in the middle of the room was a rug shaped like a giant cloud.

"Did you send someone to take photos of the nursery at my place?"

As she asked the question, she looked closer at the room.

On the rocking chair was a big fluffy yellow pillow like the one she'd chosen because she could imagine propping her baby's head on it when she was doing midnight feeds. The crib's patchwork quilt was the very one her grandmother had made for her when she was born. The bookcase was stuffed with the stuffed animals and books she'd chosen for the baby on one of her many shopping trips after she found out she was pregnant and the nesting urge hit.

"Wait a minute, you didn't copy it, this *is* the stuff from my apartment. How did you manage this?" She turned to stare up at Hawk in shock.

"Sometimes being rich is awesome. Eagle sent one of Prey's planes to collect the things from the nursery. We thought it would make this a little easier for you. I know things have been rough, and this is not how you would have expected the birth to go, so I was hoping being able to put Louie in the room you planned for him would make it a little better. While you were in labor Eagle, his wife Olivia, Raven, her husband Max and daughter Cleo, Falcon and his wife Hope, and my soon-to-be brother-in-law Ethan—he'll be marrying Sparrow early next year—were painting this."

What could she say to that?

Thank you didn't seem like nearly enough.

Hawk and his family had gone completely above and beyond to show her a little kindness.

Throwing her arms around his neck, she planted a kiss on his lips. "Thank you, thank you, thank you. This doesn't make it a little easier or a little better, this makes everything perfect. The birth didn't go how I had expected, but it was better because you were there." Maddy wasn't going to beat around the bush or play games. She liked Hawk, wanted to date him, and wanted him to know it.

His arm wrapped around her waist, anchoring her to him, and he buried his face in her neck for a moment. "You're welcome. I'm glad this made you happy, and I'm glad I was there for Louie's birth. I'm sorry I wasn't there during the pregnancy." He shushed her when she would have reminded him that he didn't even know she was pregnant. "I wanted to find you so many times. I thought about it almost every day, but I kept talking myself out of it. My job is rough on partners and families, a lot of guys wind up divorced and without their kids, I didn't want that to happen to me, so I didn't trust my gut."

"Trust your gut?"

"My gut says you and I could be amazing together. I regret that I didn't find you, that we didn't get to keep in touch, that we wasted time we could have been getting to know one another, but I don't want to waste any more time. While you're here I'd like us to spend time together. Time together that isn't just with Louie or working your case. Time where we can learn about each other and see if things could work out between us. I really like you, Maddy."

"Good, because I really like you too." Maddy had a feeling she was grinning like an idiot, but she didn't care in the least because she was here, in the nursery she'd planned for her baby, even if it was in another state, with the man she could see herself sharing a future with, and best of all, he saw that same future and wanted to reach out and grab it.

CHAPTER SIX

October 14th

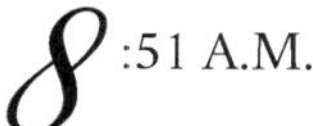:51 A.M.

"How are Maddy and Louie?" Eagle asked as Hawk entered the conference room.

"They're good, great actually. Both napping, but I have them safe in here," he said, holding up the baby monitor. Leaving them had been hard. They'd been together every second since Maddy arrived here two days ago, but Louie was sleeping after a feeding, and Maddy had passed out in bed the second Louie fell asleep. So he'd tucked his son into the bassinet and Maddy under the covers, and come down to see how things were going finding the man after Maddy. With the baby monitor set up in every room of the apartment and synced to his phone, he could check on them whenever he needed to.

Which he suspected would be often.

"As soon as Maddy feels up to it, Olivia and I would love to bring the other babies around to meet their new little cousin," Raven said. His siblings and their partners had already met both Maddy and Louie as had almost fourteen-year-old Cleo, but Maddy had been tired yesterday, and he'd wanted to keep her to himself so Luna and Roman hadn't made it up there yet.

"She'd love that. Maybe tonight everyone could come to the apartment for dinner," Hawk suggested.

"And things between you two …?" Eagle asked.

"Are great. We're both on the same page, we both want to explore this thing between us, but even if it doesn't work out —which I can't see happening—we'll be raising this baby together, which means Maddy is a part of our family now." He looked around at his siblings. Everyone had welcomed her with open arms, except for Falcon. While his brother hadn't been outright rude to Maddy, and he had helped decorate the nursery, it was clear he was still suspicious of her. But for the life of him Hawk couldn't figure out a game she could be playing. Everything she had said about why she'd come to Prey had been checked and verified, and she'd quickly agreed to the DNA test, so it wasn't like she had intended to try to keep the baby from him.

"I got the DNA test results," Raven said, holding up an envelope.

They'd pulled some strings and got the results rushed through, and Hawk found he wasn't even a little bit nervous to read them. Louie was his, he knew it deep down inside. "I already know he's mine, but Maddy asked about the results this morning, she said she doesn't want there to be any doubt that Louie is my son, that she doesn't want me thinking she sleeps around, so I'm reading these for her." He took the envelope from Raven and opened it, sliding out the single piece of paper inside. A quick read confirmed what he already knew. "The Oswald family officially has a new member."

"Congratulations again, little brother," Eagle said, giving him a slap on the back. "I know this isn't how you expected your life to turn out, but you seem happy, so we're all thrilled for you, and we all already adore Maddy."

The high he'd been riding the last two days slowly faded as reality began to sink in. He adored Maddy, too, but she was living with a death sentence hanging over her head. There was no way he was going to lose her to some deranged serial killer who was worried she'd gotten too close. "What have you guys learned so far?"

Just like that, the mood of the room dropped as everyone snapped back into work mode. "The murders started summer of last year," Eagle began. "The first woman to be found was twenty-three-year-old Holly Meyers. She was found with multiple bruises and broken bones. She'd had her eyes cut out and her ears filled with concrete before she'd been drowned. She was left on the side of a road dressed in a flowing white dress with her hair curled and dyed a golden blonde, and with makeup on. Initially, they suspected sexual assault, but there were no signs of rape. Given the unusual way the body had been treated the cops started looking into Holly's life with a fine-tooth comb, assuming she had gotten involved in something she shouldn't have or she'd witnessed something she shouldn't have."

"The killer was trying to remove what she saw and heard," he said, his stomach churning as he pictured the horrific trauma the victim had suffered before she'd been murdered.

"Maddy carried on that same theory only she took it a different way when she was brought on board. When victim number two turned up, nineteen-year-old Mia Hampton, they knew they were looking at a serial killer even though they only had two victims. So Maddy was brought in. She's one of the best victimologists around, she has a stellar reputation. She consults with various police departments across the country, works a lot of cold cases, and the occasional suspicious death where they're trying to determine if it's suicide or homicide. She agreed with that same theory, but she went right back to the victims' childhoods where she found that Mia's mother had been brutally raped and stabbed to death when Mia was only six. Holly's father had been killed in a convenience store robbery when she was twelve. Neither of the women witnessed what happened to their parents."

"So why remove their eyes and take away their hearing?" Falcon asked.

"Because whoever is killing these women did witness what happened to their parent when they were a child and is projecting onto their victims," Raven said.

Eagle nodded. "That was what Maddy profiled. What happened to the killer when he was a child is getting jumbled in his mind with the victims and their parents. He sees himself in them, removing what he can't in himself in them. He can't remove what he saw and heard, but thinks if he can do it for them, it will help him."

"Then he sets them free," Hawk said softly. "He drowns them, and then he turns them into angels. The white dresses, the blonde hair, in his mind he's saved them from the pain they've been living with and sent them off to Heaven."

"Again, that's exactly what Maddy profiled," Eagle said. "There have been another four victims since then. All of them had parents who were killed when they were twelve or younger. The cops agreed that the link was the victims' backgrounds, but not that the killer was someone involved in law enforcement. Maddy insisted that she had thoroughly looked into all of their lives and the only common denominator was their pasts. Their lives didn't intersect anywhere else which meant the killer had to be someone who was able to find out about their pasts. She theorized that the only way someone could have done that was to have access to the old case files. The women were all adults now and had all moved on. None of them attended the same doctors, dentists, gyms, or supermarkets. That is the only link, and access to the case files is the only way the killer could have known what happened to them."

"How is it that the cops didn't agree with that?" Hawk asked, mostly not expecting an answer. The cops were either incompetent or one or both of them was involved. That was the only explanation he could think of.

"According to Maddy's notes, they said that the killer might have struck up conversations with them somewhere and they had shared their loss," Eagle replied.

Hawk rolled his eyes. "Yeah, because that's the kind of thing you share with a random stranger who starts talking to you on the street or in line at the grocery store." Because of these two detectives and their failure to take the advice they'd asked Maddy to give them, her life was in danger.

There was no way he was allowing his son to grow up without a mother.

Not finding this serial killer was out of the question.

This wasn't just some case that Prey was working, this was his family they were talking about. Failure here just wasn't an option.

"What's our next step?" he asked. "I know Prey doesn't usually solve murders or hunt serial killers, but this is Maddy, the woman I haven't been able to stop thinking about. The woman that I was considering leaving the Rangers for so we could have a normal life. The woman who walked back into my world two days ago and gave me the best gift I've ever gotten."

"We're not walking away from this," Eagle assured him. "We've already reached out to contacts on the West Coast. Our team there will be speaking with the detectives who are working the case and the victims' families. Raven and Olivia are doing their thing from this end. All we need to do is find someone who had access to the case files and lost a parent as a child."

That didn't sound all that hard. After all, how many people could there be who fit those two very specific criteria? But if there was one thing that life had taught him, both through his job, and everything his family had lived through over the last eighteen months, it was that nothing was ever that easy, and anything could—and often did—go wrong.

1:11 P.M.

"So, you ready to tell me now what you guys talked about?" Maddy asked as she wiped her face with a napkin and turned her gaze full on Hawk who sat on the other side of the table in the apartment that was temporarily her home.

The apartment was nice, beautifully if simply decorated, but as well as bringing all of the nursery furniture and toys and clothes she'd bought for the baby, Hawk's siblings also packed up a bunch of her stuff. Clothes, family photos, toiletries, and a few other things they obviously thought would bring her some comfort. And they did, but not more than the sweet man sitting opposite her.

When he'd returned from the meeting with his siblings, he had been falsely cheerful and started making them both

BLTs for lunch. While the bacon, lettuce, and tomato sandwich was perhaps the best she'd ever had, the vegetables were crisp and fresh, and he'd managed to get the bacon perfectly crispy but not dried out, what she'd really wanted was information.

Had his siblings found anything out?

Had they agreed with her assessments of the victims and the man who had stolen their lives?

Normally Maddy was confident in her work and the conclusions she drew from the evidence available to her, but she was nervous this time. Maybe she wanted to impress Hawk's family, maybe she wanted them to like her because she knew it would matter to Hawk what his family thought of her. So far all of them had been really nice, well except for Falcon who seemed a little standoffish, but that was on a personal level. She also wanted them to respect her on a professional one. Everyone at Prey was intelligent, the best of the best in their field. She didn't want to be judged and found lacking.

Hawk sighed like he knew he couldn't put this off any longer. "All right, let me clear the table, you go and sit down, relax, and then we'll talk."

Maddy opened her mouth to protest, tell him they should talk now, that cleaning the kitchen could wait, but decided a few more minutes wasn't going to hurt. She pointed her finger at him and wagged it. "Don't dawdle."

The grin he shot her made her go all hot and bothered inside. Too bad it would be a couple of weeks before she would be ready to have sex again because she'd been dreaming of this man and sex for eight very long months, and when he smiled like that it made her all needy. "Don't worry, caramel, I'll be quick."

Leaving Hawk to clean up she wandered over to the lounge room side of the big open living space, where Louie was currently snoozing in his bassinet. Careful not to wake him, she brushed a fingertip along his soft little cheek, then touched her finger to his tiny hand, watching in awe as even in sleep his fingers curled around hers. It was the sweetest thing she'd ever seen, and she was sure she would never get enough of it.

Could never get enough of this perfect baby. He was strong and healthy, and she knew he would grow up to be every bit as amazing as his daddy. He had his father's blue eyes but her fairer hair, and she knew they would both impart different things to him. Maddy knew that even if things didn't work out with her and Hawk they were forever bonded, and they would raise their sweet son together.

Coming here had been the right decision. For her safety, for her son, for her, and for their future.

"He's perfect, isn't he?" Hawk asked, coming up beside her and slipping an arm around her waist.

Easily Maddy leaned into him. "Yeah, he is. I didn't know I could love someone this much. I miss him, I actually miss him because I'm not holding him, and he's right there." She rested a hand on his little stomach and soaked up the feel of him. Her world had forever changed, her priorities altered. From now on this little guy would be the center of her world. As much as she would love to just soak up the feelings of being a new mom, the most important thing she could do for her son right now was ensure he remained safe. "So, how did the meeting go? Do they know anything yet?"

"We don't know who he is, but Raven and Olivia will be searching for a man that fits your profile, and we have a team who run the west coast offices, they're former SEALs, and they're going to be interviewing families of the victims and the detectives working the case."

She'd been hoping they would already have found the killer, which was completely unreasonable, but her disappointment was tapered by the fact that it was obvious his siblings believed her and her profile. "Thank you."

"For what?"

"Believing me. Making me feel like I wasn't crazy. I knew I was right, it was the only thing that made sense, but when the cops dismissed me so easily I felt like maybe I was way off on this one."

"You weren't." Hawk's arm tightened around her. "The fact that someone has been trying to kill you is proof of that. Even if it wasn't though, I've read a few of the cases you worked on, you're good, really good, and I would have believed you off your track record alone."

His words shouldn't mean as much to her as they did. After all, she didn't know him very well, but what she knew she liked, *really* liked, and she was glad they both wanted the same things. "Think you guys can find him?"

Hawk put his hands on her shoulders, turned her to face him, and bent his knees so they were eye to eye. "That isn't even a question. You and Louie are the two most important things in my life, no way am I going to allow my son to grow up without his mother. It's not a question of if we find him only of when. And when we do, he'll be lucky if I don't kill him myself with my bare hands." There was stark fear in his eyes as he palmed her cheek. "Knowing I might have lost you before I even knew about Louie, before we got a chance to explore this thing between us, it kills me. Knowing it would have been partly my fault is even worse."

"It wouldn't have been your fault." She lifted her hand to cover his and applied gentle pressure. "We agreed on one night. If I hadn't gotten pregnant nothing would have changed that."

"Wrong, honey. I wanted more from the second I did this." His voice had dropped low. He leaned down and touched his lips to the corner of hers.

It wasn't nearly enough.

Maddy turned her head and feathered her lips across his.

Still not enough.

Not even close.

"This thing between us is real, right?" she whispered.

"As real as it gets. Nothing to do with the rugrat," he whispered back. "I was already thinking about figuring out my future and maybe not re-upping after my contract ends. I would have cracked soon and asked my sister or sister-in-law to track you down."

His words reassured her. She really wanted to find out what could grow between them, but not because he just wanted to be a permanent fixture in his son's life. He was Louie's father, he had just as much right to parent him as she did. She wanted Hawk to want her because he was insanely attracted to her and couldn't imagine not being able to see her every day, talk to her, touch her, and kiss her.

A little kissing was definitely what she craved right now.

It was obviously what Hawk craved as well because one of his arms curled around her waist, drawing her up against him, his other hand cupped the back of her head as his mouth crashed down on hers.

She kissed him back just as hungrily.

This kiss was … belonging.

When her father died, she lost her place in the world, not known where she fit in, and been afraid to let anyone else get too close because she knew the pain of losing someone far too intimately for a nine-year-old little girl.

But with Hawk there was no fear, just peace.

A sigh of contentment fell from her lips, captured by Hawk's as she shifted closer.

They couldn't have sex yet, but they could do something.

Just as she was about to say so, Louie let out a loud, offended squawk, making them both pull apart and laugh.

"Guess the rugrat thought he wasn't getting enough attention," Hawk said.

"He's probably hungry again." Maddy scooped him up and was going to carry him over to the couch when Hawk stopped her.

"You made me want something I didn't even know I was interested in, caramel. Having you here, having a chance to explore this thing between us, knowing you want me too, that's the gift. *You're* the gift. The little guy is just a bonus."

His words not only made her smile they made her know it was time to lower the fence around her heart. Loving her father had been a gift, even if she'd lost him much too soon, and loving Hawk could be a gift too.

She wasn't alone anymore, she had Louie, and she had Hawk. She'd gotten her own gift and so much more.

CHAPTER SEVEN

October 15th

9:46 A.M.

"ARE you going to watch me every time I change his diaper?" Maddy sounded amused as she buttoned up Louie's little onesie.

"Probably," Hawk agreed. He could stare at the two of them forever. It didn't matter what they were doing, if they were in the room, he was watching them. If they weren't in the room then he was watching them on his phone with a near compulsive intensity.

Maddy sighed, but when she picked Louie up and turned around her eyes were twinkling, and she was fighting a smile. "It's your turn next, just so you know," she told him as she carried Louie through to the living room.

"It sure is," he quickly agreed. He was Louie's father, it was just as much his job to change smelly diapers as it was Maddy's, and for now they were going with a taking turns system, although he was trying to do more since Maddy was the one who had to feed Louie every few hours.

"You know what I can't wait to do?" she asked. In the living room, she set Louie in his bassinet and sank onto the sofa.

"What?" he asked, sitting beside her. When he slipped an arm around her shoulders, she immediately leaned into him, and he couldn't resist leaning down to touch a kiss to her temple. They'd shared a few kisses since the one Louie interrupted yesterday, and in between caring for their son and making out they'd done a lot of talking too.

"Give him his first bath. I'm a huge fan of baths, bubbles, candles, music, some chocolate, and a good book. That's my idea of heaven. I hope Louie likes baths too. I wonder if he's going to cry the first time he goes in the water, I wish we didn't have to wait until the umbilical cord comes off."

"It'll be here before you know it," Hawk reminded her, tucking away the information Maddy had just given him. Much like their son was learning new things every day as the world around him became an exciting place, he learned new things about Maddy every day, and she definitely made his world a more exciting place.

"I can't believe two days have gone by already. It's like I just blinked, and we went from giving birth to this. I can't wait to watch him grow and experience the world through his eyes. There are so many firsts that will come in the next few weeks, months, and years, and I'm just so honored to be his mom and get to enjoy them with him."

Tears welled up in her eyes, and even though Hawk knew they were happy ones his gut clenched at the sight of them. No guy liked to see his woman crying, and Maddy was his, that he knew with absolute certainty. They still had a lot to learn about each other, and they hadn't talked about the future yet, what Maddy planned to do after they found the killer hunting her, but he knew they would figure it all out.

"Come here," he said, lifting her over so she sat in his lap. Framing her face with his hands, he swiped at the tears trickling down her cheeks with his thumbs.

"Sorry, I don't know why I'm so emotional," Maddy said, her voice trembling.

"I do. You found out you were pregnant, thought you would be raising a child alone, battled against someone trying to hurt you, were ignored by the cops, and then had a baby a mere two days ago. Of *course* you're emotional." Hawk tucked her close against his chest. His chin rested on the top of her head as he cocooned her in his embrace. He could stay like this forever.

"Hawk?"

"Yeah, honey?"

"I was thinking, maybe we should get Louie used to feeding on a bottle. Just in case."

His chest was suddenly too tight. "Just in case what?"

"In case the killer does get me. If he does, then you'll be all Louie has. I think it would be wise that he's used to a bottle so he'll be okay with you feeding him."

"Maddy," he muttered, pained. That was the last thing he wanted to be thinking about right now.

"I'm scared," she admitted in a soft whisper. Her hands moved until they were tangled in his shirt. "It's so weird. On the one hand, I'm so excited about the future and watching our son grow. But on the other, there's like this dark shadow looming over me, constantly murmuring in my ear a reminder that I might not be around to watch him grow up."

"You're not going anywhere. I won't let anything happen to you."

She lifted her head and touched a light kiss on his jaw. "I love that you think you have that kind of power, but I'm more of a realist."

"I am too. Trust me. I'm a practical person. You know how I grew up. On an off-the-grid farm where we had to completely provide for every single one of our needs. You think there was a lot of time for dreaming? Our whole lives revolved around work and planning ahead. Then I joined the military and worked hard to become a Ranger. Do you think the Army is full of naïve dreamers? It's not. I'm practical, and I'm skilled, and when I tell you that I won't allow anything to happen to you I mean it," he finished fiercely.

Maddy huffed a small chuckle. "When you say it, I almost believe it."

"Believe it. Do you really think I'm going to let anything happen to the mother of my son? The woman I'm falling for." Hawk touched his forehead to hers, then pressed his lips to hers in a gentle kiss. "You want to nap while the rugrat is out?"

"No, I'm too wired for sleep." Her eyes brightened suddenly. "Want to make fudge?"

"Fudge?" he asked a little doubtfully. He enjoyed cooking and would even consider himself a reasonable cook, but he was more a meat kind of guy, he wasn't so good when it came to making sweets.

"Yeah, you know, that deliciously soft candy that's so sweet it feels like it's going to rot your teeth on the spot but tastes like heaven anyway," she teased.

"If my girl wants fudge, then we'll make fudge." Hawk stood with Maddy still in his arms, and then released his hold on her legs, letting her body slide slowly down his until her feet touched the floor.

"Your girl, huh?"

"You got a problem with that?"

She cocked her head, studied him for a moment, then grinned. "No. No problem with that." Then she turned and headed for the kitchen where she began rummaging through the cupboards.

"Don't we need a recipe?" he asked as he followed and watched as she started setting ingredients on the counter.

Her cheeks pinked slightly. "I may have made this one enough times that I know the recipe by heart."

"Fudge addict are you, caramel?"

"Maybe," she admitted. "This one is my absolute favorite though. You can make it in the microwave, so you don't have to worry about the candy thermometer and over or under-heating it. It's super creamy and has the most delicious caramel flavor."

"Just like you if I remember correctly," he said, moving behind her and nuzzling her neck.

She shivered in his arms and tilted her head to give him better access. Hawk kissed and nipped at the slender column of her neck for a moment before stepping back. Neither of them was ready for more than kissing yet, not just because they needed to wait a while for sex since Maddy had just given birth, but because right now they were building a deeper connection. They were kind of doing this relationship all haphazard, moving from sex, to a baby, to getting to know one another, but he wanted to do things right from here on out, and that meant nothing more than kissing until they were both ready, and Maddy wasn't there yet.

"Okay, what else do we need?" he asked.

"A big glass bowl," Maddy said. "We put everything in the bowl except the white chocolate and then stick it in the microwave. We also need a whisk and a wooden spoon. We heat it in bursts, and then stir in between each one. When I was a kid, and I made this with my mom, I always used to sneak little bits of the fudge from the whisk and spoon when the bowl went back in the microwave. After my dad and sister died, she didn't want to make it anymore so I would do it on my own before I got sent to boarding school anyway."

"Tell me about it," he said as he set a glass bowl on the counter beside the ingredients she had collected. So far Maddy had been pretty tight-lipped when it came to talking about her parents. He knew her dad had been killed when she was nine and that it was why she had gotten into the field she worked in, but she hadn't said much about its impact on her family.

Maddy shrugged. "Not a lot to tell. My dad and little sister were murdered. My mom didn't like being alone, met this wealthy guy, he proposed, she said yes, he creeped me out, and not just because I didn't want a replacement dad. He wasn't a kid kind of guy, so he sent me to boarding school. The end."

He doubted that.

But it was obviously all Maddy was willing to share at the moment because she grabbed kitchen scales and began to measure out the ingredients. That was okay though. He just needed to be patient and prove to her that she could trust him with all of her, including her pain. Hawk had meant what he said earlier, Maddy was his girl, and he would show her that he was her guy, all she had to do was reach out and let him be there for her.

* * *

10:29 A.M.

"DEEDEE LOVED THIS FUDGE," Maddy said softly as she smoothed the thick, gooey fudge with the back of the wooden spoon, then set the baking tray on the counter to cool for a few hours at room temperature before it went into the fridge overnight.

Earlier when Hawk had asked her to tell him about what her life had been like after her father and sister's deaths, she'd clammed up. It was a time in her life she never talked about, and she had immediately shut down without even thinking about it, but now she was regretting that. She could talk to Hawk, of all the people in her life he was the one person she trusted implicitly.

"DeeDee was your sister, right?" he asked, capturing her hand when she would have turned on the tap and filled the sink with hot, soapy water to wash the dirty dishes, and leading her into the living room.

"She was only four when she and my dad were killed, just a baby. I used to get so angry with her. I was five years older, a big girl, and she used to follow me around *all* the time. Used to drive me crazy," she said softly. After her dad and DeeDee were killed, Maddy would have given *anything* to have her annoying little sister back.

"Sometimes you don't realize what you have until it's gone."

The pain in Hawk's voice had her snuggling closer as they sat side by side on the couch. "I'm so sorry about your parents. I only lost my dad. I can't imagine losing both and at the same time. And you all had the added burden of adjusting to a whole new way of life."

"In a way you did too." Hawk's arm was around her shoulders, his hand tracing a line up and down her arm, the motion soothing, and she settled closer and rested her head on his shoulder.

"I guess it did. My mom wasn't the same anymore. She wanted to pretend that my dad and DeeDee never even existed. She got rid of all their things after the funerals and took down all the family photos. I … I stole one of my sister's teddy bears and the smallest of my dad's stargazing telescopes and hid them under my bed, and I managed to get one photo of us all together. It was taken the summer before they died when we were on vacation at the beach. My dad, he loved stargazing, DeeDee and I used to beg him to let us stay up late in the summer to go out once it got dark and look at the stars with him. After he died and I was all alone, I used to pretend he was a star staring down at me. That's all I have left of them." The familiar pang in her chest stabbed at her. She tried to think of her dad and DeeDee often to keep them alive, but it still hurt even all these years later.

"I'm sorry, that's rough. I know people cope with grief in different ways, but she should have packed that stuff up and had it left for you when you were older."

Hawk's hand stroking her arm continued to calm her, and she shifted for a moment to reach out and smooth the soft fuzzy hair on Louie's little head before curling up against Hawk again. "I hated her for it," she admitted. Maddy had always wondered if that made her a bad person, hating her mother who had only acted out of grief, but it was how she felt. "I hated her even more when she got married again so quickly. She didn't care how I felt about it. She didn't ask my opinion or ask if I wanted to leave my home and move to Ireland with her new husband. Didn't care that the man terrified me to the point I would move my dresser in front of my door every night so he couldn't come in while I was sleeping, and she didn't care that he sent me away to boarding school."

By the time she'd finished her outburst, she was breathing heavily and trembling all over. She'd longed to say those words out loud to someone for so long, but she'd kept them buried away inside her believing that they were mean and selfish, but she was in a safe place now, safe with Hawk, and she couldn't hold them in a second longer.

"Shh, honey, come here." Hawk slid an arm under her knees and maneuvered her sideways, so she was sitting on his lap. His legs were muscled and firm beneath her, a solid foundation, his arms strong, encircling her in stability that had been lacking in her life since she was a little girl. His lips lightly touched her temple, murmuring a string of soothing nonsense, reminding her of what it felt like to have someone care about you.

Because he hadn't judged her, hadn't reminded her that she wasn't the only one grieving, and that her mother hadn't meant to hurt her, she allowed a few tears to fall down her cheeks. They were quickly soaked up by Hawk's shirt, and she couldn't help but feel as though in some way he was soaking up part of her pain, making it his own, sharing her burden.

Was this what it was like to be in a serious relationship?

Because as much as she was battling her own pain right now, in her mind standing beside her nine-year-old self was a ten-year-old little boy with black hair falling over his bright blue eyes. Hawk had only been a year older than she had been when he lost both his parents and her heart wept for his loss as it wept for her own.

"Shh, caramel, it's okay, let it out. You shouldn't hold those things inside, it's not healthy. It's okay to hurt, honey. It's okay to be angry too. It's okay to feel however you want to feel."

As Hawk held her, rocked her, and continued to murmur in her ear, Maddy felt herself relax. She couldn't help but feel that this was where she was supposed to be.

When someone knocked on the apartment door she went to move, but Hawk tightened his hold. "Not ready," he whispered. She wasn't sure if he was talking to her or himself, but she relaxed back against him anyway. "Come in," he called out.

The door opened a moment later, and she lifted her head to see who it was. One of the receptionists she remembered meeting that first day was standing there with what looked like a package in her hands.

"This was just delivered, it's for Maddy. I wasn't sure if it was something for the baby, so I brought it right up," the young woman explained.

"Thanks, Ellen," Hawk said. "Could you pop it down on the table by the door?"

"Sure thing, Mr. Oswald," Ellen replied.

"What did I tell you? No need to call me Mr. Oswald, that's Eagle, I don't even work here. Just call me Hawk," he said, shooting that charming grin at the pretty receptionist.

Maddy might have felt a spark of jealousy, but she and Hawk had just had a baby, and he was still holding her on his lap, his hand draped possessively across her thighs, gripping one of her hips. They might not have been together long, but she knew Hawk wasn't a cheater. If they were together, they were together. She knew he would never bring anyone else into their relationship for any reason.

"Okay, I'll try to remember that, Mr. Os … I mean—"

The rest of Ellen's sentence was cut when the room suddenly exploded.

The force of the explosion knocked both her and Hawk off the couch. Her head hit something as they fell, and unconsciousness danced around her, but she fought it.

Louie.

She needed to get to her son.

She tried to move, but the pain intensified, and she couldn't fight the darkness any longer.

The next thing she knew she was waking in a panic.

"Louie!" she screamed. Or tried to but it came out a hoarse croak.

"He's okay, Maddy. Don't move."

Hawk's voice.

Normally that would make her relax, but she needed to see her baby.

"Louie, I need him, need him," she mumbled, trying vainly to sit up even though Hawk was holding her down.

"You hit your head and were knocked out. You need to stay still until you get checked out."

She blinked, tried to clear her cloudy vision, and saw that she was lying on the floor with Hawk kneeling above her. There was dirt, grim, and a trickle of blood on his forehead, but he looked okay. One part of her heart relaxed, but the other part screamed for her baby.

Maddy reached for Hawk and clutched at him. "Louie, please, I need him."

Obviously sensing her growing distress, Hawk nodded once. Then he very carefully picked her up and set her on the armchair in the corner, one of the few pieces of furniture in the room that remained upright. Then he moved to the bassinet, picked up the precious bundle inside, and brought her Louie, resting their son in her outstretched arms.

She squeezed the newborn as hard as she dared and planted desperate kisses all over his face. Somehow, he was still asleep, and the craziness of that had her huffing a borderline hysterical laugh that turned into a sob she had to choke down.

"What happened?" she asked, sure her memories of an explosion had to be wrong.

Hawk perched on the arm of the chair, holding her close as he rested a hand on their son's head. "Someone just tried to blow you up."

3:12 P.M.

. . .

"That's it, I'm done," Hawk announced as he glanced over to find Maddy still sitting in the same armchair he'd put her in when she first regained consciousness, still staring sightlessly into space, her face a blank mask of shock.

Over the last four hours or so, they and Louie had been checked out by paramedics. They'd given statements to the police, and they'd spoken at length with his family about the explosion. Well, he had done most of the talking. Maddy had managed no more than single-word answers to most of the questions she'd been asked.

It was obvious she was in shock, and the paramedics suspected she might have a mild concussion. When the EMTs said they wanted to transport her to the hospital he'd put his foot down and said he would hire someone to watch her. There was no way he was allowing her to go to a hospital which would be a logistical nightmare as far as security went.

Now he was rethinking that.

Maybe she needed more care than he could provide.

What he did know was that she couldn't sit in this room any longer.

"Where are you taking her?" Eagle asked. Concern was written all over his brother's face, and he knew Eagle didn't like the idea of taking Maddy away from Prey, but as far as Hawk was concerned it was already compromised for her here.

"My place. It has good security. If we can pull in a few of Prey's men to help watch the place we'll do that, if not, I'm sure we have contacts we can ask to provide extra security. I wanted to move her into my place from the beginning anyway, but I was worried it was too soon and would scare her away. Now I don't care about that. All I care about is keeping them safe, and they're not safe now." It was a miracle that Maddy and Louie hadn't been hurt, but Ellen who had brought the package up had been killed. They had speculated that the bomb had triggered when she set the box on a small table near the apartment door. The blast hadn't been big enough to do any structural damage to the building, but the living room of the apartment was a mess. Had she not been directly in the bomb's path then Ellen probably would have survived.

He could so easily have been the one to get up and take the package from her, triggering the bomb when he set it down or opened it.

Or worse, Maddy could have been.

"If he found her here he can find her there," Falcon warned.

"And I wasn't able to find a tracker in any of her belongings, on her car, or on her," Raven reminded him. "But so far he's been one step ahead. He could find her at your place, especially if he knows your Maddy's baby's father."

"How would he know that?" Hawk asked.

"I don't know, but so far he seems to know what she's going to do, just be careful," Raven warned.

"Of course. I'm not going to let anyone hurt Maddy or Louie. Once we get to my place we won't leave. I'll have the place locked down, we won't order anything, and we won't let anyone but you guys come up." Unfortunately, Hawk had the feeling that there was no safe place for Maddy right now, but at least at his place he had the hometown advantage.

"Be prepared," Eagle warned. "I thought Olivia would be safe at my place and we were attacked there. And Sparrow was abducted from her place just nine months ago. Don't let your guard down, even when you feel safe and everything in you urges you just to enjoy your new son and the woman you like."

"I won't let my guard down," he promised.

"Call if you need anything," Eagle said.

"I will."

"Take care of your woman," Falcon said, nodding his head in Maddy's direction. It seemed his brother had softened a little when it came to Maddy. Hawk understood Falcon wasn't trying to be difficult, but someone was out to get their family and using other people—both innocent and not—to do it.

"I intend to." With that, he said goodbye to his siblings and walked over to crouch before the armchair, cradling Maddy's cheek in his hand, and smiling when she immediately nestled her face closer. "You ready to get out of here?"

"Yes," she answered immediately. Her voice was soft, a little shaky, and she was still trembling despite the fact he'd wrapped her in one of the quilts that had been packed up and brought over here. But she was at least capable of interacting with him so wasn't that far buried in her shock.

"Let's go then." He set her on her feet, wrapped an arm around her waist to steady her, then picked up the baby car seat carrier where they'd put Louie after Maddy had fed him earlier.

Taking his family down to the underground parking lot he bundled them into a car, and they were driven to his penthouse. Although he hadn't asked, he knew Eagle would have someone following them, making sure no one was tailing them. He also knew that there would be someone watching over his little family, which meant while his focus would always be on their safety, he could also attend to Maddy's needs.

The drive to his penthouse took less time than he had anticipated, and a mere twenty minutes later they were stepping out of the private lift and into his living room. He'd chosen this place specifically because of the views, but because he was still active military he didn't spend a lot of time here. Still, the place was home, and seeing Maddy here made him imagine what their future could look like.

Hawk guided her over to the sofa and eased her into it, lifting her legs to turn her around so she could recline more comfortably, and propped some pillows behind her, tucking the blanket around her to keep her warm. Then he took Louie from his car seat and set him in his mother's arms, knowing Maddy needed the reassurance right now of holding her baby. He knew that was what she needed because it was what he needed.

"You want something to eat, to drink?" he asked, smoothing back a lock of hair that had fallen free of her hair tie and tucking it behind her ear.

"Not hungry."

"What about some hot tea? I'll put a little lemon in it. It will help soothe you, warm you up a little."

When Maddy nodded, he took her face between his hands and planted a long, slow kiss on her forehead and then one on her lips.

Leaving her—even to go to the kitchen—was hard, but he quickly made them both cups of tea, then grabbed a few cookies and some chocolate and put it on a plate, returning to the living room with both.

There he found Maddy had fallen asleep, Louie still cradled in her grasp, and he set down the cups and plate on the coffee table and then just stood and drank in the sight of them. He could have lost them today. In reality, he could have lost them at any time during the last few months. The man after Maddy could have succeeded in his attempts, but that was before.

Before he knew she was pregnant.

Before they'd spent more time together.

Before he'd learned more about her and come to like and respect her so much more.

Before she gave him a family.

Before she was his.

As carefully as he could, Hawk gathered her up and took her place on the couch, settling her and Louie on his lap.

Maddy stirred, but he touched a kiss to her temple and whispered, "Go back to sleep."

She gave a sleepy nod and settled back down against him, tucking her head beneath his chin and burrowing into him like she couldn't get close enough.

Hawk knew the feeling.

Even holding his woman and son on his lap he felt like they were too far away, their position in the land of the living too precarious.

Tightening his hold, he pressed his lips to the top of her head, willing his senses to believe that she was here, safe for now, and right where she belonged. No longer was Hawk approaching this thing with Maddy with a wait-and-see approach. He already knew she was it for him, knew he would protect her with his dying breath, and knew he would do literally anything to keep her safe and happy.

"Mine," he murmured.

Maddy stirred again, pressed closer against him, one hand coming to rest above his heart. "Don't leave me," she murmured.

A smile touched his lips. "Wouldn't dream of it, caramel. Wouldn't dream of it. Nowhere else on earth I'd rather be than here with you and our rugrat in my arms."

CHAPTER EIGHT

October 16th

1:12 A.M.

"UMM, what is that supposed to be?" Maddy giggled as she watched Hawk fumble to paint the mural on the wall in one of his spare bedrooms. Third time was the charm, at least that's what she hoped. Even if things didn't work out with Hawk—and she was deluding herself if she thought they wouldn't—Louie would still be living here half the time.

"It's a lion," he said, his brows scrunching into the most adorable frown.

Maddy giggled again. "That's supposed to be a lion?" she asked doubtfully.

"Yeah, he looks good," Hawk said, looking from the mess

of a lion on the wall to her and back again like he couldn't figure out what her problem was.

"Uh, no he doesn't. You didn't do any of the painting in the room at Prey did you?" She tried not to allow images of the explosion to creep into her mind. Today was about bonding, hanging out with Hawk, and doing something together for their son.

"No, the others did the room. I was with you because you were in labor."

"You're not an artist, are you?"

"I'm good at art," he said defensively, but she could tell by the spark in his eyes that he knew he wasn't and was not offended being called out on it.

"Sure you are." Maddy patted Hawk's hand leaving a smudge of yellow paint behind.

"Who's the bad artist now? Do I look like the wall to you?" he teased as he grabbed the paintbrush he'd been using to attempt to give the lion a face and swiped it down her arm.

"Hey!" she squealed, darting away from him. "No fair, mine was an accident."

Hawk shrugged. "Mine was too."

"Liar." She flicked her paintbrush in his direction sending paint spots raining down across his face.

"Oh, it's on now, caramel." One of his large hands snaked out, and with surprising speed, he managed to snag a hold of her wrist even as she attempted to dodge out of his reach. He yanked her against his chest and smeared pain down the front of the old shirt he'd loaned her to wear while they painted the new nursery.

"Ha-ha," she said as she tried to wriggle free from his hold, "this is your shirt, so you only painted your own clothes."

"Wise guy, huh?" he said. Hawk shifted the brush until it was right by her face.

Maddy squealed. "You wouldn't dare."

"Wouldn't I?"

"You do it, and you'll be sorry."

"Oh yeah?"

"Yeah."

"Oh yeah?"

"Yeah."

"Oh yeah?"

Maddy giggled again. "We going to do this all day, or are you going to let me go before you do something that will guarantee payback?"

"Payback, huh?" His voice had dropped, gone low and sexy, making her body instantly respond. Her thighs clenched together at the sudden tingling between her legs, and her nipples pebbled. All of a sudden, her skin felt hyper-sensitive, and the air around them seemed electrically charged, like the spark simmering between her and Hawk would ignite and consume them both.

Not that she would be complaining.

After all it was inevitable.

Sooner or later things were going to explode between them, and she couldn't wait for when it did.

But she wasn't sure now was the right time. Now they were building trust and a foundation. If they jumped right back into bed then she was worried that the bond they were creating would break. She was enjoying having fun with Hawk, talking to him, and sharing a few simple kisses.

As though sensing now wasn't the right time, Hawk swiped the brush down her cheek leaving a trail of wet, slimy yellow paint in its wake.

"I can't believe you did that," she shrieked.

"Got you that time. You, not my clothes," he added, and his chest rumbled with a laugh.

"Ooh, you're going to be sorry you did that." When he went to get her again she grabbed his hands and pushed up, causing him to paint himself instead of her.

"Hey!" Hawk exclaimed, releasing his hold on her.

Maddy sprung away from him, then turned and laughed when she saw the streak of yellow along his black hair, making him look like some sort of weird skunk. He looked ridiculous and hilarious, and she couldn't not laugh at him. She doubled over as she laughed so hard tears began to stream down her cheeks and she planted her hands on her knees.

"Oh, you think that was funny, do you?" Hawk said in a mock growl, but soon he was laughing too, and it felt so good to be free for a moment, not worrying about a serial killer hunting her or raising a baby alone, just enjoying life.

By the time their laughs died down they were both breathing hard, with wet cheeks. Their eyes met and she felt it.

Felt it right down deep inside.

A little voice—that sounded surprisingly like her father's—telling her it was okay. That it was time.

It didn't matter that even though they'd met almost nine months ago, they had shared only one night with no expectations, then hadn't seen each other again until a couple of days ago. It only mattered that they were here together now, and that they both wanted the same things.

Time was relative. Sometimes it only took one moment to know you'd met the right person. That was what Maddy had felt in February when she and Hawk first met. It was why she hadn't been able to forget him even before she knew his baby was growing inside her. She felt it now too, a pull she couldn't ignore. Something was drawing her toward the man standing before her.

When he reached for her, she stepped toward him. Wrapped her arms around his neck and drew him down so she could kiss him.

Kissing him was like setting off a firestorm inside her. Her body burned with a need she hadn't experienced before, a desire unlike anything else, one that consumed her almost entirely. His hard length pressed against her body and suddenly that was all she could think about.

She needed to touch it, stroke it, taste it, feel it inside her.

Hawk took control of the kiss, backing her up against the wall. Curling one hand behind her head, his other moved to claim one of her breasts, fondling the needy mound through her shirt.

"More," she begged, just like she had that night they'd shared. The best night of her life. Not only had she met the most amazing man, but he'd given her the most amazing gift. And now she had both of them, and there was no way she was letting them go.

"You sure?" Hawk asked, lifting his head to look down at her.

There was a heavy dose of lust in his eyes, but along with it was a genuine concern for her mixed with genuine affection. He cared. It was evident in the way he fussed over her after Louie was born and yesterday after the explosion, in the way he was attentive to her needs, the way he had listened and reassured her when she talked about her father and sister's deaths.

He wanted her, she wanted him, they weren't doing anything wrong.

Yeah, she was sure.

"Never been more positive of anything in my life."

As though her words were all he needed, he crushed his

mouth to hers, kissing her hungrily. Although she had shared a few kisses over the last several days this one felt different. It was hotter, deeper, there was more between them now. Okay their relationship had kind of been fast-tracked, but that didn't make it any less real.

Her hands fumbled with the zipper on his jeans, she knew they couldn't have sex yet, but that didn't mean she couldn't use her hands or mouth to make him come. Hawk's hands were just finding their way inside her pants when Louie's cry came over the baby monitor.

"Again?" she said, both frustrated and amused.

"Guess the rugrat doesn't want to see mom and dad have any fun," Hawk said with a chuckle as he shifted uncomfortably, trying to get his jeans to accommodate his hard length that was now not going to get any relief.

"I guess his vote is no for a little brother or sister," she said without thinking. Then turned panicked eyes on Hawk. They both wanted to make this work, but talking about having more kids was a little presumptuous. Hawk might not have wanted kids at all, and although he was happy to be a father to Louie it didn't mean he wanted more.

Tipping her chin up he kissed her hard and fast. "I definitely want to give Louie siblings."

Maddy relaxed. "Guess I better go feed him."

As she started walking Hawk barked out a laugh. "I'd say I got you back for the hair thing."

"What?" She looked over her shoulder at him and saw her back was now smeared with yellow paint from the wall. "Oh, man," she muttered. "You are so dead. Don't you worry, Hawk Oswald, I will get you back for that one."

His laughter followed her out of the nursery and into Hawk's bedroom where they'd set up Louie yesterday. She had slept with Hawk in the bed, and although they hadn't done more than sleep, she'd been exhausted after the explosion. But now as his laughter washed over her, soothing her, warming her, stirring up all these feelings in her heart, she couldn't wait to get the nursery ready and move Louie into it because as soon as her body was healed, she couldn't wait to make love to Hawk again. This time she knew it would be even more amazing.

* * *

1:22 P.M.

"WHY DON'T you go and lie down for a while? You look exhausted," Hawk suggested. Despite the fact that she seemed to have bounced back well after yesterday's explosion he knew Maddy was taking it harder than she was letting on. Last night she hadn't slept much, and when she had, she'd been tossing and turning. From the whimpers coming from her, she had likely been having bad dreams. It was clear she didn't want him to know she was struggling because she hadn't mentioned it, but he'd slept beside her in his bed so he'd noticed how unsettled she was.

As wonderful as it had been having Maddy in his bed, he'd been wired about how close he'd come to losing both her and their son, and hadn't gotten much sleep himself. Most of the night he'd spent watching her chest rise and fall, and then getting up to check that Louie was also still breathing, giving him a front row seat to her distress.

This morning he hadn't brought it up, and neither had she, they'd had fun together making Louie nursery number three, and he hadn't minded Maddy pointing out that his graphic design skills left a lot to be desired. On the other hand, she was a brilliant artist and had been able to paint several of the animals freehand while he'd struggled to use the stencils. Another thing he'd learned about her, and every time it happened, he got a little thrill. Hawk wished he'd chased her down eight months ago, but at least they were together now.

"I guess I could," Maddy replied, not looking particularly excited about the idea. She stood and carried her plate to the sink, rinsed it, and stashed it in the dishwasher, but instead of heading for the bedroom, she lingered in the kitchen looking lost.

Leaving his plate where it was, he crossed to her and drew her into his arms. "What's wrong?"

Maddy sighed like she didn't want to admit any weakness to him, but then she nestled closer and wrapped her arms around his waist, resting her head on his chest. "I can't stop thinking about yesterday. How close we came to dying, how close our son came to dying. And Ellen, she died because of me. That package had my name on it. Someone knew I was there and sent it to me. It was meant to kill me and yet she died instead."

Her words were accompanied by a small shudder, and he held her tighter. "No, honey," he said, smoothing a hand down her hair hanging loose around her shoulders. "Ellen didn't die because of you, she died because some psycho thinks it's okay to steal other people's lives."

"But …"

"No buts," he said firmly. Looping her hair gently around his hand, he tugged lightly until her head lifted and tilted so she looked up at him. Then he planted a soft kiss on her lips. Each kiss they shared he felt the pull between them grow. Earlier when they'd been fooling around in the bedroom things would have gone a whole lot further if Louie hadn't interrupted them.

Although he had intended this kiss to be comforting, Maddy quickly deepened it, moving her hands to curl into his hair and opening her mouth to let his tongue swoop inside. The hand not tangled in her hair moved to cup her backside, anchoring her against him and his growing erection.

Hawk had thought it was a good thing Maddy couldn't have sex for a few weeks because it would give them time to connect on a deeper level, but now all he could think about was plunging inside that sweet heat of hers he remembered so well. Just a week ago he was waffling over tracking Maddy down and plagued by thoughts that marriage never worked out.

Now he kept thinking how he couldn't wait to fill a home with more kids and build a life with the gorgeous woman kissing him like she couldn't get enough of him.

His phone dinged to alert him to the fact that someone was in the lift and on their way up and he groaned as he pulled back. "Interrupted again."

Maddy laughed. "It seems like the Universe is really insistent we don't do anything more than a little kissing."

"Have I told you how much I hate the Universe?"

She laughed again. "Well, it brought us together even though we agreed on only one night. And it did give us Louie."

He heaved a dramatic sigh. "Okay, then I guess I do love it after all." Her sweet laugh rang out a third time, and, boy, did it have him, hook, line, and sinker. "Go, get a little rest. It's my brothers and sister to discuss the case."

Maddy looked like she was going to disagree. He knew she was itching to be involved, but she was the victim here, and she'd already given them everything she had. It was time for her to step back and let them do what she'd come here to ask them to do. But instead of arguing she stood on tiptoe to kiss his cheek. "All right, I'll try to take a nap, only if you promise you'll call if you need me."

"Deal."

They sealed it with a kiss before the lift doors opened and his brothers, Raven and Olivia filed out.

"Hi, Maddy, how are you feeling?" Eagle asked as he came over to kiss her cheek.

"I'm okay," Maddy replied.

Raven gave her an appraising once over before pulling her into a hug. "If you need to talk, I'm always available." When she stepped back, she gave a wry smile. "Oh, and Cleo is already asking when she can come and visit Louie again. Apparently, having a baby brother in her house is not enough to satisfy her baby craving. So when you feel up to it we'd love to bring dinner over one night."

"We'd love that," Maddy said.

"If it's not too overwhelming, Eagle, Luna, and I would love to tag along. We'll bring dessert," Olivia said as she hugged Maddy.

"If you're bringing dessert I'm never going to be overwhelmed," Maddy said.

Olivia laughed as she stepped back. "Good, when you're ready we'll set it up. I'm sure Hope and Falcon will come too, and Ethan, he's missing Sparrow, so he'd probably love to come and hang out with us."

Maddy cast Falcon a surreptitious glance. He knew she was picking up on Falcon's suspicion and was a little intimidated by his older brother. It wasn't unusual. Most people were intimidated by Falcon, particularly when he did nothing to appear even remotely friendly. Hawk was going to have to talk to him and tell him to ease up around Maddy. The last thing he wanted was anything to drive a wedge between them as things were going so well.

"Go lie down," he said, giving Maddy a little nudge toward the bedroom.

"Maybe I should make coffee for everyone first?" she suggested.

"I can do that. If you don't take a nap now, Louie will be up and hungry again before you get a chance."

"Okay." Still, she moved somewhat hesitantly toward the bedrooms, and he knew it was killing her to take a step back, but that's why she had come here. Because she trusted Prey's reputation. Now she had a personal stake with him, he prayed that trust had only grown.

Once she was gone, he gestured to the kitchen table, and the others sat while he started making coffee. "Please tell me you guys found something." Living with a threat hovering over Maddy's head was not what he wanted—ever, but especially when they were getting to know one another.

"Actually, we did," Raven told him.

"Don't leave me in suspense." With the coffee percolating, and mugs on the table, Hawk joined the others.

"One of the detectives working the case lost his mother to a horrific car accident when he was twelve. A drunk driver took out six cars and killed fifteen people, including two families with two young children each. Not exactly a violent crime per se, but it definitely fits with Maddy's profile, and could be why the detectives were so dismissive of her. He's the more experienced of the two and could have influenced his partner to shut down that line of investigation," Olivia told him.

"That's not all we found," Raven added. "There is also a crime scene tech that attended two of the scenes and has quite a tumultuous past. He's an older man, close to retirement age, he's actually been offered retirement twice before, but both times his replacement suddenly backed out at the last minute. When he was seven, he lost his entire family to a violent home invasion. He was spending the night at a friend's house. If he'd been home, he likely would have been killed too. The family was brutally stabbed to death. The mother and both sisters, aged thirteen and five, were all raped. Father was badly beaten before they moved on to stabbing him. Growing up with that hanging over his head would have been difficult, plus there was no family to take him in so he spent the rest of his childhood in the foster system."

"Both of those sound like viable suspects," he said, the weight on his shoulders lifting slightly. The coffee was ready, so he got up to grab it, and filled each of their cups as his family added cream and sugar. "So, what's our next step?" he asked as he stirred his coffee.

"We keep looking into our suspects," Eagle said. "We'll find what we need."

"We also need to look into the possibility that whoever is after her has nothing to do with the serial killer case," Falcon said. He was leaning back in his chair, his arms crossed over his chest, a frown on his face. "Whoever is after our family hasn't been successful going after the rest of us. Maybe they decided it was time to focus on you. Someone could have been following you, if they were, they would have seen you go to the hotel with Maddy. Did you drive her home after?"

"No, she took a cab."

"So, she'd be an easy mark. He could have followed her back and learned her name. If he was watching her to find out if she could be leverage, then he would have eventually noticed she was pregnant. The timing would be logical that it was yours. Then he tries to either get to her or scare her enough that she comes here. Now you have a child, he's something that can always be used to get you to do what he wants."

Hawk wanted to refute what Falcon had just said, but unfortunately, the man after their family had proven to be ruthless and to use others to try to manipulate them.

Was it his fault that Maddy and Louie had been in danger?

The thought left him barely able to drag oxygen into his lungs.

* * *

1:49 P.M.

EAVESDROPPING WAS WRONG.

Maddy fully agreed with that sentiment.

But this was *her* life they were discussing. She wanted to know who was after her, and while she hadn't intended to go in and let Hawk and his family know that she'd been listening in, when Falcon started to talk about whoever was after her being related to someone after the Oswalds, she knew she had to go in.

While Hawk hadn't mentioned that someone was after his family—something he definitely should have mentioned given that her son was an Oswald—she knew he would be panicking over the possibility.

Even though she was a little annoyed he hadn't enlightened her to that possibility, the urge to comfort him was stronger. When she'd arrived, she'd told them it was a serial killer after her because that was what she had believed. She hadn't known there were any other options on the table and couldn't really be mad at him for believing her.

"You need to tell me about this person after your family," she said as she re-entered the kitchen and went straight to Hawk, wrapping her arms around him in a brief hug before pulling up a chair beside him.

"I thought you were taking a nap," he said, a little accusation in his tone.

"I know, I shouldn't have been eavesdropping, I'm sorry, but I wanted to know what was going on. This is my life remember, and if someone is out to get your family, it impacts me and our son. I have a right to know." There was a little accusation in her own tone as she spoke.

"I agree," Eagle said. "Hawk was trying to protect you, but this person has been after us for years, and so far, we haven't made any progress finding them. I personally would love to have your thoughts on this, see what you think."

She felt better now that she had something useful to do. Being sidelined was a lot harder than she had anticipated, even if she had come to Prey because of their reputation and her belief that they could help her. "Hawk hasn't told me anything about this, so why don't you tell me what you know, and I'll see if I can offer some insight."

Hawk's lips brushed her ear. "Sorry I didn't tell you. You just had enough on your plate, and I didn't really think it could be related."

Maddy turned her head so she could kiss him. "It's okay. I was more thrown than angry. So does this have anything to do with your parents' murders?"

Falcon narrowed his eyes at her. "Why would that be your first thought?"

She shrugged. "Hawk told me they were murdered, and I guess since I've been thinking a lot about childhood trauma impacting adult behavior it was the first thing to come to mind." She met his gaze squarely, trying not to let his glower intimidate her. She hadn't done anything wrong and had no need to be squirming like a naughty child caught with their hand in the cookie jar.

"Until a few years ago we always thought it was a random thing," Eagle informed her. "I'm sure Hawk told you we grew up on a remote off-the-grid farm." When she nodded, he continued, "I'd left to join the military, but the others all lived there. Our parents were in the house alone when two men who had recently escaped from prison broke in, tortured, and killed them. When they got back to the house my siblings realized something was wrong. Raven was the oldest at home, so she sent the others to hide in the barn while she went in to try to eliminate the threat. Which she did." There was pride in Eagle's voice as he looked at his little sister, but Falcon had stiffened, and she suspected he carried some guilt over his sister being the one to go in after the threat.

"I was badly hurt," Raven said, taking over the narrative, "but Falcon, Hawk, and the others got me to help. We ended up moving to Manhattan afterward, we learned that our mom had been crazy wealthy, but she'd run away with our dad because they were in love, but neither family approved of the union. Our parents were a little odd, but they were kind, loving people, and we had a good, albeit weird upbringing. We thought that was the end of things, but when Cleo was three, she was kidnapped and sold on a black-market human trafficking website. It took me a decade to track her down, but I did a year ago, and while we were there, I learned that her abduction wasn't random, she was targeted because someone has a grudge against our family. The same person who ordered a hit on our parents. A hit that was supposed to take out all eight of us, but all of us kids survived."

"A woman who had been at the same auction where Cleo was about to be sold again was taken before rescue could come, and when Falcon and one of Prey's teams went in to rescue her, he learned that the person after our family is someone related to us. The woman was Hope, she's now Falcon's wife," Eagle told her. "Then when Sparrow and Ethan were kidnapped by a drug trafficking warlord earlier this year, she learned that this relative is a weapon trafficker. So far, we haven't been able to find him, and we have some of the best computer experts in the world working on it." Eagle waved a hand at his sister Raven and his wife Olivia.

"Our mom came from old money. Her family had several businesses that were extremely profitable and were worth billions," Hawk explained. "Mom was an only child, but our dad's family were immigrants from Ireland, they were catholic, didn't believe in birth control, and he had a lot of siblings. Raven and Liv have been trying to track them all down, but there were twelve of them, and they scattered once they were adults. Dad's father worked as a gardener on Mom's family's property, it's how they met."

"Are you sure your parents ran because their families disapproved of their relationship?" Maddy asked the first question that sprung to mind.

Four faces frowned back at her. Okay, so they had never considered that option.

"What do you mean?" Falcon asked.

"I was just thinking that going off-grid is an odd option for someone with a lot of money who had grown up surrounded by luxury. Now it's totally possible they were both survivalists at heart, or they were running because they were afraid. If it was just because their families didn't approve there were lots of other things they could have done. They could have just married, your mom probably had a trust fund, so they could have supported themselves. Your dad could have gotten a job. But they didn't do that. Instead, they hid."

Eagle stared at her in shock for a beat. "We didn't think of that. We never met either set of grandparents, both were deceased by the time we left the farm. Our father was the youngest of his siblings, so his parents were older. And mom's parents had recently died in a car accident, that's why we inherited everything. Some of the money went to hiring someone to look after my brothers and sisters while I was away, then we used a lot of it to start Prey. We met a few of our aunts and uncles at the funeral but never kept in contact. We don't really know a lot about our parents' lives before they ran, but it's possible that what you suggested could be true."

"Let's say it is," Raven said slowly, half lost in thought. "Who could it be? We could try to track down aunts and uncles, but I've already struggled to find them all. There are two that seem to have completely disappeared off the face of the earth."

"I'd start with those two then," Maddy said. "People only disappear for a reason." She hesitated before asking her next question, not wanting to upset them but wanting to follow her train of thought. "Can you tell me a little about the assault on your parents?" she asked gently.

"Why do you need to know details about that?" Falcon all but growled, and Olivia reached over to rest a calming hand on his forearm.

"I'm sure she has a reason," Olivia said. "Remember this is what she does. She studies victims to form theories on who might have hurt them."

"I definitely don't mean to pry or bring up bad memories," Maddy agreed, "but I can't do what I do without some details."

"It's okay," Hawk assured, taking her hand and entwining their fingers while throwing a glare at his big brother. "What do you need to know?"

"Were their injuries the same, equal, or was one hurt more than the other?" she asked.

"Both were fairly badly cut up," Hawk replied.

"Do they know who died first?"

"I'd have to look up the reports to find out, we never asked, never had reason to," Raven said.

"I hate to ask this, but it could be relevant. Was your mom raped before she was killed?"

They all stiffened, and if looks could kill then Falcon's death stare would have her keeling over, but Eagle nodded. "Yeah, she was. We assumed with two escaped prisoners, sex was high on their mind, even after we knew it wasn't random. You think that's significant?"

A lot of what she did was forming assumptions. Of course, you could never really know what someone was thinking or why they did what they did. You could only make logical guesses based on the evidence you had. "I think it could be. Could mean it was personal, someone with a specific grudge against her, not a lot of better ways to hurt a woman, punish her, or make her pay for perceived wrongs than to have her sexually assaulted. Or it could be exactly what you thought it was, two men who hadn't had sex in a long time getting off with an available body. Still, I would focus specifically on someone interested in your mom and wasn't pleased that she married someone else. If your parents disappeared for a reason then that means you can find that reason, and if you find it, you'll find the person after you now."

Whether it was that same person who had also been stalking her or not, she wanted Hawk and his family to finally have peace and be able to live in safety. She hoped that one day these people might be her family too, that they might accept her into the fold, and she wanted all of them to be able to live in peace.

* * *

6:35 P.M.

. . .

"EAGLE, we have to go. We have to pick up Luna in twenty-five minutes, and it will take us about that long to get back to Prey," Olivia announced.

His sister-in-law's announcement broke up what had been an hours-long brainstorming session. They'd ordered pizza, which Falcon had gone downstairs to collect since they weren't allowing anyone to come up to his penthouse. Hawk had enjoyed seeing Maddy relax and start to assimilate into his family, even if the topics they had been discussing were dark and grizzly ones.

"I should go too, Max was picking up Roman and getting Cleo after school, but they'll both be wondering where I am by now," Raven added. "Do you think you're going to be staying in Manhattan or going back to California, Maddy?"

She cast a glance his way, and when he smiled she returned it. "Well, since Hawk is here, I guess I'll be staying. I have enough money saved to stay for a little while, but the city is expensive, so I'd have to find a job almost right away as I'll be using my trust fund to pay you guys so …"

"Honey, if you think you're staying anywhere but right here in my house you're crazy," Hawk told her. "And if you think we're taking your money you're even crazier."

Maddy gave him an adorable frown. "I don't expect you to help me for free just because of Louie."

"You're cute when you try to disagree with me, but no way are we taking your money. What if this is all because of us anyway? What if whoever has been after you is doing it to get to me? Letting you pay us to help with a problem we caused wouldn't be fair."

"What if it's not because of you? What if it is the serial killer like I thought? Having you work for free because we share a child wouldn't be fair."

He loved the smug little smile she gave him. Couldn't wait to kiss it off her once his brothers and sister left. "Caramel, we're not working for free because you and I share a child, we're working for free because you're mine."

A shiver rocketed through Maddy. He could feel it because they were sitting close side by side at his table. Heat flared in her hazel eyes, and it was all he could do not to take her here and now.

"Stop trying to fight it, Maddy," Olivia said with a laugh. "It's a lost cause. The Oswald brothers are all alphas, and Hawk is so charming and adorable and easy-going you won't be able to say no to him."

"Hey!" Eagle protested. "Did you just call my brother charming and adorable?"

"I also said he was easy going which you are not, love of my life." Olivia reached up to ruffle Eagle's hair.

Eagle snagged her wrist and tugged her into his lap where he kissed her thoroughly. "You saying you'd rather charming and adorable over that?"

Olivia pretended to think about it. "Well, you are a good kisser I'll give you that, and you can be charming when you want to be, but you're too sexy to be adorable."

Eagle smirked and then kissed his wife again.

"All right," Olivia mock sighed. "I guess I'd pick you over anyone else. Except maybe Luna, she's pretty cute and doesn't pout as much as you do."

Raven rolled her eyes at the couple. "What I was going to say is if you're staying, when you find a new job and go back to work if you're looking for a nanny for Louie, Max and I share one with Eagle and Olivia, I'm sure she'd be happy to take on a third baby Oswald."

Maddy smiled like she liked the idea. "Then the cousins can grow up more like siblings."

"Exactly," Raven said. "You can let me know when you decide and we'll talk to Katie."

Everyone said their goodbyes, and once he was alone, he

turned to find Maddy with her hands planted on her hips and that adorable little frown back on her face. "I don't want you going all caveman over me. I like that you want to help me, and I'm glad it's not just because of Louie, but I think we need to see how things are developing between us once this mess is cleared up before we decide if we're ready to move in together."

"You really want to make Louie a fourth nursery when there's a perfectly good one down the hall?" he asked as he stalked toward her.

Maddy rolled her eyes. "The one down the hall is a mess thanks to you and your antics."

"My antics?" He arched a brow as he backed her up against the edge of the counter. "Pretty sure you were the one who started it."

"By accident," she reminded him, her eyes on his lips.

"Didn't you hear what Liv said? It's no use arguing with me. I'm charming, adorable, and the sexiest man alive."

Maddy laughed like he'd hoped she would. "She didn't say you were the sexiest man alive. She said you were easy-going and that her husband was sexy."

Hawk shrugged and grinned. "I paraphrase." Then he grew serious, reached out, and swept his knuckles across her cheek. "I don't want to let you go, Mads. We lost eight and a half months, and I missed out on a lot. I didn't get to experience pregnancy with you. I don't want to miss out on anything else."

Her gaze softened, and she leaned up on her tiptoes to kiss him. "I guess we can move in together. I mean properly, once this is all sorted out and I have all my things, and we don't have anything hanging over us."

"Got you to come around pretty quickly on that one," he teased. His hands rested on her shoulders, and he trailed his fingers lazily down her arms. When he got to her hips, he changed track and let his fingers trace a line up her sides.

"Mmm," Maddy moaned. "Don't get used to getting your way all the time."

"Sure thing, beautiful," he said. When his hands reached her hips again, he lifted her easily and set her on the counter, nudging her knees apart so he could stand between them. Trailing his fingers over the top of her thighs he brushed a single fingertip along her center. She was wearing a pair of leggings, but he could feel her heat through the material. "You sore, caramel?"

"Not much." She shivered when he stroked again, a little firmer this time.

"I don't want to hurt you." Even though she was doing something that billions of women had done throughout the course of history watching her in pain as she brought their son into the world had been hard. More than hard. The sight of her in pain shredded him. As much as he wanted to fool around, he wouldn't if it was going to hurt her.

"If it hurts we can stop." The glint in her eyes told him she wasn't going to back down. That she wanted this as much as he did only turned him on more.

"Wrap your legs around my waist," he instructed. Once she had he lifted her and carried her over to the sofa where he gently laid her down. "Let's get rid of these." He pulled off her socks and leggings and tossed them aside, then he took one of her feet in his hands and began to massage it.

"Hmm," Maddy hummed her approval as he slowly worked his way up her calf and onto her thigh. When he made it to the apex of her thighs, he paused to swipe a thumb across her panties, causing her hips to rise, seeking more stimulation, but he brushed his thumb against her once more before moving down to her other foot.

Again, he worked slowly, kneading each muscle thoroughly, relaxing her, preparing her. By the time he gave her what she wanted she had to be ready, thinking of nothing else, so nothing he did hurt.

By the time he reached the apex of her thighs again, Maddy was shifting restlessly beneath him. Her eyes were locked on his hands watching as they slowly made their way to where she wanted them, but when he finally eased her panties down her legs, doubt entered her beautiful eyes.

"Doctor said I might not be able to come for a while," she told him. "So don't be surprised if I can't orgasm."

"Shh, stop worrying." Hawk leaned over and kissed her. He'd thought he had her all relaxed, feeling instead of thinking, but obviously he had a little more work to do. Keeping his mouth on hers, he let one of his hands dip between her legs. They couldn't do penetration for a few weeks, but the doctor said if Maddy wanted to they could try some external stimulation.

She was wet, and he coated a finger in her juices then swirled the pad of his thumb across her sensitive bundle of nerves. Hawk was sure he could get her to come but only if she didn't try to put too much pressure on herself to do it.

Keeping her attention split between the kiss and what he was doing between her legs Hawk hoped he could get her to let go, allow her body to feel natural sensations without trying to force it.

Working her up slowly, he increased the pressure and speed, and she began to squirm beneath him. Bit by bit he got faster and harder, always aware not to go too fast or too hard and cause her pain. But from the breathy moans she was making, he was pretty sure she was feeling the opposite of pain.

Knowing she was close, hovering on the edge, he took her little bud and rolled it between his thumb and forefinger, and she exploded beneath him. Her hips bucked, her body trembled, and a scream was caught by his mouth. Hawk prolonged it for her for as long as he could, working her bundle of nerves until he felt her sag against the couch cushions.

"I came," she said, wonder in her eyes when he managed to tear his mouth away from hers.

"I saw," he said, feeling somewhat smug.

Apparently, she saw that because she swatted lazily at his shoulder. "I see you want to take all the credit for that."

"Heck, yeah I do." Maddy's eyelids looked heavy, and she stifled a yawn, she should be trying to nap while Louie was asleep, and he'd be up soon enough for another feed. Scooping her up he started for the bathroom, he'd clean her up then tuck her into bed.

"Hey, I didn't get to play," Maddy said sleepily.

"Next time, honey," he assured her. He was hard as a rock and throbbing with need for release, but he'd gotten his girl to come, and that was all he cared about.

CHAPTER NINE

October 17th

5:43 A.M.

Last night she hadn't gotten a chance to touch Hawk, and Maddy intended to make up for it now.

The orgasm had wiped her out. After he'd cleaned her up in the bathroom, he'd tucked them both into bed and she'd immediately fallen asleep. She'd been so relaxed, so exhausted, that she'd slept without dreaming, and while Hawk had woken when she did for Louie's first two feeds, he hadn't woken for the last one.

Full, dry, and tucked safely into the bassinet in a corner of Hawk's bedroom—*their* bedroom she supposed if she was going to stay here—Louie was fast asleep and would be for a couple of hours. This meant there wouldn't be any distractions this time.

Slipping back under the covers, she reached down and ran a finger along his length. He was big, *really* big. Had he been that big back in California last February? Somehow it seemed like he had grown during that time, but that was probably because she had been dreaming about him ever since. Some mornings she had woken all hot and bothered. Dream Hawk couldn't really bring her any satisfaction, and she didn't sleep around. Besides, she hadn't wanted to just get laid, she wanted him.

This sweet, charming, easy-going man sprawled in the bed beside her.

He'd been so attentive last night, reading her body to perfection and giving her the best orgasm of her life. Although she'd thought the same thing about the ones he had given her the night they conceived Louie. Maybe every time with Hawk was going to be better than the one before.

This time though, it was all about him.

Her finger trailed up and down his length again, and she felt him start to harden beneath her touch. His thing might be awake, but as of right now, Hawk was still out, snoring softly. He usually woke at six if the last few days were anything to go by, but she wanted to be the one to wake him and give him something because right now it seemed like he was constantly the one giving her things.

Reaching inside the gray sweatpants he'd worn to sleep in, she found him bare and curled her fingers around his oh so impressive length. When she gave him a gentle squeeze, she felt him stir.

"Good morning," she murmured.

"I'd say it is, honey," he drawled, his voice husky from sleep.

Running her hand up and down him, she enjoyed the way

he hardened under her ministrations. Because he seemed to possess the ability to read her so well, Hawk folded his hands behind his head and left her to do what she wanted.

Maddy tossed aside the covers so she could move into a better position. She couldn't wait until they could have sex, but for now she'd enjoy bringing him the same pleasure he'd given her last night. In her hand he began to twitch, his body grew tense, and just as Hawk had on the couch in the living room, she took her time, increasing her speed slowly, watching him as he watched her hand inside his pants.

When she felt like he was trying to hold back, she wanted to snap that control and make him fall apart. So, she squeezed him hard, moving her hand as fast as she could up and down his shaft, and was rewarded with a groan as his pleasure exploded through him and out of him all over her hand. She kept going, trying to make it last as long for him as it had for her last night.

"Mmm, I could get used to waking up like that," he murmured when his body stopped thrusting into her hand and finally relaxed.

"Me too," she agreed. It almost didn't feel real that she actually could get used to shared moments like this every morning. For so long, she hadn't had a connection like this to anyone else. Her mother had created emotional distance between them after her dad and sister were killed, and then that emotional distance became physical distance when she was sent off to boarding school. There she was just one of many lonely girls. They bonded over being away from home, but for her it was different, she didn't *have* a home anymore. The house she'd lived in with her family had been sold, and her stepfather's house had never felt like a home in the short time she'd stayed there.

But here felt like home.

Hawk felt like home.

His whole family did.

She liked it here, wanted to stay, wasn't even upset that she'd caved so easily, and agreed to stay in Hawk's penthouse.

Why would she want to leave the very thing she'd craved for most of her life?

"You're thinking awfully hard over there." Hawk reached out and tugged on a lock of her hair.

"Just thinking how lucky I am to have met you in the bar that night."

"I'm the lucky one, caramel."

"See, that right now is why I feel so lucky. You're almost too good to be true, you know. You're charming, funny, and really sweet. And you're sexy and handsome, and did I mention that this body looks like it was chiseled from stone?"

Hawk laughed and pulled her over so she was draped across him. "You are smart, you care about people, you're strong and tough, you weren't too proud to admit you needed help and got yourself safely here. You have hair like spun gold and eyes that seem to change color every time I look at them. You have the most adorable little nose and the most perfect pair of breasts. You smell good, you taste good, and holding these perfect curves in my arms is what heaven must be like. So, I'm definitely the lucky one."

"Maybe we can agree that we're both lucky." Her head rested on his rock-hard chest, and she traced circles with one finger around his nipple.

"You keep that up, honey, and we'll be onto round two, and that's not fair, it's my turn next."

He was even managing to find a way to make not being able to have sex fun. She rolled off him and climbed out of bed. "Why don't you go grab a shower? I'm going to go make breakfast, and then we can work on the nursery some more." It was taking longer with just the two of them doing it than it had when his whole family had chipped in to decorate the one at the apartment, but she liked this, doing it together just the two of them, laughing and teasing one another. This is what a normal couple would have done, and the more time they spent together the more she started to feel like they were a normal couple.

Hawk came up behind her, wrapped an arm around her stomach, and pulled her up against him. He kissed the side of her neck, and she relaxed against him. "Thank you," he said.

"For what?"

"Being here, trusting me to keep you safe, and saying you'll stay. I wanted you to know that I'm not going to be re-signing with the Army when my current contract is up. I want us to be together, a real family, and that means being here. I don't know what exactly I'll do yet, but something at Prey. I have an idea I wanted to talk to you about later."

"Can't wait to hear it," she assured him. "And thank *you* for being here when I needed you, looking after me and our son, and wanting a future with us."

Hawk kissed her neck again and then headed for the bathroom while she picked up the bassinet and took it with her to the kitchen. She set it down on the counter and leaned down to kiss Louie's cheek. "He's pretty great, isn't he?"

Of course the baby couldn't reply, but he did stir, his long lashes fluttering against his round, chubby little cheeks. He was just the most precious thing, and as much as he was a tie that bound her and Hawk, she suspected that if they'd managed to cross paths again, they would have reconnected even without him.

"I know we could have made it, just the two of us, but this is so much better. I know what it's like to grow up without a daddy, and I'm so glad you won't have to go through that. No matter what happens you'll always have a mom and a dad who love you, and a family there to support you. But I think it's going to work. It's kind of crazy, but I'm almost grateful that someone was after me because it brought me here. I'm so glad I decided to come to Prey for help, if I hadn't, I never would have found your daddy again, and we wouldn't be here, safe and sound in our new home. We're pretty lucky, aren't we?"

Despite the threats still hanging over both their heads as Maddy began to gather ingredients for pancakes she started to hum. Lucky. It was all perspective, some might not agree with her, but she knew what it was like to be loved, she knew what it was like to lose that love, and now she knew what it was like to find love again.

It was a precious gift and one she had no intention of squandering.

* * *

2:38 P.M.

"LOOK AT THIS," Raven said in a tone that immediately had the hairs on the back of his neck standing up.

When she turned her laptop around so the rest of them could see the screen, Hawk felt his blood turn to ice. "That looks like dad, only I know it can't be because he has a scar on his cheek that dad never had." Something in the man's eyes said he was bad news. He'd seen that empty, cold look before, in the eyes of men he had killed, men who thought nothing of killing anyone who got in their way, who would use women and children as shields and distractions, who would do anything to get the upper hand.

"Who is it?" Eagle asked.

"His name is Sean Murphy, but I would swear on my life that he's related to us. He looks exactly like dad did. It has to be one of his brothers who I hadn't been able to track down, one of them was called Sean," Raven told them.

"How did you find him?" Falcon asked.

"I didn't. I mean not on purpose anyway. I was looking into Maddy and her family, trying to gather as much information as I could because I wanted to see if I could figure out if the serial killer might be after her because she was onto him or because she herself lost a parent to a violent crime when she was a child. Wondered if that was how she ended up on the killer's hit list, and as I looked into it, I found a picture of her at her mother's second wedding. This is the man her mom married. Sean Murphy. Irish, just like dad's family. Looks just like dad. Has the same name as one of dad's two brothers I haven't been able to find."

Acid burned in his gut.

Could Maddy's stepfather be his uncle?

Could Sean be the family member who had organized his parents' murders? The man who was now after him and his siblings?

"What does Sean Murphy do?" he asked. The man must be wealthy because Maddy had mentioned that she was sent to boarding school, and that she had a trust fund she hadn't touched but had intended to use to pay for Prey's services. Her mother wasn't wealthy, she'd been a stay-at-home mom, and Maddy's father had been a cop. They weren't poor but weren't rich enough for boarding school and trust funds.

"Imports and exports," Raven replied.

"Perfect cover for dealing weapons," Eagle said thoughtfully. "We need to find out if he is the missing uncle, the one who wants us all dead."

If he was, what did that mean?

Was it a coincidence that Maddy had been in that bar that night?

Was it a coincidence she had wound up pregnant with his child even though they'd used a condom?

Was it a coincidence that she'd shown up here right as she was about to give birth begging for help?

Hawk massaged his temples where a headache was currently pounding.

Just a few hours ago he had been laughing at his painting skills as he and Maddy worked on their son's nursery. It was almost done, another day and they'd have it finished, another after that for the paint to dry and the smell to dissipate, and then they'd be able to move Louie into his room. A room he had already been picturing changing as Louie got older. Maybe he'd want dinosaurs on the walls when he was in preschool, and then sports motifs as he got older still. The crib would change to a single bed, and then probably a queen as Louie grew bigger. The stuffed animals would become basketballs and baseball bats, and instead of adorable onesies folded in a drawer in the dresser there would be jeans and shirts tossed haphazardly on the floor.

Now everything felt different.

Tainted.

The DNA test proved he was Louie's father but was Louie's mother who she claimed to be or had Madeline Montgomery fooled everybody, including him?

"What does it mean if he is?" Hawk asked, his voice strangled. Had it been the woman he'd been falling for who'd had her hands on him just this morning, or the hands of an evil con woman working with the man who wanted his entire family destroyed?

"It doesn't necessarily mean anything," Raven said in a soothing voice. "Don't go getting ahead of yourself. Even *if* Sean Murphy is really our uncle Sean Oswald, and even if he is dealing weapons and after us, it doesn't mean that Maddy knows anything. So far, we've been able to verify everything she's told us. There is a serial killer in San Francisco, and he has been murdering women who lost their parents to violent crimes. She also was almost killed, witnesses backed up her story. I also checked into the motel she said she stayed at and there were reports of a broken door on her room and shots fired the night she left. Nothing she's said has been untrue, so there's no reason to believe she might be here for any other reason than for help."

Yet the doubt didn't leave him.

He'd never believed in forevers. He'd seen too many of his friends' marriages end in disaster to believe that there was any such thing as true love. But then Maddy had come along and changed everything.

At least that's what he'd thought.

Only now he was facing the possibility of a very different future than the one he'd believed was ahead of him this morning when he'd woken with Maddy's hand wrapped around him.

"Could she be the killer?" Falcon asked quietly.

Hawk's mouth dropped open as he turned to stare at his brother.

Believing that Maddy was involved somehow in the plot to take the Oswald family down was one thing, but to think she was a deranged serial killer was quite another.

Acid burned inside him.

Falcon shrugged. "Just saying, she fits her own profile."

"She's not," Raven said with such confidence Hawk found himself relaxing. "She wasn't in town for the first two murders. She was on the other side of the country consulting on a completely different case. No way she did it."

Hawk nodded, sagging into his chair, feeling like he had just run a marathon.

"What do we know about her father and sister's murders?" Eagle asked.

"Maddy was nine, at softball practice with her mom. Her dad was taking little sister Deirdre to get snacks for the team. They never showed up. Mom got a call on the way home to say their bodies had been found discarded at the side of a road. Theory was the dad had stopped to help someone and been taken out by a killer working the area at the time who killed cops. They assumed the sister was taken out simply because she saw the killer's face. Their working profile of the police officer killer was a young male, eighteen to twenty-five, recently arrested or incarcerated, taking out his anger on the police force. Maddy changed that. Even at nine, she possessed the ability to read people and situations. She insisted her dad would never allow himself to be vulnerable to a man, not when one of his daughters was with him. Said he wouldn't have pulled over to help a stranded man, he would have called in for help instead, but he would have stopped for a woman. Said she'd seen a woman hanging around him in the park the previous week at softball practice. Turns out she was right. The killer was a middle-aged woman whose husband had been shot by a stray bullet during a convenience store hold-up," Raven told them.

While part of him ached to feel sorry for the little girl who had lost so much so young and yet still been brave enough and strong enough to help the cops solve the case and save lives. Another part of him wondered if all she had been through had hardened her, changed her, turned her into a woman who could easily betray and manipulate people.

"Was Maddy in any financial trouble? Drugs or alcohol problems? Any boyfriend who could have been used to force her hand? Is her mother safe? Could her stepfather have threatened to hurt her if Maddy didn't do what he wanted?" Hawk was clutching at straws, and he knew it, looking for ways to excuse Maddy's betrayal before they even knew anything concrete.

"I'll look into everything, I promise," Raven assured him.

"What we need first is proof that Sean Murphy is Sean Oswald. Once we have that, we can start digging into his life, see if we can find proof that he's trafficking weapons. Then we'll look and see if it's at all possible he sent Maddy here as a mole as part of his plan to get to us," Eagle said, casting him a pitying look.

"And if she is?" he asked, already knowing the answer.

"If she is we do what we always do," Eagle replied. "Whatever it takes to protect our family."

Whatever it took.

Was he really capable of that when it might mean hurting or even killing the mother of his child?

* * *

5:47 P.M.

MADDY HUMMED off key as she bustled about the kitchen, cooking dinner. She might be good at painting and drawing, but she was a terrible singer, not that Louie seemed to mind, he was in his bassinet snoring away. It was such a cute little snuffly sound, one that she would be quite happy to listen to all day every day.

Hawk had gone into Prey's offices for a meeting around lunchtime, and while she'd expected him to be back before now the extra time just meant she could make sure everything was extra special. She'd found a nice tablecloth buried in the back of a china cabinet and put it on the table, she'd found candles and good crockery and had the table all set. She's called Raven to ask her what Hawk's favorite food was, and although the older woman had seemed a little off on the phone, she'd told her Hawk loved fried chicken, steamed vegetables, and mashed potatoes, so that was what Maddy was making.

The chicken was almost finished in the air fryer, the vegetables were just soft without falling apart, and the potatoes were ready for mashing. If Hawk wasn't home soon the dinner was going to ruin. Louie had been fed, so hopefully he'd get home and they'd have a couple of hours to enjoy together before the rugrat woke and interrupted them.

Turning off the stove, Maddy carried the pot of potatoes to the sink and drained them, then just as she added some butter and got the masher ready, the lift dinged.

Perfect timing.

"Hey, you're home," she said brightly as footsteps sounded a moment later and a shadowy figure filled the doorway.

When the figure didn't reply she looked up mid-mash to find Hawk channeling his inner Falcon and glowering at her.

Was something wrong?

"What is it?" she demanded, letting the masher fall from her hands where it hit the granite countertop before clattering to the floor.

Instead of answering, he stalked across the room, only not in a sexy way like he had last night after his siblings left. This was a scary kind of stalk, like a predator approaching its prey.

He set a photo down on the counter in front of her and then stared at her.

With a shaking hand, she reached out and picked up the picture, startled when it was the one of her, her mother, and stepfather taken at their wedding.

"Why do you have this?" she asked thoroughly confused. And why was he acting all angry with her? She hadn't done anything wrong.

"Who is he?" Hawk asked.

"It's my stepfather. His name is Sean Murphy. Why?"

"Sean Murphy, huh? Not Sean Oswald?"

"Oswald? As in your family? My stepfather is related to you?"

"You tell me. Is he?"

"I have no idea. Why would I? I barely know him. I lived in that house for less than four months before being sent away to boarding school. In the next eight years, I came home a total of maybe ten times. I haven't seen him or been back to Ireland since I graduated high school. And why are you asking me questions about ...?" Maddy trailed off as a horrible thought occurred to her. Of all the coincidences in the world could it really be true? "Is he the relative after your family?"

"You tell me," Hawk said again. "Is there a reason you entered my life right around the time someone was trying to kill my siblings?"

She had to force the words out past the lump in her throat. "Are you accusing me of being in collusion with my stepfather to destroy your family?"

"Pretty big coincidence, don't you think? Someone tries to abduct my sister Raven and her daughter Cleo, they manage to escape, but when Falcon goes after Hope they're almost killed. Then Sparrow was threatened, and her helicopter shot down. Then all of a sudden there you are, hitting on me, and getting pregnant with my child, turning up here with a sob story about being stalked. Got you easy access, didn't it?" he sneered.

Maddy didn't even know what to say to that. "You can't honestly believe that."

"I don't know what to believe right now."

"I didn't even know who you were that night, and *you* hit on me."

"So you say."

"We used protection. How could I have known I'd wind up pregnant?"

"Maybe you did something."

"It was *your* condom." She couldn't even believe they were having this conversation. Tears threatened to spill down her cheeks, but she held them back. This had to be some sort of horrible nightmare. Maybe she'd fallen asleep after she put Louie down. There was no way the special night she'd planned could turn out like this. No way could the man she was falling for, had already been thinking she would spend her life with, accuse her of doing such awful things. "You really think I would do that? Work with Sean to infiltrate your family, use my own son—*your* son—to do it? That I would come here to help get you and your siblings killed? If you think I'm capable of that then you don't know me at all."

"I'm beginning to realize that."

She nodded sadly, her heart breaking into a million pieces.

She'd been wrong. Here wasn't home and it wasn't safety. It was like everything else. An illusion.

"If you truly believe that then I think it's a good idea that Louie and I leave."

Faster than she'd ever seen anyone move, Hawk was between her and the bassinet holding their son. "You are not taking my son anywhere."

Her heart stuttered in her chest. "I'm Louie's mother."

"And I'm his father. You even think about taking him from me, and I guarantee you won't like the consequences. I will do anything to keep him in my life. *Any*thing. Including using my money to pay off a judge to grant me custody."

Her stomach dropped at his cold words. Right now, the man she'd been falling for was gone. In his place was a man chillingly similar to the stepfather who had terrified her. Sean had thought he could throw his money around to get what he wanted too, and he hadn't cared who he hurt as long as he got his way.

"Y-you wouldn't d-do that," she stammered.

"Try me, sweetheart." The endearment was said with a sneer, and the man before her wasn't even recognizable as her Hawk. This man was a stranger. One who was threatening the one thing she loved the most in the world.

Stepping closer she met his gaze through tears that made him shimmer, only these tears were part sadness, part terror, and part anger that he would threaten to hurt their child by cutting her out of his life. "You try to take my son, and I will claw your eyes out. I won't let my baby be bought and sold like a piece of meat. He's a person, a sweet innocent little baby, one who needs his mother. I haven't done anything wrong. I didn't know that Sean might be your uncle and I certainly haven't been working with him. I had no idea who you were when we slept together, and I certainly didn't come here to get people killed. I came because Prey was the best, I trusted you to keep me and my unborn baby alive. Now I know better. Prey isn't the best. They're just a bunch of spoiled rich people who use their money to get what they want, not caring who they hurt in the process. I thought you were different," she said softly. "I thought you cared, that you liked me, I thought you were a good guy. I felt safe with you. Now I see you're just like Sean. I guess he really is your uncle."

"I am *nothing* like that man," Hawk hissed.

"Keep telling yourself that, but all I know is right now you're acting exactly like him. I heard him buying people off on the phone one night when he thought I was sleeping. Making deals, and threats, throwing money around like it was the most important thing in the world. But it's not. Love is. Family. Belonging. I thought you were going to be my family, I thought I belonged here, but this isn't any place I want to be. I'd rather spend the rest of my life alone. I'm taking Louie to a hotel. When you calm down, we can work out a schedule for who gets him on what days. If you try to take me to court, I will fight you. I might not have your name or your money, but that is my baby, and he is all I have. I will fight for him until my death. He is everything to me, don't cause him pain by taking him from me, one day he'll hate you for it. I'm going to pack us a bag."

As she walked past him and into the hall, she couldn't hold back the tears any longer. They flooded down her cheeks as a cyclone of pain raged inside her. Now she was back on her own, fighting off a serial killer who wanted her dead, fighting her stepfather who might use her to hurt the Oswalds, and fighting for her son.

She'd had it all only to lose it a second time.

* * *

6:07 P.M.

As Hawk watched Maddy walk off down the hall to pack a bag, he couldn't help but feel he was making a huge mistake.

One there might be no coming back from.

Did he really believe that Maddy had come here to betray him? That this had been a setup from the very beginning?

He thought back to that night almost nine months ago. Maddy hadn't once glanced his way when she entered the bar, nor had she seemed particularly comfortable being there. If she had been sent in as a lure to hook him, then she hadn't come in with the right attitude. Normally he was attracted to confident, self-assured women, and that wasn't the Maddy who had entered that bar.

Hawk couldn't even say what had caught his attention,

there was just something that drew his eye to her, and the rest was history.

The Maddy of that night had explained to him that she had a job that took up most of her time, but her friends had insisted she needed a night off which was why she was there. She'd told him she didn't date much, and he suspected she wasn't very experienced, making him reluctant to take her to bed for the night which was his usual custom when he went out looking to hook up.

Those suspicions she wasn't experienced had been confirmed when they had sex.

The morning after had been awkward as expected, but was it because Maddy had wanted more and been upset that he hadn't offered more, or because she was feeling guilty or had she just been acting, and he was yet to meet the real Maddy?

A headache was battering around inside his head. His gut told him that he knew Maddy and that she would never do anything like this, but his head screamed at him that facts were facts.

What were the chances that Maddy's stepfather was almost definitely his uncle and the man who had tried repeatedly to kill his siblings, and she turned up in his life, pregnant with his child, but wasn't here to do her uncle's bidding?

He didn't believe in coincidences that big.

Yet, he couldn't shake the feeling that Maddy wasn't that kind of person.

She had to have been blackmailed into this. She made a decent living, and while she wasn't wealthy, she certainly wasn't wanting. She would have been able to swing being a single parent without struggling too much. There had been no boyfriend in her recent past—he knew that because Raven and Olivia had gone through Maddy's life all over again once they knew who her stepfather was and hadn't found anyone—so if her stepfather had threatened someone in her life it wasn't a partner.

Which left her mother.

By Maddy's account, she wasn't close with her mother anymore, and again what Raven and Olivia had dug up suggested that to be true, Maddy hadn't been to Ireland since she graduated high school, just like she'd said, but that didn't mean she didn't love her mom. Nor did it mean she wouldn't do whatever she had to to keep her mom safe.

That had to be it.

And if that was the case, then all she had to do was tell him, and he'd make sure that nothing happened to her or her mother.

He looked up as Maddy re-entered the kitchen. She had a suitcase handle in one hand, and her other arm was wrapped around her middle as though protecting herself from further pain.

Pain *he* had caused.

Coming home tonight when his emotions were all over the place hadn't been a good idea. In fact, his siblings had told him that if he couldn't handle himself right now around Maddy to make an excuse and not go home at all.

But he'd come because he needed to confront her, needed to hear what she was going to say, needed to try to figure out if she had betrayed him or not.

Only here he was, standing beside her and he had no idea.

All he knew was that Maddy was hurting, and he wanted to fix it. It was stupid, she could be a dangerous woman, and while he could have handled things better—threatening to pay off a judge to secure custody of their son was not one of his finer moments and something he regretted—he was pretty sure there was no fixing things between them, even if she was innocent.

Which means he could have just lost the best thing to ever happen to him.

In his world, marriages always ended in disaster, but this had to top the list.

"Maddy," he started.

"Don't," she said, interrupting him. She wouldn't meet his gaze, but he didn't know if that was from guilt or because she was hurt and upset. "I can't."

Hawk nodded because what else could he expect from her right now?

The longer he spent in her presence, the less he believed she'd done what he accused her of. Maybe her staying at a hotel was for the best right now. It would leave him with a level head so he could figure this out without letting his feelings for Maddy sway him.

Logical.

This required him to be logical, and he just couldn't do that when he looked at the pain in those pretty hazel eyes that had hooked him the moment they'd met his.

Without another word, he moved Louie to the baby car seat and picked it up. Letting his son leave felt wrong, but for now, Louie needed Maddy, and as much as he hated that, he wasn't going to hurt Louie by keeping him here. It was only for the night, Raven and Olivia were working on looking for anything that suggested Maddy was guilty, and he'd see Louie tomorrow, and spend some time with his son.

Still, there was always a chance if Maddy was guilty she would run, so he surreptitiously stuck a tracker on the baby car seat as they headed for the lift. If Maddy ran, she had to take the car seat with her, and if she did, he'd be able to track them down.

Hating feeling this way about the woman he'd been falling for, hating doubting her, hating hurting her, hating letting her go, hating letting his son go, hating every single thing about this mess, but hating his uncle most of all, Hawk followed Maddy into the lift.

The ride down was quiet, the air crackling with tension, and not the good kind, not the sexual tension that had crackled between them every second of the last few days. This tension was the kind that made your stomach roll, your head pound, and the world feel like it had spun out of control.

The car ride to a nearby hotel that had good security was filled with the same tension, and it was almost a relief when he pulled up outside it.

Almost.

But not completely because he was about to let Louie and Maddy walk away.

If Maddy wasn't dangerous, if she had come to Prey simply to seek help dealing with a psychotic serial killer stalker, he was leaving her alone and unprotected. Hawk had to remind himself that there was no tracker on her—except the one he had planted—so if she was being stalked then there was no way the killer could track her here.

She would be fine here for the night.

Maddy climbed straight out of the car and then opened the back door to get her suitcase and the baby car seat out. She shut the back door but paused before closing the passenger one. Her eyes met his squarely, the tears shimmering in them about destroyed him, but her voice when she spoke was clear.

"I didn't do anything wrong, Hawk. I don't even know my stepfather. He was never really part of my life, it's why I never touched the trust fund. I didn't want anything from him, but my baby's safety took precedence, and I was willing to spend it to hire Prey. All I was looking for that night in the bar was someone to chat with for a few hours. If it had been anyone but you, I wouldn't have gone home with them. I thought you were special. My mistake, but one I won't repeat. I hope you're able to find whoever has it out for your family, and if it's Sean, I hope you make him pay. I'm rescinding my request for Prey's assistance, but I would never keep you from your son, all I ask is for the same respect. I don't have money for a fancy lawyer so I'm hoping we can come to a fair arrangement. Whatever you think of me don't hurt Louie. He deserves his mom and his dad in his life."

Maddy closed the door without waiting for his response, and he battled his seatbelt to scramble out of the car. "Wait."

She stilled but didn't turn around.

"Prey will pay for the hotel room, and we'll continue working the serial killer case," he assured her.

She was right, if nothing else they shared a son, and despite the accusations he'd flung at her, she wasn't threatening to take Louie away from him. Shame at his own threats earlier beat down upon him. It was obvious she was hurt, but she was trying to be the bigger person, set it aside, and put Louie first.

"Thank you for the offer, but I no longer trust Prey," she admitted, still without turning around.

He wasn't fighting with her about it, but he intended to make sure that Prey kept working the case whether she trusted them—or really him—or not. "Can I say goodbye to Louie?"

"Of course, he's your son." She finally turned and held out the car seat.

Hawk reached in and picked up his son, cradling the baby in the crook of his arms. "Hey, rugrat, you're going to spend the night in another new place, but your mom is with you, so there's nothing to worry about. I'm going to see you real soon though. There's one thing I always want you to remember, and that is that your daddy loves you and will never be going anywhere. Never. I am always going to be there for you, and I will never let anyone take you away from me. I love you so much." He pressed a kiss to his son's soft little head before setting him back in the car seat.

Maddy didn't wait, just turned, and walked inside without looking back.

Earlier when she had walked out of the kitchen to pack, Hawk had worried that he was making a mistake.

He was no longer worrying about that.

He was sure he was.

Either Maddy was innocent, or she had been blackmailed into helping Sean. Whichever it was, he was pretty sure their chance at happiness had been disintegrated.

CHAPTER TEN

October 18th

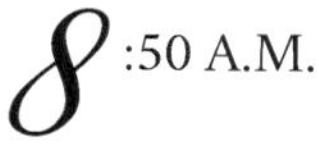:50 A.M.

"Good morning, Maddy," Olivia Oswald greeted her as she walked in the front door to Prey's offices.

She'd been summoned.

A phone call at eight this morning asking—although it felt more like an order—her to come down to the office at nine to answer a few questions.

Her trust in these people had been shattered.

Decimated.

It had taken everything she had not to run last night. If she'd had somewhere to go she might have.

No.

That was a lie.

As much as she longed to get as far away from Hawk and his family and the heartache they'd brought her, she wouldn't do that to her son. She was serious about sharing custody with Hawk. She would never hurt her child by denying him his father. Maddy knew that loss far too personally, and she would never inflict that kind of pain and suffering on Louie.

So, she was stuck here.

For now, she couldn't leave the city, but she absolutely would be leaving these offices as soon as humanly possible.

"Morning," she said because it had been drilled into her as a child to be polite, so manners were ingrained enough to be automatic.

"Want me to look after the little guy for you until Hawk gets here?" Olivia asked.

Instinct had her tightening her hold on Louie's stroller, not quite as good as holding her son himself but better than nothing. Trust was gone between her and the Oswald family, and while Olivia might not be blood-related, she had married Eagle and given him a daughter. Her loyalty was to them, not to her and Louie. Hawk's threat had replayed in her head all night as she tossed and turned. Would he really do it? And if he tried, how could she stop it from happening?

"It's okay, I'll stay here where you can see me," Olivia said as though sensing her hesitancy to let Louie go. But that was something she was going to have to get used to. Even if Hawk didn't steal him, she was going to have to share custody, which meant there would be a lot of handing her baby off and leaving him.

With a slow nod, she handed the stroller over to Olivia. May as well get used to this feeling now. "Where am I going?"

"In there." Olivia pointed to the same room she'd been taken to the first time she came here. She already knew that none of Prey's clients were allowed off the first floor, so it seemed she was back to a nobody again in the Oswald family's eyes.

No, not a nobody.

A traitor.

"Why don't you go in? Eagle, Raven, and Falcon will be in soon," Olivia suggested. "I'll stay right here with Louie until Hawk comes."

"I fed Louie just before I left, and I pumped some breastmilk, it's in a refrigerated bag, so Hawk can give him his next feed." Touching a lingering kiss to Louie's cheek, she walked into the room and took a seat at the table. Hawk had asked to spend the afternoon with Louie, and she suspected that the interrogation she was about to endure would last all day.

Straightening her spine, she pretended she wasn't terrified out of her skin.

If only she hadn't come here.

Maddy had known what she was missing out on. She'd been old enough when she lost her family to have plenty of memories of them, so she'd known that being alone sucked. Hawk and his family had given her a little taste of what it was like to belong again, but then just like it had when she was nine, the rug had been ripped out from underneath her.

If Hawk believed that she was capable of the things he'd accused her of then he didn't know her at all, and all her dreams of a happy future had been just that; dreams.

From her seat she watched as Olivia tapped away on a laptop keyboard, her foot gently rocking Louie's stroller. She was so busy watching the somewhat soothing movement that she didn't notice the others enter the room until a door closed.

Startling, she turned to find Eagle, Raven, and Falcon taking seats. While there was no outright hostility from any of the three of them, they had to believe the same things that Hawk did. They'd called her down here after all, which meant right now they were the enemy. Between the serial killer, worrying Sean would come after her because of the connection she now had to his family, and worrying the Oswalds would steal her son, she was wound as tightly as it was possible to be.

Somehow, she managed to wait them out, not blurting out something stupid that they would likely twist until they spoke first.

"You know this man, correct?" Eagle asked, setting down a different photo of Sean than the one Hawk had shown her last night.

"It's Sean Murphy, my stepfather. Although Hawk told me you think he might be your uncle," she replied.

"He is," Raven said with a decisive nod. "Once I had a name to work with, I was able to find when he petitioned the court to legally change his name. He's Sean Oswald, our father's brother."

"What do you know about him?" Eagle asked.

"He's in import and export. He's rich, lives in an old castle he converted himself. It's a beautiful building. He met my mom just two months after my dad died when she got stuck in the rain when our car broke down. She was immediately enamored by his wealth. I don't know what he saw in her. He doesn't like little kids, or at least he didn't like me. Has no kids of his own. Sent me off to boarding school to get rid of me, but he did set up a trust fund that I had never touched but will use to settle your bill. Sean is well-liked where he lives. He donates a lot of money to charity, has done a lot for the town where he lives," she said, rattling off some facts she was sure they already knew, but they had asked so she had answered.

"That's not what I meant," Eagle said. "I meant, what do you *know* about him from the time you spent with him."

"I didn't spend much time with him," she prefaced. When

Eagle nodded, she continued, "He terrified me to the point I would drag my dresser in front of the door every single night I spent in his house, and I was somewhat relieved to be shipped off to boarding school."

"What made him scare you?" Raven asked not unkindly.

Maddy shrugged. It was hard to put it into words because it had been more of a feeling. He hadn't hit her, hadn't sexually assaulted her, hadn't even yelled at her, but he made her skin crawl, her stomach churn, and something tingle in her very young and developing gut instincts. "I don't know exactly. Something about him just told me he wasn't a good guy. He didn't spend much time with me when he was dating my mom, and they were married six weeks after they met, just over three months since my dad and DeeDee had died. I didn't want a new dad, and I certainly didn't want to leave our house and move to Ireland, but Sean lived in a castle, and even I had to admit it was cool. I would spend hours exploring it."

"You heard or saw something," Falcon said, speaking for the first time.

She nodded. "There were these secret passages, and I was exploring them one day. One must have had a door that led to Sean's office because I could hear him on the phone. He was yelling at someone, saying he would get what he wanted, and he didn't care how much it took to get the job done." Apparently, the apple didn't fall far from the tree because Hawk had also threatened to throw money at something to get what he wanted. Only the thing he wanted was her baby. Maddy cast a look out the window to see Olivia still rocking the stroller and typing away on her laptop. Reassured she continued. "A couple of weeks later I had moved on to exploring outside. The woods surrounding the castle were magical, and I was kind of hoping I would find fairies or something. I mean, I was nine, so I knew there was no such thing, but that place kind of made you believe in magic. Anyway, I didn't find fairies. I found a huge stash of guns."

"He was trafficking weapons, just like Sparrow was told," Eagle said.

"I assume he was," Maddy agreed. "Only I was nine back then so I just thought he used them when he couldn't use his money to get what he wanted. About two days after that Sean suggested that I go to boarding school. I didn't want to leave my mom, but I also didn't want to stay. I was afraid he would get past the dresser and into my room one night and shoot me." Maybe there had been more to it than that. There was something in the way Sean looked at her that made her feel uncomfortable only she had been too young at the time to realize what it was. Now she knew though. Lust. It had been lust. "I was a reminder of what she'd lost, so my mom didn't argue. I think she wanted to get rid of me. So, I was sent away. The boarding school sent everyone home over Christmas, so I went back over the holidays for those eight years, and I think I went home for two birthdays. That was it. After I graduated, I moved back here and haven't seen Sean since. So, I know you all think I'm working with him, but I wouldn't do that, and he wouldn't reach out to me. I don't know how else to convince you of that."

And that was the root of her fear.

How did you prove yourself innocent of something you didn't do?

These people were Oswalds. They were rich. Why would she believe they were any different than their uncle? He used his money to get his way, they would too. They could have her charged with crimes she hadn't committed, locked up, and then they would snatch her baby, and Maddy had no idea how to stop it from happening.

* * *

10:32 A.M.

He and Maddy agreed he would pick Louie up at Prey at eleven and spend a few hours with him, but Hawk couldn't wait a single second longer.

Maddy had been asked to come to Prey to answer some questions about her stepfather, and it bothered him that he wasn't sitting there beside her, supporting her.

Not that she'd want his support after the way he'd acted the day before.

That bridge was burned, and the best he could hope for going forward was that they could co-parent Louie without argument because he wasn't sure he could cut his son's mother out of Louie's life. It didn't seem fair to Louie, who hadn't done anything wrong. And if Maddy had done what he'd accused her of he was sure it was because she had been backed into a corner.

Maybe what bothered him most was that she hadn't confided in him and come to him for help.

Okay, so when she'd first arrived at Prey they hadn't known each other very well, but they'd spent days together, making out, caring for their son, surely she had figured out that if she was in trouble he would have moved heaven and earth to help her. Yeah, he would have been mad about her manipulating him, but he would have understood that she was protecting someone, probably her mom the only relative she had left. After all, there wasn't anything he wouldn't do to protect his family.

Instead of finding Maddy waiting with the baby, he found Olivia sitting on one of the couches in the foyer, tapping away on her laptop, a stroller beside her, gently rocking it with her foot.

Guess he wouldn't be seeing Maddy today.

Regret hit him hard. He missed her. Last night he hadn't been able to sleep without her soft body snuggled beside him. How could he have become so accustomed to her in just a few days?

It defied logic, but it was what it was.

"Where's Maddy?" he asked Olivia as he headed straight for the stroller and immediately scooped up his son, snuggling the baby close and feeling a piece of his soul settle.

"Still in there," Olivia replied, nodding her head at the conference room while she shut her laptop.

"Still?"

"Guess she has a lot to tell them."

"Has she admitted to working with her stepfather?"

"No, she's sticking with the same exact story she told you. She says she barely knows her stepfather, he scared her, and she was banished to boarding school to barely return. Hawk, it's not my place … and we don't know each other as well as I know the rest of your siblings … but we're family and …"

"It's okay, Liv. Tell me what you need to say."

"I've been through her life with more detail than any other case I've ever done since I came to Prey because I know Maddy is important to you, and I can't find any evidence that she's had any contact with her stepfather since she graduated high school. Even while she was in school neither he nor her mom called, wrote, or emailed. They sent money on her birthday, and on two of those birthdays she went home, and that was it. She gave me her phone and laptop. I went through them, there's no evidence on there that she contacted him. Could she have used a different email address just for contact, or a disposable cell for contact, I guess, but her financials don't show that. Other than when she took cash to run, she only uses her debit and credit cards, and there is no record of a disposable cell on either. Sean hasn't left Ireland in years, and neither has Maddy's mother, so they didn't meet in person. It's possible he sent someone else after her, but again I just don't think so. I don't think she's involved."

His sister-in-law had no idea how much he prayed she was right.

As much as he knew that Maddy was right when she said that fighting over Louie was only going to hurt him, if she really had played a role in trying to take down his family, how could he in good conscience consider himself a good father if he allowed her to be around his son? Wouldn't that wind up hurting Louie more? He only wanted to allow good influences around his sweet little boy, so his son grew up to be the kind of man who protected others, who was loyal, and compassionate, and honorable.

"I don't know, Liv. I want to believe that so badly, but what if I'm wrong? What if she has us all fooled? What if she's working with our uncle and winds up hurting Louie?"

"You really think she'd hurt her baby? Because she was almost in a panic leaving him here with me to wait for you to visit with him. Her eyes … there was betrayal in them. She doesn't trust any of us now, and she thinks you're the one who hurt her not the other way around. Remember how Eagle and I started? He was majorly wrong about me. Maybe you're majorly wrong about Maddy." Olivia gave him a smile and stood. "Maddy fed him before she brought him here. She said she pumped some milk and left it for you to try bottle feeding him."

His brow furrowed. "How did she pump milk? She didn't have one on her when I dropped her off." Hawk swore when he realized she must have ordered it last night and had it sent to the hotel. Doing so had risked her—and Louie's—safety because if there was a killer after her and he was tracking her then she'd just set off a flare alerting him to her location.

"Why would she do that? She had to have it sent to the hotel. Now she's back in the firing line."

Olivia shrugged and rested a hand on his shoulder. "Guess she was thinking about making it easier for you, so you can care for your son without her."

But had she done that to be nice or because she knew that she would end up dead if she betrayed Sean, or in prison if she had betrayed his family?

Her words from a few nights ago replayed in his head. She'd made a comment about moving Louie onto a bottle. At the time he'd thought it was just because she was afraid that the man after her would get her. Now he had to wonder if she had always known she would eventually be leaving Louie.

Collecting her laptop, Olivia disappeared up the elevator, no doubt to work in her office and try to find him proof that Maddy was clean. Really, the only way to do that was to find Sean and get him to confess the truth. Alone now, he rocked Louie, who still hadn't stirred. "You'll sleep through anything, huh, rugrat? Even a visit with your dad."

Hawk hated that that's how life with joint custody of Louie would go. It would always feel like his son was visiting him rather than living there. While he hadn't thought he'd wind up with a kid, if he did, this certainly wasn't how he'd envisioned it being. He'd thought he'd give his child a family like he'd had. His parents might have kept them completely off-grid, but their home had been a happy one, filled with love and laughter, and lots of time spent together.

He'd wanted to give Louie everything including a home with both his parents. Parents who loved one another and were happy together

What if he *was* wrong about Maddy?

What if she was telling the truth and had no idea about

the connection between him and her stepfather and he had accused her of something awful with absolutely zero proof?

If he was wrong and Maddy had come here for help, only to be treated the way she had, he would never forgive himself. He wouldn't blame her if she thought he was a bad influence on Louie and sought full custody.

Only he didn't think Maddy would do that.

She was too sweet, too attuned to other people. It was what made her great at her job but also set her up for heartbreak.

His mother had told him that his fiery temper might get him in trouble one day. Hawk didn't get angry often, ninety-nine percent of the time he was laid back and easy-going, but when he was set off he was like a firecracker. Eagle was the brother who always said things like he saw them, Falcon was the brother who kept his emotions on a tight rein, and he was the one who lost his temper and put his foot in his mouth.

Which he had done in epic proportions with Maddy last night.

CHAPTER ELEVEN

October 19th

:17 A.M.

"ASLEEP AGAIN ALREADY, HUH." Maddy huffed a small chuckle as she snapped the studs closed on Louie's little onesie. It was one of the ones she had bought back in San Francisco when she'd gone on a huge shopping spree for everything she'd need for the baby. She wished that sweet guy who had organized to have the baby things brought to Manhattan, along with some of her stuff, had stuck around.

Too bad Hawk wasn't the man she thought he was.

Still, he was Louie's father, which meant that they were bound together for the rest of their lives, so she was going to have to find a way to get along with him.

She was pretty sure she could do it. All she had to do was keep the focus always on their son. That meant not engaging if he decided to start yelling at her again, not letting it get personal, and if it came down to it, getting a lawyer to make sure everything was in writing.

Maddy prayed it didn't come to that. There was no way she could afford the kind of lawyer Hawk could, and his threat to take her son, lying and paying off a judge to do so, continued to play on a loop in her mind.

Would he really do it?

Yesterday after being grilled for hours by his older siblings, when she'd gone to collect Louie, she and Hawk had managed civility, and she could have sworn she saw regret in his eyes. But Maddy no longer trusted her ability to read people, she had to wonder if this new lack of confidence would affect her job, so she was sure she must have imagined it.

Wasn't like he had apologized.

Or really said anything other than to thank her for the breast milk so he could feed Louie, tell her she shouldn't have placed an order on her credit card, and then tell her that if she was in trouble, she should have told him.

Well, she had told him, and look how that had turned out.

She'd come here for help, thought she'd received it, only to be treated like a criminal by the family she'd thought might become her own.

Maddy supposed she ought to be grateful at least that he seemed to believe now that she had been blackmailed into helping her stepfather because he'd threatened her mom. Well that was the impression she'd gotten from Hawk's brothers and sister. That was marginally better than him just believing she was a bad person.

Still, it felt like cold comfort when she'd cried herself to sleep, the feelings of betrayal running so deep she was almost surprised she wasn't bleeding real blood.

"Okay, Mommy's little sleep monster, you going to be good if I leave you here and walk to the trash chute?" She had a room almost down the end of a corridor, and the trash receptacle was only four rooms down, no further really than taking trash out to the garbage bins if she lived in a house.

Even though he was a good sleeper, Maddy didn't want to chance waking him because she intended to take a long hot bath, hopefully relax enough to take a nap, so that when Hawk came at noon to pick Louie up she looked at least reasonably human and not the mess that she felt like. She also had to pump some more breast milk so Hawk could get Louie through the few hours he'd have him. Maddy was pretty sure it was only the fact that Louie was a newborn and needed nursing so often that Hawk had allowed her to bring their son to the hotel with her, but Louie wouldn't stay a newborn for long, and Hawk's attitude could spin on a dime.

Feeling slightly uneasy leaving Louie in the hotel room, even though she'd be gone all of a minute, she locked the door behind her. At least she could keep the door to their room in her line of sight the entire time. Maddy hurried down the hall to the trash chute. She dumped the dirty diaper and was almost back to her room when the door to the room next to hers opened. Not really expecting to see anyone she knew, Maddy was about to go on past when the figure stepped in front of her, blocking her path.

A moment of panic that something was between her and her son passed quickly when she realized that she did indeed know this person.

"Officer Martinez?" she said, recognizing the officer who had attended one of the serial killer crime scenes. It had been the first one Maddy had gone to after she was asked to consult, and she had interviewed everyone who had been there. When she was working on a case it became the focus of her life until it was solved, and she never forgot the face or the name of anyone involved, so she knew the woman even though they'd only met once.

"Good morning, Ms. Montgomery."

"What are you doing here?" There was no way it could be a coincidence that Maddy had fled San Francisco with a serial killer hunting her, only for someone connected to that very same case to show up in the hotel room next to hers.

"Detective Arlington asked me to come and collect you, there's been a break in the case, and he believes that you're in danger," Officer Martinez explained.

Maddy had to wonder why Detective Arlington would send a random officer to come and get her, but then she had suspected there was something romantic going on between the younger detective and Officer Martinez, so maybe that was why. "Detective Arlington and Detective Winters believed that my profile on the killer was incorrect. What changed that?"

"Detective Arlington found out some information on his partner. Apparently, Detective Winters lost his mother in a terrible car accident when he was twelve. She was killed by a drunk driver who killed fifteen people. When he learned this and realized that his partner had been the one who was adamant that they weren't looking for a cop he became suspicious. Found out that his partner had a whole file on you and hadn't wanted you to consult. He believes there's a chance that you could be in danger."

"Why not call me himself?" she asked. Something didn't feel right, and while she usually trusted her gut, it had been a little rusty lately, so she wasn't sure if this feeling was just because her nerves were so strung out.

"He would have, but Detective Winters has disappeared."

Panic clawed at her, and the need to see her baby was

overwhelming. Rushing past Officer Martinez, she unlocked the door to her room and hurried inside, relief flooding her when she saw Louie still safe and sound and fast asleep in his bassinet. "Does Detective Arlington think that his partner is coming after me?"

"Yes. He wants me to bring you back to San Francisco where he can put you into protective custody until his partner is found and apprehended."

Maddy's immediate response was that this was a fabulous excuse to get away from Hawk and his family. It was also proof that she hadn't lied and there had been someone after her, this wasn't all just some ploy made up by her stepfather. She no longer trusted Prey to protect her or keep her safe, and if Detective Winters was the killer, then this case would be closed as soon as he was found and arrested.

And yet she couldn't leave.

Bottom line was Hawk wouldn't let her take their son out of state, and she was afraid to do anything to antagonize him and cause him to lash out.

"I can't go with you," she told Officer Martinez.

For a moment the woman just stared at her as though the possibility that Maddy would decline protection was insane. "Why not?"

She gestured at her son. "Louie's father is here, and we're not together, he won't let me take him out of state, and I can't leave him behind. Maybe I should talk to Detective Arlington to see how progress is going to find his partner. And maybe he could talk to some local cops to see if they would be willing to post someone outside my hotel room?" The last thing she would do was go crawling to Prey and ask them to protect her. They'd probably laugh in her face and use it as evidence that she shouldn't be around Louie. No way was she going to give them ammunition to use against her.

"I'm sorry, Ma'am, my orders were to collect and bring

you back with me. I'm sure your child's father would understand that these are extreme circumstances."

Yeah right. Hawk definitely would not understand.

His words yesterday ran through her mind.

He had insisted that she reach out if she was in trouble, and although she knew he had meant to admit that her stepfather had blackmailed her, maybe she should tell him about this. After all, if she was in danger then Louie was in danger, and she would do anything to keep her son safe. Including sucking it up and telling Hawk and Prey about this new development and asking if they could help until Detective Winters was apprehended.

"I need to call Hawk," she announced, heading for the bedside table to get her cell phone.

Officer Martinez heaved a sigh like Maddy was deliberately trying to be annoying. "I'm sorry, Ms. Montgomery, I can't allow you to do that."

"What do you mean you ...?" The rest of the question died on her lips when she turned to find the officer holding a gun on her.

Her gut was definitely broken.

Maddy had been so worried about Hawk and the situation with their son that she hadn't noticed that the biggest threat of all was standing in the room with her.

11:48 A.M.

Once again, Hawk had held off for as long as he could, but the need to see his son had him heading up to Maddy's floor of the hotel early. More than twelve hours was a long time to go without being able to hold and kiss your baby.

If he wasn't lying to himself, Louie wasn't the only one he was desperate to see.

He'd messed up, he was willing to admit that. Maybe he could give himself the excuse that he had been trying to protect his family but he had gone about things all wrong. He should have sent a car, brought her to Prey and asked her questions calmly in a more neutral setting, rather than accusing her of horrible things in a place that had been becoming *their* home, not just his.

He also should have used his ears, listened to what Maddy had said, and given her the benefit of the doubt.

Hawk had let his belief that all marriages ended in betrayal and divorce cloud his judgment.

And he wasn't even basing his beliefs off all of his experience. Nothing but death would have separated his parents, nor could he imagine anything less than death ending his siblings' marriages. While he had several friends who'd had their spouses cheat on them while they were overseas serving their country, that hardly constituted all relationships.

He'd jumped to conclusions, let fear fuel him, and convinced himself of the worst even before he'd walked in the door and asked Maddy to give her side of things.

It was a mistake and one he was here to attempt to make the first step in rectifying.

Hawk was praying that what he held in his hands would be enough of a peace offering to at least get Maddy talking to him again.

As he approached Maddy's room he heard crying. Sounded like Louie was not a happy camper at the moment. Maybe the little guy missed his daddy. If Hawk played his cards right perhaps a reunion with Maddy wasn't completely off the table.

Reaching her room, he knocked on the door and waited.

When he didn't hear any sounds of her moving about in there, and Louie continued to wail, he felt his hackles rise.

Something wasn't right.

He knocked again, and when there was still no response, he swiped the card he'd sweet-talked the woman at the front desk into giving him and opened the door.

The room was empty. Maddy's suitcase was over by the window, her purse sat on the desk, her cell phone on the nightstand, the bed was unmade, and Louie lay in his bassinet on the couch, crying his little eyes out.

"Maddy?" he called as he dropped the envelope on the bed and picked up the baby. Where was she?

A horrible thought struck. Maddy wasn't …?

No.

Surely not.

And yet, she'd been under a lot of strain lately. She'd found out she was pregnant, thought she'd be raising the baby alone, then become embroiled in a serial case that had threatened her life. She'd run across the country, found him, then had things turn so disastrously wrong. Was it completely out of the realm of possibility that she might harm herself?

Unfortunately, it was not.

Making sure the baby's head was tucked against his shoulder—Louie might be a newborn and would never remember this, but if it was worst-case scenario, he still didn't want his son seeing his mother like that—Hawk hurried to the bathroom and threw open the door.

Empty.

Instead of feeling relief his anxiety only ramped up. Even if he still considered it a possibility that Maddy might have been coerced into helping her stepfather he believed she was at heart a good person. And certainly a good mother, there was no way she would walk away and leave Louie behind.

No way.

Which meant she hadn't walked out of here willingly.

Balancing the baby—who had stopped crying—with one hand, he fished his cell phone out of his back pocket. Before he could use it to call his siblings it began to ring.

Eagle's name was on the screen.

This couldn't be good.

"Maddy is gone," he said as soon as he answered.

"What?"

"I was supposed to be spending the afternoon with Louie. When I turned up, I could hear him crying, she's not in the room, and she wouldn't just leave him here alone."

"Not even if she knew you were coming and he wouldn't be alone long?"

"Eagle," he growled. After spending the last day and a bit trying to convince him that Maddy wasn't involved, his brother was suddenly jumping ship.

"Sorry, little brother, just want you to be sure, to know where your head's at."

"You were calling me, why?" His siblings knew he was spending the afternoon with his son, and they knew about his peace offering to Maddy. Eagle wouldn't be calling now unless it was something important. Something that couldn't wait.

"One of the detectives working the serial killer case disappeared two days ago. Just vanished without a trace. No signs of him at his house, hasn't been into work. Car is gone, cell phone and wallet inside, doors locked. It's like he just vanished into thin air. No unusual activity on his credit cards, nothing. He's just gone."

"The one who lost his mother to a drunk driver or the other one?"

"The one who lost his mother to a drunk driver."

"Did he leave to come after Maddy or foul play from

someone who wants us to think he left to come after Maddy?"

"We're looking into it," Eagle promised. "I'll have Olivia and Raven go through security footage from the hotel. If Maddy left we'll pick her up, hopefully get some answers."

Hawk was positive that Maddy had left. It was *how* she had left that was still in question. Would she really walk away and leave their newborn son behind? Hawk didn't believe that she would. Which meant she had either been forced into leaving or she had been taken out of here.

It was the taken out of here that left him near breathless.

She could already be dead, her body stuffed in a suitcase and removed from the premises or any number of other things.

"Hold it together, little brother," Eagle said, his voice a calm anchor in the raging storm inside Hawk's head.

"You hold it together when Olivia was taken?"

"No way. Totally lost it, ended up hitting Falcon."

Hawk huffed a laugh. "Falcon is annoying with his refusing to argue attitude. Wouldn't mind taking a swing at him myself right about now." While he certainly couldn't blame the way he'd treated Maddy on his older brother, Falcon's persistence in remaining wary of Maddy certainly hadn't helped. Falcon had been suspicious of her from the very beginning which made it so much easier to believe she might not be as innocent as she seemed.

"There you go," Eagle encouraged. "We're already getting ready to head out. Olivia is calling the hotel to ask for access to their security footage, it's quicker if we do it with their cooperation. Raven is calling the cops to report Maddy as missing. And Falcon is talking to Fox, checking in with him on the missing detective." Owen "Fox" LeGrand was a former SEAL whose wife had almost been killed because of a mole at

Prey. Now Fox and the team he'd served with in the SEALs ran Prey's West Coast offices.

While Hawk appreciated that his family, extended Prey family included, were coming together on this, it didn't ease the tightness in his chest.

Maddy thought he hated her.

She didn't know that he'd come today to try to apologize and do a little groveling.

She might never know that.

"We have everything covered. For now, all you need to do is take care of Louie and not fall apart," Eagle said.

"Easier said than done."

"Of course it is. But keeping faith right now is important as is keeping a level head. Maddy needs you, hold on to that thought when fear threatens to overwhelm you."

Holding onto Eagle's words, Hawk hung up and dropped down onto the bed, holding his son in his arms. "Can we do that, rugrat? Can we hold on to the fact that Mommy needs us to be strong for her right now?"

Fingering the envelope, he opened it and slid out the custody papers. He'd wanted Maddy to know that no matter what happened he regretted using their son as a weapon—would for the rest of his life—and that he wouldn't try to take Louie away from her. He'd had the papers drawn up last night, putting in writing the fact that they would share joint legal and physical custody. If she was able to find it in her heart to forgive him, the papers could be torn up as they'd wind up married anyway, but if she couldn't then at the very least he wanted to give her peace of mind knowing that he wouldn't try to take her baby from her.

Now all he prayed for was a chance to hold her again and tell her how sorry he was.

* * *

12:00 P.M.

THE CAR BUMPED over something sending Maddy flying up into the top of the trunk and then slamming back down again.

She'd been tossed about so much that her body felt like it was a mass of bruises.

Not that that was her main problem right now.

The plastic zip ties bit painfully into the tender skin of her wrists. At first, she'd thought having her hands slick with blood would help her slide them out of the plastic ties, but it hadn't. All it did was coat her fingers with blood making her attempts to locate the release button she knew was here somewhere that much more difficult.

A couple of times she'd thought she had almost found it, but the car had turned a corner or bumped over something, tossing her about and meaning she had to start all over. The fact that the car was traveling fast didn't help, even if she could get the trunk open, she was going to have to jump, and that wasn't going to be pretty.

Still, she'd do it.

She had to.

There were no other options.

Maddy would do whatever it took to get home to her son. Nothing else mattered to her. She would kill, maim, and make a deal with the devil if that was what it took. Nothing was more important than her sweet little baby boy.

There was no way she was going to continue the curse of making him grow up without a parent.

At least she had been nine when her dad was killed. She'd been old enough to remember him, how much he loved her, the fun times they'd had together, what it felt like to be part of a family and know you were safe and loved. But if she died now then Louie would never know her. She would just be the woman who gave him life, nothing more. There weren't even any photos of the two of them together because while she had taken probably at least a thousand photos of him already, none of them had her in them. She hadn't even thought about it. At the back of her mind she had probably thought there was plenty of time for family photos later, and she'd just taken a picture of him any time he'd done something cute. She couldn't even count on Hawk to talk about her to their son because he hated her and wanted her out of Louie's life.

He might actually get that wish.

Maddy shifted again, searching for the release switch that would save her life. Supposedly it would illuminate itself, but she couldn't see anything, making her job that much harder. If Officer Martinez had bound her hands in front of her, she'd have a better chance, but arms tight behind her back, in the dark, constantly thrown about, this felt impossible. It always sounded so easy when someone spoke about getting out of the trunk of a car, you just pull the release and voila, but in reality it was so much more difficult.

Reaching out with her fingers where she'd thought she felt something earlier, this time they connected. She pulled, the trunk lid lifted, and for once luck was on her side because the car slowed.

There was no time to think about it, run through scenarios, or worry about the pain that was about to come. Maddy had to act now if she didn't want to lose what might be her only chance to escape.

In a way, it was a blessing because it didn't give her time to freak out and talk herself out of it.

Using her shoulder to shove the trunk open, she swayed as the car swerved but didn't tumble back down.

Although the car had slowed, it was going fast enough

that she knew it wasn't going to be a pleasant landing. Hopefully, she wouldn't break any bones or knock herself out.

Or kill herself.

Maddy jumped.

The landing was harder than she'd thought it would be.

Tires squealed.

She had no time to worry that Officer Martinez was stopping the car, that she was armed, and was a cop so she would be a good shot. Maddy staggered to her feet, not an easy feat with her arms behind her and her body bruised and battered from being tossed around in the trunk.

They weren't out on some remote country road like she thought she would be. Instead, it seemed like they were in an abandoned industrial estate. There were no trees to hide her, and she couldn't see a road, just dilapidated buildings everywhere.

She ran as fast as she could. For the moment adrenalin was masking the pain, and for that she was eternally grateful. Still, she was a little uncoordinated and swayed as she ran toward the closest building.

It was that very incoordination that saved her when a bullet whizzed past.

Her heart couldn't beat any faster, at least that's what she had thought until that bullet slammed into the wall beside her.

She stifled a scream and shoved through a partially broken door, finding herself inside a large mostly empty room. Trash was strewn about, and it looked like druggies hung out there frequently if all the empty syringes were anything to go by. There was a door on the adjacent wall, and Maddy headed for that.

That door led to another room similar to the one she had just left, only this one had a staircase that led to what looked like an office of some sort, a large roller door that no doubt led outside, and another door on the opposite wall that probably led to another room.

Outside was her best bet.

Heading for the roller door, Maddy twisted so she could grab it with her bound hands, but it wouldn't move.

"No," she whisper-sobbed.

This wasn't fair. She had only been doing her job when she worked that case, and now she was going to die because she'd gotten too close to the killer.

"I know you're in here, Madeline, and we really don't have time for this," Officer Martinez called out from somewhere behind her.

Upstairs or downstairs?

Surely Officer Martinez would think she wouldn't want to trap herself by going up, so if she hid up there, the cop should keep checking from room to room, eventually assuming she'd headed outside and into one of the other half dozen or more buildings on the estate.

Maddy was halfway to the stairs when her ankle suddenly gave out.

Stifling a scream of pain, she clamped her teeth into her bottom lips and began to hobble for the stairs. She had to get up there. Had to hide and pray that Officer Martinez didn't find her.

Somehow, she made it to the top and into a large office. There was a large pile of discarded flattened cardboard boxes lying in the middle of the room, and she headed for them, dropping to the floor and piling them on top of her.

Her chest was heaving, her breathing loud and echoey in the empty room. Tears stung the backs of her eyes, but she held them back, not wanting to do anything that would give her location away.

"Come on, Madeline. Where are you?"

Time seemed to stand still.

Seconds ticked by with excruciating slowness.

Questions chased themselves around her mind. Why was Officer Martinez in such a rush? Where was the woman taking her? If she just wanted her dead, why not shoot her at the hotel? Maybe she didn't want a mess to clean up. Maybe the cop was going to make it look like Maddy had been mugged. Or worse, maybe she intended to make it look like Maddy had committed suicide.

The worst part about that was that Hawk might actually believe it.

Believe it and take it as an admission of her guilt.

"Aha." The word was accompanied by a swift kick that sent the boxes—her only layer of protection—scattering around the room, and Officer Martinez stood above her.

"Please," Maddy begged, scrambling backward, away from the cop. "You don't want to do this."

"Oh, I want to do it." Officer Martinez stepped closer, her eyes devoid of emotion, the gun in her hand steady as it pointed at Maddy's head. "You're one of us. One of the kids who grew up in the shadows of losing a parent to a monster. You lost your dad and sister, I lost my mom. My dad beat her, but she saved every cent she could and ran taking me and my baby brother with her. Those six months we were free were the best of my life, but he found us. Mom locked me and Timmy in the bathroom, but I heard everything, watched through the crack in the door as he raped her and beat her until she wasn't even recognizable anymore. The pain ..."

"Never goes away," Maddy finished softly. "Killing me won't change that. Nothing will. No matter how many kids like us you kill you'll still see those images inside your head, hear your mom's screams echo in your mind."

"Killing you would help, would give me a moment of peace, but he wants to use you first. He said if I brought you to him, he'd help me escape before I'm caught, give me a new identity, and help me get out of the country."

Maddy's stomach dropped. An awful feeling brewed inside her. She feared she knew exactly who had offered to help Tiana Martinez escape justice in exchange for Maddy's life.

Before she could ask who Officer Martinez was working with, the answer stepped through the door.

"Sean," she whispered. Unwitting though she'd been, she *had* been a pawn in her stepfather's game of revenge against Hawk and his family. He must have known she was pregnant with Hawk's baby—which was creepy in and of itself—then identified the serial killer before she could and sent Officer Martinez after her, hoping she would go running to Hawk.

"Where's the baby?" Sean asked Tiana.

The cop shrugged. "I don't like babies. I left him at the hotel."

"You left him?" Sean raged. "I needed them both. Her and the child. The perfect bait to finally get them where I wanted them." He raised a weapon and fired.

Tiana Martinez dropped.

Dead before she hit the floor.

It took Maddy a long moment to realize the screams she could hear were coming from her.

"Time to go home, Madeline," Sean said, looming above her, his blue eyes colder than ice. As terrified as she was of what Sean would do to her, worse was the fear that knowing if he got his hands on Hawk it would be all her fault.

* * *

5:39 P.M.

. . .

IT SUCKED BEING LEFT OUT, and yet Hawk had to admit that at the moment he was no good to Maddy.

Fear and guilt and regret had him in a choke hold, paralyzing him until he could barely function. All his efforts were going into taking care of Louie and trying not to fall apart. He was going to have to trust his family to do what they did and locate Maddy before it was too late.

If it wasn't already.

It all hinged on who had taken her and for what reason.

He had driven himself crazy all day, playing the what-if game. What if she had betrayed his family and her disappearance was related to that? What if the serial killer she had been running from had finally caught up with her? What if something completely unrelated to either, something completely random, was what had happened to her?

There were no answers to be found in that game, and all he'd ended up with was a raging headache. If it wasn't for Louie, for the fact that his son needed him, he would have already gone off the deep end, armed himself to the teeth, and gone hunting for his woman.

His woman.

No matter what had happened over the last few days, it didn't change anything. Maddy was his, and he would get her back. He'd made a mistake in accusing her without having all his facts, and that one mistake might wind up costing Maddy her life. If he hadn't been such an unreasonable jerk then she would have been safe here at his home, not alone and vulnerable at a hotel.

The lift doors opened, but he didn't bother lifting his head. The only person he wanted to see wasn't going to come walking through those doors so what was the point?

"You wouldn't answer my calls," Eagle said as he and Olivia, Raven, her husband Max, Falcon and his wife Hope, and Sparrow's fiancé Ethan all filed into his living room, filling the chairs but not *filling* the room.

The only one who could truly fill any room was his Maddy. She filled him, patched a hole inside himself he hadn't even known existed. Without her, his life, his future, and his heart felt empty. Never before had Hawk felt so alone in a room full of people.

"Been taking care of the rugrat," he said, nodding his head at Louie's bassinet on the coffee table. The only silver lining to the horrible storm cloud hovering above him was that his son was much too small to understand what was going on around him.

"We have news," Raven told him.

"Yeah?" he lifted his head to look at his big sister.

"We know who took Maddy," she told him.

"Serial killer or Uncle Sean?" he asked, a tentative flicker of hope igniting inside him.

"You know the woman on the hotel security footage?" Raven asked.

"Yeah. The one who held a gun on Maddy, you know who she is?" The footage Raven and Olivia had reviewed showed Maddy leaving the hotel with a woman around six-thirty this morning. The woman was walking unnaturally close behind Maddy, leading them to think she might be holding a gun on her, and after playing around with the film, Raven had managed to enlarge it enough to give them a glimpse of the weapon. Knowing that Maddy hadn't left of her own free will, that he hadn't hurt her so badly she'd taken her own life, that she hadn't left because of guilt or because she'd done what she'd come here for, had filled him with relief, but just as quickly with shame.

Shame for ever doubting the woman he had been falling in love with, and shame for his own actions and behavior that had driven a wedge between them.

"We IDed her as Tiana Martinez, an officer for San Francisco PD. She had a link to one of the cases, she was first on the scene for the third murder, and when we did a little digging into her past, we found out that her dad was an abusive drunk who beat her mom. Mom ran, taking Tiana and her little brother Timothy, but the dad tracked them down, raped and beat her to death while Tiana and her ten-month-old brother hid in the bathroom," Raven informed him.

"She's the serial killer," he said.

"No proof yet," Eagle said, "but a likely conclusion. SFPD is on it, searching for anything to tie her to the murders. For now, we know that the same day Maddy left to come here Tiana called in to take time off work. She claimed there was a family emergency. We're looking for footage from the shooting at the motel where Maddy spent the night before she met with us to confirm that Tiana followed her there."

"We're also checking to see if her prints match the partial found on the bomb that blew up the apartment at Prey," Olivia added.

"Seems like Tiana thought Maddy might be on to her, followed her here to try to take her out, but once you brought Maddy here she lost access to her would-be victim. She must have stayed in the city, and when Maddy ordered the breast pump and bottles the other night she got a hit on the credit card and checked into the hotel and waited for an opportunity to strike," Raven said.

"Detective Winters' body was found a couple of hours ago. He'd been shot, his body dumped in the trunk of his car, his car left at a shopping mall parking lot," Eagle told him.

"Tiana Martinez?" Hawk asked.

"She might have been trying to set up a scapegoat to take the fall for her crimes," Eagle agreed.

All of that information answered a lot of questions, but not the one he wanted the most.

None of it told him where Maddy was right now or if she was still alive.

"Why take Maddy instead of killing her in the hotel room?" he asked, more to himself than the others.

"Maybe she wanted to find out if Maddy had any proof she was the killer, or maybe she …" Eagle paused, met Hawk's eyes straight on, "maybe she needed space and privacy to do what she usually does to her victims."

Hawk gagged on the bile that burned his throat.

Lurching to his feet, he stumbled across the room.

Images of what Tiana Martinez had done to her victims flooded his mind.

Eyes cut out.

Ears clogged with concrete.

Drowned.

Turned into a macabre version of an angel.

Is that what the deranged serial killer had done to his beautiful, sweet Maddy?

"She wasn't working with Sean," he mumbled, unable to look at the others. He hated himself for thinking she had been for even a second.

"Of course she wasn't," Falcon said fiercely.

"You were the one who was wary of her in the beginning," he growled, whirling on his brother.

"It was the sensible thing to do. But I read every case file she ever worked on. She did a lot of good, was dedicated and hardworking, and fought more than once for the truth, going against what others believed to fight for the victims. No one who does that would suddenly turn traitor. Even if Sean had threatened her mom, she would have found a way to get help. She would have told us when she arrived, pretended to be doing what her stepfather wanted," Falcon said.

"I said horrible things to her." Hawk dropped his head to his hands, struggling to keep his lungs inflating with air. "She might have died believing I thought she was nothing but a traitor."

"You can't change the past, Hawk," Hope said quietly, crossing the room to stand before him. "All you can do is fight for her now. This was waiting for you downstairs." She handed him a box before ushering the others to the door. "You'll call us if you need us," the redhead said, an order not a suggestion and he found himself nodding.

Alone, he opened the box, already knowing what was inside. When Maddy had told him about how she had hidden one of her dad's telescopes and her baby sister's stuffed animal, so they didn't get thrown away with all the rest, he'd had someone find them at her place and send them to him, intending to surprise her with them.

Fury at his own stupid arrogance and bruised ago raged through him, and he threw the now empty box across the room. It hit a framed photo of him and his siblings, sending it crashing to the floorboards, the glass shattering.

The sound woke Louie, who startled with a wail.

Gathering up his son, he sat on the couch with Louie, the faded stuffed dog, and the telescope on his lap. All he had left of the woman he adored. Hawk picked up his phone from the coffee table and pulled up a picture of Maddy and Louie he'd taken just after their son was born. Maddy was still in bed, Louie had been checked out, cleaned up, wrapped in a pale blue blanket, and set in his mother's arms. Maddy hadn't realized he'd snapped a picture, but the look of awe, adoration, and pure unadulterated love on her face as she gazed down at her baby in her arms was a moment he couldn't resist capturing on film.

It was the only picture he had of Maddy and Louie together.

A sob built in his chest, gathering pace as it collected every emotion, every shred of guilt and shame, every ounce of fear until it exploded out of him in gut-wrenching sobs. Hawk didn't cry, not since he was ten years old and his parents had been murdered, but his very heart had just been ripped away from him, was possibly already gone for good, and it was all because of him.

CHAPTER TWELVE

October 20th

2:24 A.M.

THE CABIN of the plane was nice. Luxurious, beautifully furnished, comfortable leather chairs, plenty of room, and even a bed in the back. Maddy had flown first-class several times, although he hadn't cared about her, her stepfather had still paid for first-class tickets every time she'd gone back to his house for Christmas, but first-class had nothing on this private jet.

Too bad she couldn't enjoy it.

Her wrists were still bound with plastic zip ties, but now in front of her, another zip tie fixing them to the seat. She was still wearing the same leggings and oversized t-shirt she'd been wearing last night, and the sneakers she'd shoved her feet into when she'd headed out into the hotel corridor to take Louie's dirty diaper to the garbage chute. Only now her clothes were covered in blood, both hers and Officer Tiana Martinez's.

Maddy couldn't get the image out of her mind of the woman's dead, empty eyes staring sightlessly back at her.

Of course she'd seen dead bodies before. In her line of work it was inevitable. She'd even seen bodies tortured and mangled. Comparatively speaking, Tiana's body was relatively clean, just a single bullet hole between her eyes. But Maddy had never seen someone die before and she couldn't stop thinking about it.

Even now, hours later, her body still trembled, and her jaw ached from clamping her teeth together to stop them from chattering.

It was bad enough she was bound and injured. She didn't need to show even more weakness in front of her stepfather because he would definitely take advantage of it. Sean wasn't a good man, not even close. While she'd had no idea he was into weapons trafficking she wasn't surprised to find out. He'd built his imports and exports business from the ground up as a young man, he was wealthy, but he seemed to crave money and power. He also liked to make sure people knew he was superior. He had a high IQ, was good at reading people, and took pleasure in playing with people, giving them just enough rope to hang themselves.

Well, she had no intention of handing him any rope to hang her.

She wasn't going to play the mouse to his cat.

Maddy shifted slightly in her seat wincing as her aching body protested. The skin on her left forearm had been torn off when she'd jumped from the car, she'd messed up her left ankle, and her left hip throbbed. The side of her face stung as well, and she was sure she'd scraped off a few layers of skin there too. No doubt she looked like an extra in some horror movie, but the more worrying thing was that she might be too injured to escape if an opportunity presented itself.

It took everything Maddy had not to shy away from Sean when he walked slowly down the plane and took the seat beside her. So far, he had left her alone, allowing one of his men to manhandle her to his limo and then later onto the plane, and she'd been pleased. Now she had no idea how to handle the man who was married to her mother, and who hated her son's family enough that he had sent a serial killer after her.

"Drink," he said, holding a bottle of water to her lips.

Although she wanted to pull away from him, her need for water won out, and she opened her mouth and swallowed a few mouthfuls. Too soon he moved the bottle away, and she had to clamp her lips together so she didn't cry out. She needed more water, but she knew Sean was offering her only a little water on purpose. Playing with her was his MO, and it seemed nothing had changed over the last decade.

"It's been a long time, your mother misses you," Sean said, lounging in his seat and taking a long drink from the same bottle he'd just given her, no doubt to taunt her, remind her of her place.

Now though it wasn't the water she was craving it was her mother's love. She had lost her mother—at least the one of her early childhood—along with her father and sister. It had been too hard for her mom to be around her, a reminder of their loss, so her mom had shut her out. It had hurt a lot, and she'd had to develop tough skin when dealing with her mom, but right now she was vulnerable, and his words struck a nerve. The last time she had spoken to her mother was last Christmas. They spoke on the phone every Christmas Day for exactly thirty minutes. That was it, the only contact she had with her only living family member.

Well, only family member before she had Louie.

Now she had someone who would love her unconditionally, and she would fight with everything she had to get back to him. Which meant not allowing Sean to mess with her head.

"Then it will be nice to see her when we get to Ireland. That is where we're going, I assume?"

He set the water bottle down on the chair across from hers where it could taunt her, but Maddy was already in survival mode and barely spared it a glance. "We are going to Ireland, but I can hardly take you home in your current condition. I'm sure seeing you like this," he waved a hand to indicate her bloody appearance, "would worry her, and I don't like for my wife to be worried."

"Where are we going then?" She tried not to let her disappointment show. In the event that Hawk and his family figured out she had been taken by their uncle then they would go to his house, the one she'd told them all about, she'd hoped he would have taken her there. Seemed like she wasn't that lucky.

Sean merely smiled. That same creepy smile that had made the hairs on the back of her neck stand up the very first time he used it on her when she was nine years old. "It was certainly a shock when the man I had tailing Hawk Oswald reported that he had taken my own stepdaughter to bed. I was disappointed when you two didn't keep in contact, but imagine my surprise when I received a report that you were pregnant. It is an Oswald baby, am I correct?"

Maddy kept silent, no need to paint an even bigger target on her son's back.

"Congratulations, your mother will be pleased to be a grandmother. And I believe she always wanted a son." His fake charm slid away, and the viciousness she knew he was capable of seeped into his voice. "We can do this the easy way or the hard way. If you make this easy on yourself, do what I tell you, and I won't kill your son. The rest of them have to die, but if your mother takes custody of your son, I get what I want anyway, access to the family fortune. It's up to you, Madeline, either you sign your son's death warrant, or you agree to help me."

In this moment she had a choice to make.

Either she could be the woman she wanted her son to remember her as, strong, courageous, loyal, and honorable. She could do the right thing, tell Sean there was no way she was working with him, that she wouldn't help him kill six innocent people, their spouses, and children, including two babies only a few months older than her baby.

Or she could agree to be Sean's pawn and pray that he followed through and spared Louie's life.

She couldn't do it.

There were no guarantees that Sean wouldn't kill Louie along with the rest of his family. He wanted control, and even if he let Louie live, he would mold the boy into his own image. Destroying her sweet little baby.

After defending herself against Hawk and his family's accusations it felt like it would all have been a lie if she ended up acquiescing and helping Sean with whatever he had planned. In the end it was a moot point anyway.

"They already think I'm working with you, Sean. They think I'm a plant, that you threatened my mom to get my compliance. Hawk hates me. He won't care that you took me, he won't care if you kill me, I hold absolutely no value to you whatsoever," she finished, suddenly completely wiped out. Maddy hated that it was true, that she meant nothing to Hawk, that he was probably relieved to have her out of the way because now he could keep Louie. His family knew about Sean, knew he was a threat, they'd be vigilant, keep her son safe, but they wouldn't come running to her rescue.

Depressing but true. Maddy was in this on her own.

* * *

7:33 P.M.

THE LARGE EMPTY New Jersey industrial estate looked like something out of a horror movie.

Given why they were here, Hawk figured that wasn't far off.

Currently, he lived in his own personal horror movie. Maddy was gone, she hated him, and no doubt thought he wouldn't be looking for her. His son might grow up without a mother, and while he knew that his family would rally around his son, nothing and no one could take the place of Louie's mother. Things had seemed like they were improving for a while. They had a suspect and they'd solved Maddy's serial killer case. All they had to do was figure out where Tiana Martinez would take Maddy and then go and get her.

Only like in a movie, a plot twist had come along.

One that guaranteed that Maddy had almost definitely gone from the frying pan into the fire.

Eagle parked the car, and neither he nor his brothers spoke as they followed the police activity through one of the dilapidated warehouses.

Had Maddy run this same path in a desperate bid for escape?

Had she been injured?

He knew she would have been terrified, fighting for her life, alone, abandoned, betrayed, but with a determination no fear could steal because Maddy had something to live for, something to fight for. Her son. Hawk knew without a shadow of a doubt that she would never give up because she wasn't going to let her baby suffer the very same loss that she had as a child.

That was what he had to hold onto.

Maddy would fight, so he had to fight. He couldn't give up on her. For her, for their son, and for himself he would do whatever it took to find her and bring her home. Then he would face perhaps the greatest battle of his life, trying to win back Maddy's heart.

Even if he couldn't do that, even if all they would ever be to one another was co-parents to their son, he would make sure that she was home, that she was taken care of, and that she knew without a shadow of a doubt that he regretted the harsh words he'd throw at her.

They walked through one room and into another, and then up a flight of stairs and into what had obviously at one time been the office for the warehouse. Now it was empty save for several large, flattened cardboard boxes scattered about.

His attention immediately zeroed in on the large puddle of blood and the figure lying face down in it.

Tiana Martinez was dead.

A single bullet hole in her forehead.

Whoever had killed her was a good shot.

Maddy had been kidnapped by Tiana, but he knew that someone else had shot the woman. If Maddy had killed her abductor, the first thing she would have done was find her way to the nearest police precinct or to a phone to call him and check on Louie. She wouldn't still be out there somewhere, and the body before them had been dead for over twenty-four hours, more than enough time for Maddy to make contact.

"How long?" Eagle asked the medical examiner who was crouched beside the body.

"Twenty-four to thirty hours," the middle-aged woman replied.

The look Eagle shot him said that the ME's words had confirmed what he believed as well. That Maddy hadn't killed the woman who abducted her. Which meant that whoever had shot Tiana Martinez had taken Maddy.

If she'd been saved by a good Samaritan, then again, she would have immediately called the cops and him because the first thing on her mind would be her son.

Had whoever killed the cop turned serial killer stumbled upon them by accident, taken advantage of an opportunity to kidnap a beautiful young woman, or had this been planned? Had Tiana been bringing Maddy to someone?

Hawk feared it was the latter.

Feared he knew exactly who currently had Maddy in their clutches.

"You say this woman was a San Francisco cop?" an older man in a suit asked. They knew he was Detective Kennedy, the man assigned to this case. They'd put out an APB on Tiana Martinez and used Prey's sway to make sure they were notified if the woman was located, only this was not how they had expected her to be found.

"Wanted for seven murders including a cop who was working the case," Eagle explained. "We have her on security footage holding a gun on Madeline Montgomery and forcing her out of the hotel."

"Could your kidnap victim have gotten her hands on the gun and done this?" Detective Kennedy asked, nodding his head at the body.

Before Hawk could reply, Falcon answered for him. "No," his tone offered zero room for doubt. "If Maddy had done this and gotten free the first thing she would have done was make contact. Tiana Martinez left Maddy's week-old son alone in the hotel room. She would have wanted to check on him."

"Could have been afraid of the ramifications of taking a life?" Detective Kennedy suggested, not looking convinced.

"Maddy has been involved in law enforcement for years, she would know this was self-defense," Eagle said.

"Unless she wasn't taken against her will," the detective suggested.

Hawk saw red.

He didn't even realize that the low, dangerous growl he could hear was coming from him.

Didn't know he was moving either until Falcon clamped a hand around his arm, holding him back.

"It's not worth it," his brother said, shooting the cop a look that could kill. "Maddy needs you focused and there for Louie. Getting yourself arrested means you can't do either."

Eagle stepped into Detective Kennedy's personal space, his voice all the more menacing for its calm. "Maddy has dedicated her entire adult life to profiling victims to help catch killers. She was stalked by this woman, and when she went to the cops she was ignored. Given no choice but to run for her life she came to us. She is one of the most honest, compassionate, and big-hearted people I have ever met. Now she's missing again. I want you to work this case like your life depends on it because it does. You don't find her, and I'll make sure your career is ruined. Nobody messes with my family and gets away with it."

With that, Eagle turned his back on the cop and walked over to one of the cardboard boxes. The ME followed and gestured to what had caught Eagle's attention. "Blood on there, I tested it, it's a different blood type than the victim. I'm guessing it's from your kidnap victim."

Still struggling to get his anger under control, Hawk dragged in a deep breath, more grateful than he could express to his brothers, not only for doing everything they could to find Maddy, but also for considering Maddy family. While he was sure Maddy thought his whole family hated her, in fact they had been lobbying for her from the beginning, and unlike him, had never believed she was working with her stepfather.

Knowing Maddy had been bleeding in this very room didn't help him get himself under control, not when he was sure he knew who had killed Tiana Martinez and taken Maddy.

"Sean," he said quietly.

Everyone looked over at him. "You think Sean is involved in this?" Eagle asked.

"Who's Sean?" Detective Kennedy asked, but everyone ignored him.

"You don't think he's involved?" Hawk asked his oldest brother. "He's tried going after all of us and not been successful. What better way to finally get what he wants than to take her, use her as bait? He has to know that will guarantee we're going to either negotiate with him or go in after her. Who else could it be? Even if someone happened to be out here and stumbled upon Tiana and Maddy, why kill one and not the other? Either they'd both be dead or they both would have been taken."

"If Tiana was working with someone, why kill her?" Falcon asked.

"Because she didn't hold up her end of the bargain," Hawk said his stomach dropping. "Maybe she was supposed to deliver Maddy and Louie but for some reason she didn't bring the baby. Sean killed her as punishment." From the looks on both his brothers' faces they agreed with his theory. It was really the only thing that made sense, and all of a sudden Hawk needed air.

Shoving away from Falcon who was still hovering nearby,

no doubt in case he decided to do something stupid like hit the cop who had badmouthed Maddy, he made his way outside, where he planted his hands on his knees and drew in several near gasping mouthfuls of air.

Maddy was gone.

He'd come so close to losing Louie as well.

If Maddy was in Sean's hands—and he had no doubt that she was—then her life was in grave danger. Sean wouldn't go easy on her because she was his stepdaughter, he would use her for his own ends, hurt her, and maybe even kill her.

And Hawk didn't know how to get her back.

The last week had been insane. He'd gone from considering life away from being a Ranger, wondering if he should track down Maddy, to her bursting into his life with his son in tow. He'd thought he had everything, but now he had almost lost it all. While he still had his son, his family wasn't complete without Maddy.

His heart wasn't complete without Maddy.

CHAPTER THIRTEEN

October 21st

9:53 A.M.

EXHAUSTION WEIGHED HEAVILY upon her and yet she was buzzing with adrenalin.

It was a strange feeling and one Maddy was completely unfamiliar with. She didn't live her life on an adrenalin high. Sure, her job was stressful, she traveled a lot and saw and heard many horrible things. She had seen humanity at its worst, but it was always from the comfort of behind the scenes. She wasn't a cop, she didn't hunt down criminals, she occasionally testified in court and that was as close as she came.

Adrenalin-pumping sports weren't on her radar. She didn't want to go sky diving or bungee jumping. She didn't go mountain biking or white-water rafting. Her idea of fun was usually working, and if she managed to get a break between cases she might go shopping, to see a movie, or out for dinner. The riskiest thing she had done in her entire life was the one-night stand with Hawk that had given her the most amazing gift she'd ever received.

Louie was her everything, and while she would do whatever she could to get back to him, she was starting to lose hope.

She was hurting, injured, still bound, and there had been at least two of Sean's men around her at all times. There was no way she was going to get an opportunity to run like she had before. There had been no locking her in the trunk. They'd gone from the plane to a limo, to the house where her mother lived—although they hadn't gone inside just to one of the outbuildings where she had been told to change her clothes—and back to the limo. At no time had she been left alone, and while Officer Tiana Martinez had been unstable, which led to her making mistakes, Sean wasn't like that, he was too levelheaded. There would be no mistakes that gave her even the slimmest of chances at freedom.

At least she could take solace in her son being safe.

Who would ever have thought she would be grateful for the fact that Tiana's baby brother had been locked in the bathroom with her, screaming his lungs out, while their father had killed their mother? Obviously, that had stuck with Tiana to the point where she couldn't seem to stand to be around infants. It had worked in her favor, although not Tiana's because she hadn't kidnapped Louie and Maddy like Sean had ordered her to.

It hadn't worked in Sean's favor either because now he wasn't going to get what he wanted. She was terrible bait, no one would be coming for her.

Not that she cared.

If it meant Louie lived, she would gladly sacrifice her own life.

The limo turned and stopped outside large iron gates. The gates were intricately carved, and she had no doubt that whatever house he had here would be grand. Sean liked to put on a good show, he liked the prestige of showing off his wealth. It was why he'd sent her to boarding school, it got rid of her, but he also liked telling people his daughter went to one of the most expensive, elite schools in the world.

The driver got out, unlocked the gates, and then returned, driving them onto the property. While he stopped again to lock them behind them, Maddy looked around taking in the grounds. This place was remote, she hadn't seen another car on the quiet, winding roads in hours, and sheer cliffs with the ocean crashing beneath them lined the road.

Even though he hated her, she knew Hawk would take good care of their son, and since she didn't want to be selfish, she hoped one day he would fall in love so Louie could have a mother. It hurt her heart to think it because *she* wanted to be her baby's mommy, but she couldn't deny him that kind of love. She wouldn't.

Her son came first, and Louie needed a mother even if it couldn't be her.

"Let's go," Sean said, snapping her out of her reverie.

Having spent most of the last twenty-four hours tied up, trapped in the trunk of Tiana's car, and then sitting, unmoving, in Sean's limos and jet, her muscles were tight from lack of use, and her bumps and bruises had stiffened up. She bit back a groan as she forced herself to climb from the car. Her right hip and ankle threatened to buckle almost immediately. With her bound hands, she couldn't do much to stop it from happening, and she certainly wasn't reaching out to grab onto Sean or one of his bodyguards to steady herself.

Wobbling precariously, somehow, she managed to remain

upright, and staggered after Sean as he headed up steps to the front door of what could only be described as a magical castle out of a fairytale. She'd thought the house he lived in was something special, but this was something else. The inside was every bit as magnificent as the outside. She felt like she had stepped back in time, surrounded by exquisite antiques.

"I see you are impressed with the furnishings," Sean said, pride shining from his blue eyes. The family resemblance was uncanny. She saw Hawk in those eyes, his siblings too. It was obvious the Oswald siblings had taken after their father, the genes dominant, they all had the same blue eyes and jet-black hair. She would love to think that was where the similarities ended, but she'd seen the same self-righteous anger in Hawk when he'd accused her of being in cahoots with her stepfather.

"It's a beautiful home," she said, suddenly overwhelmed by the need to lie down. Her body must have run out of adrenalin because the hyped feeling had faded, leaving her with heavy eyes and an even heavier body.

"It could be your son's home. Just remember this doesn't have to be horrible. You can play along, and things will go well for you," Sean said.

He could say it, but she didn't believe it.

"This way."

Her stepfather led her up a flight of stairs, and then another, and a third, and finally a fourth. Her body was screaming at her to rest, her hip burning with pain, her ankle barely able to support her weight, a headache pounding at her temples. When they eventually reached the top, one of her stepfather's goons cut her bindings sending pain screaming down her limbs as normal blood flow resumed.

Sean unlocked a door and gestured for her to go inside. She did because there wasn't really any other option. The room she was sent into was every bit as nice as the rest of the castle, a comfortable-looking rocking chair by a window, an open fireplace with a fire already crackling in it. There was a large canopy bed, a wardrobe, an armoire, and nightstands on either side of the bed. Everything looked to be antique, and she could just as easily be standing in a five-star hotel as her prison.

But it *was* a prison.

That was something she could never allow herself to forget.

Sean was toying with her, trying to bribe her with pretty furniture and a warm, comfortable place to rest her head. That was all it was though, a bribe meant to entice her to work with him instead of against him. In the end, the result would be the same. She wasn't walking away from this alive. The only thing she would save herself if she agreed to try to help Sean was a little pain and suffering.

It wasn't worth it.

Her self-respect and knowing that with her dying breath she had been the mother her son deserved, one he could be proud of, was worth more to her than saving herself from whatever torture he had in mind for her.

"There is a bathroom through the door there," Sean said, pointing to a door on the far side of the fireplace. "Meals will be served at noon, seven in the evening, and seven in the morning. You are welcome to put in a request, and if the chef has what you want it will be prepared. If you cooperate you can stay here, in this beautiful room, well fed, warm, clean, comfortable, until I have what I want. If you do not cooperate, I think you will find your accommodations will drop significantly."

With that, he closed the door behind him. She heard the distinctive clunk of it locking, and then the sounds of footsteps descending, leaving her all alone.

Too exhausted to consider cleaning up and tending to her injuries, all Maddy could manage was dragging herself to the bed and collapsing on top of the covers.

Sleep was what she needed now. Maybe with a clearer head, she could figure out a way to keep herself alive, buy some time, for what she wasn't quite sure, but she knew that she wasn't going down without a fight.

Closing her eyes, she drifted off into slumberland imagining her son snuggled safely in her arms and wondering if she would ever see him again.

* * *

6:54 P.M.

THE LAST TWO days had been excruciating.

Everything seemed to move in slow motion, and Hawk hadn't felt like he was doing anything concrete to bring Maddy home where she belonged.

Now, finally, they were in Northern Ireland, just a mile or so away from Sean Oswald's remote country estate, where they hoped Maddy was being held. Sean had taken her for the specific purpose of using her as bait so it made sense that he wasn't going to hide her away someplace where they wouldn't be able to find her.

Hawk kept expecting a little voice in the back of his mind whispering to him that Maddy could still be setting him up. It taunted that she might have played him for a fool, used him, pretended to be upset over his accusations, but walked out of that hotel room with Tiana Martinez of her own free will. That even now she was safe and happy with her stepfather simply waiting for him to swoop in and save her only to have him walk straight into a trap.

He kept expecting to hear that little voice, but it never came.

Maddy was innocent, his gut declared it. His family all agreed it didn't fit with her personality, and he would forever regret the accusations he'd hurled at her, even if believing she was working with her stepfather had been a logical assumption at the time.

Now he knew how wrong he was, and he was determined to right those wrongs and bring Maddy home to her son.

Leaving Louie behind had been difficult. Okay, it had been more than difficult, but he knew his son was safe with Olivia, Raven, and Hope. All three women had bodyguards, and Raven's husband Max, and Sparrow's fiancé Ethan, were there with them. They were all well protected, and this was something he needed to do.

Since they knew this was a trap, they were coming well prepared. Prey's Alpha team would be working the perimeter while he, Eagle, Falcon, and a Delta Force team comprising of seven of the most highly trained, skilled operatives the US military had ever produced would breach the house. While it was likely Sean had more men at his disposal, Hawk was confident none of them were as intelligent or skilled as the men sitting in the back of the truck with him.

Eagle pulled the truck over to the side of the road and into the trees surrounding Sean's property. They'd already received a report from Luca "Bear" Jackson, Prey's Alpha team's leader, that the estate was protected by an electrified fence and that while there were guards stationed at several points around the perimeter, it wasn't being patrolled as heavily as they had feared it might be.

An electrified fence wasn't anything that was going to slow them down. They'd go under it, or over it, or find a way through it. He didn't care which, all he knew was nothing was going to keep him from getting to Maddy.

Sean was going down.

Uncle or not, the man had put his family through so much, from what he'd done to Hawk's siblings to what he'd done to Maddy. Sean had set a serial killer on Maddy's trail just to scare her into coming to him. Tiana hadn't known that it was all a game to Sean to get what he wanted, she believed Maddy had to die and likely would have followed through if Sean hadn't killed her first.

Hatred for the uncle who had caused his family so much pain burned brightly inside him, and he took that hatred and used it to his advantage. It would make him fight harder, smarter, and stronger, meaning the threat to his family would finally be eliminated, and they could live in peace.

"I'm going in the front door," he announced to the others.

Eagle leaned over to glare at him from the driver's seat. "That wasn't the plan."

"It's the right thing to do, and you know it," Hawk said. "He knows I'm coming. He knows Maddy is important to me, that we share a child. He's expecting me to come here, but he doesn't need to know that I came with an entire Delta team and you and Falcon. I go in, his focus is on me, then you guys can breach the property, surround him, and then this is over."

Before Eagle could protest, Walker "Trigger" Nelson spoke up. "It's not a bad idea. The place isn't heavily guarded, and he knows for sure Hawk will come. He's been planning this for a long time, been after you all for years, he's going to be giddy when he sees Hawk, all his attention will be on that. From what you know of him, he enjoys grandstanding, he's not going to be able to shut up, he'll be bragging about his perceived victories, too busy to expect the rest of us."

"I don't like it," Eagle muttered.

"Because it wasn't your plan," Hawk shot back. His oldest

brother liked to be in control and didn't do well when things didn't go his way.

"Falcon and I should go with you," Eagle countered.

"No. It has to be me. Just me. We don't want him to think it's over, we just want him to think that this part of his plan worked. No doubt the plan is once he has me, he uses that to get the rest of you. We want him cocky and confident, but not thinking he has everything he wants already. Have a little faith in me, big brother. I can do this. I have all the motivation in the world to make it work because Maddy's life is on the line. Besides, we have these guys," he nodded at the Delta team.

"We have a little experience dealing with hostage situations," Trigger said wryly. That was a massive understatement. The man had actually met his now wife, Gillian, when she and a plane load of people had been held hostage. Hawk's faith in the Delta team was unshakeable, they were the best of the best, and although there was healthy rivalry between the various special forces groups, there was no doubt that Delta was one of the most elite.

Hawk could see his brother's internal debate, but finally Eagle nodded. "Okay, but I'm sending one of the guys to shadow you. Sean won't know he's out there, but you will, and I'll know you have backup if you need it. The rest of us will split up into two groups, Trigger, Brain, and Lucky you're with me. Lefty, Oz, and Doc, you're with Falcon. Grover, you shadow Hawk, you don't let him out of your sight."

Although the Delta team worked independently, this was Prey's mission, and none of the men disagreed with the plan. They all climbed out of the truck, and while the others faded into the forest around them, Hawk allowed himself to be seen by anyone watching. Even though he couldn't see

Clarkson "Grover" Groves, he knew the Delta operative was out there, watching over him.

When he reached the front gates, Hawk expected to find them locked, but they weren't. When he pushed them, they swung open. None of the guards approached him, and he felt like maybe in coming here they were barking up the wrong tree.

It seemed the most logical conclusion, given that Sean actually wanted them to come to him, but now it felt wrong.

He made his way up a long, winding driveway. Someone was watching him, someone other than Grover, but since no one made a move to stop him, he had to assume that something was waiting for them at the house.

It emerged from the forest like it was part of the landscape, and given how old the building was it made sense. According to what Maddy had told his siblings, the castle was hundreds of years old. Sean had bought it when he made his first million and poured several million dollars into restoring it.

A beautiful building but one that hid dark secrets.

Hawk approached boldly, walking up the few stone steps, carved lions sitting guard at either side, to the huge heavy wooden door. The door was open, and he knew immediately that no one was home. Sean had left a few guards behind, no doubt to confirm that Hawk was in Ireland and on his way after Maddy, but he wasn't here.

There was a single light on inside and a candle chandelier hung from the ceiling of the ornate foyer. Several pieces of what he assumed to be expensive and authentic pieces of art dotted the room along with a shiny black grand piano. A huge split stairs staircase went up on either side to the floor above. On the hardwood floorboards right at the bottom of the stairs lay a pile of clothes.

As he got closer, he saw they were bloody clothes.

And he knew who the clothes belonged to.

Hawk immediately recognized the unicorn leggings and oversized t-shirt with a picture of a panda on the front.

They were Maddy's.

She'd been here, but he would bet his family's entire fortune that she was no longer on the property.

She might be gone, but Sean wanted him to know how close he'd been to finding her. The first battle might have gone to his uncle, but Hawk intended to win the war. He had to, his heart and his future depended on it.

CHAPTER FOURTEEN

October 22nd

:38 P.M.

WITH NOTHING ELSE TO DO, Maddy sat in the rocking chair by the window, staring out at the cliffs and the ocean below, watching the sun work its way slowly across the sky, watching as white puffy clouds floated across the wide blue expanse. The sky in Northern Ireland, especially at this time of year, was a pale blue, not the brighter blues of a Californian summer.

As a little girl, Maddy would lie on the grass in her backyard beside her dad, and the two of them would watch the clouds and try to find shapes in them. To pass away the time and try to calm her almost severed nerves she'd been searching for shapes, imagining her dad was beside her like he used to be. Like even mother nature wanted to beat her over the head with it, all she kept finding were animals. Lions, elephants, bears, monkeys, all animals she had so lovingly painted on Louie's nursery wall at her place in San Francisco. They'd been stenciled again in the apartment at Prey, then once more on the walls in Hawk's penthouse. She hoped that would be the last place her son would move.

She wanted him to have a stable life.

Wanted him to be happy.

Hoped he might grow up not allowing the weight of her fate to stifle him.

Acceptance had finally come. She wasn't getting out of here alive. Maddy knew that, and with that acceptance came a certain level of freedom. When you had nothing to lose you weren't constrained by anything. She would take advantage of any opportunity she could because she wanted to live, but she knew full well there were no guarantees and likely no opportunities.

When the door opened, Maddy shifted to see who was there. Her aching body protested, and she barely managed to bite back a moan. After sleeping yesterday she'd taken a long, hot shower, carefully washing the deep wounds on her wrists and the gravel burns on her forearm and cheeks. If she survived, she would have horrific scars circling her wrists. Too many hours with the zip ties cutting into her skin and fighting against the unforgiving plastic had basically shredded her flesh. Plus, her entire left side was black and blue from the jump from the trunk of Tiana's car. She was sure she had a couple of cracked ribs, her ankle was sprained at best or broken at worst, and her hip still throbbed, there was no position that was comfortable.

Basically, she was a mess, but a mess that was somehow managing to hold it together so far.

Expecting to see the same guard who had brought in

lunch and dinner the day before, and this morning's breakfast and lunch, she was surprised when instead she saw her stepfather standing there. As always, he had his bodyguards with him, and she couldn't help but think that for all his bravado and self-confidence, in fact Sean was nothing more than a coward. He hid behind his money, letting others do his dirty work, paying people to stand between him and any danger that might present itself.

He wasn't strong he was weak.

"You lied to me," Sean said, his blue eyes narrowed, dark brows slanted.

"About what?"

"You said you would not be good bait. That Hawk hated you and would not come after you."

"How is that a lie? He *does* hate me. He accused me of working with you and threatened to buy a judge to get custody of our son."

"Then why did he show up at my house yesterday looking for you?" Sean demanded.

Maddy's heart stuttered in her chest. Hawk was here, in Ireland? He'd come looking for her?

No.

That couldn't be.

He might have come after Sean, but it had nothing to do with wanting to save her. If someone had found Tiana Martinez's body, and he knew that was who had kidnapped her, then maybe he had assumed that she was in Ireland with Sean. He and his family had probably decided it was time to take down their nemesis, set their family free once and for all.

She hoped they succeeded.

Apparently, he read that in her face because he closed the distance between her and backhanded her. The force of the blow had her head snapping to the side, and a fresh wave of pain joined the others already coursing through her battered body.

"He's not here for me," she repeated, and she believed it, she truly did.

"Then how do you explain this?"

Sean thrust a photo at her, and if ever a picture told a thousand words this was it. She immediately recognized the setting as the foyer at her stepfather's house, only all the lights were out except the candle chandelier that hung from the ceiling. At the bottom of the grand staircase were a pile of what she recognized as the clothing she'd been wearing when she was abducted three days ago. Hawk was down on one knee beside the clothes, his head hung, resting in his hands.

Despair.

That was the immediate emotion that bled off the picture, but surely that despair wasn't aimed at her. Was it?

A tiny flicker ignited inside her.

Could he have come to Ireland looking for her?

She hardly dared to hope it was true because she wasn't sure her heart could take the battering of finding out he couldn't care less if she lived or died.

Doing her best to mask her bubbling emotions, Maddy handed the photo back. "I thought you wanted him to come to Ireland looking for me. What's the problem?"

"The *problem* is that I don't appreciate being lied to. I thought you would have remembered that."

Of course she knew exactly what he was referring to. Not long after she had moved out here, he'd found her sneaking through the castle's secret passages. That had been forbidden, she was supposed to stay out of them. At the time she'd had no idea why, now she assumed it was because he used them for his less than legal business. He'd yelled at her for what seemed like hours, then taken her favorite toys, brought her out to the yard, dug a hole, buried her toys, and told her ominously that problems were easily buried.

Now she was a problem.

Sean's sneer suggested that what was running through her mind might actually be true.

One of the bodyguards grabbed her arm, and she was dragged unceremoniously down the four flights of stairs. The man was much taller than her, his legs taking bigger steps than hers, and she stumbled more than once, her bad leg giving out underneath her, only to be yanked continuously forward.

They didn't stop when they got to the ground floor. Instead, she was led through a maze of halls and corridors and then down into a basement. Maddy thought they would stop there, but they went down again, and then again, and once more until it felt like they were down in the bowels of the earth.

The room was eerily lit with candles in the walls, around the edges of the large open space were white crosses.

Grave markers.

Beside the closest grave marker to the door was a large hole.

A hole meant for her.

Her grave.

As utterly terrified as she was in this moment, she was even more grateful that her son was safe at home.

With a boldness she only had to slightly fake, Maddy met her stepfather's gaze. "I'm glad Tiana didn't bring you my son. You'll never get your hands on him, you'll never destroy his family. I don't believe Hawk is here for me, he's here for you. To destroy you. And I'm glad. Finally, my mother will be free of you, and you won't be able to torment your own family any longer. You're no match for them, Sean."

Not used to anyone talking to him that way, she could see

him fuming. He nodded at the bodyguard still gripping her arm in a bruising hold, and she was forced over to hole's edge.

One shove was all it took.

Maddy cried out as her already bruised body hit the hard dirt ground, about ten feet down.

Her chest constricted.

Buried alive.

Wasn't it most people's worst fear?

While she might not say it was her worst fear, it was certainly up there along with drowning and spiders.

Automatically her fingers clawed at the dirt walls as she clambered to her feet, but there was nothing to grab onto. The hole walls might be dirt, but they were tightly packed. There was no way she was digging her nails into them enough to climb out of here.

"You want to know the best part?" Sean asked.

No, she did not, but she didn't tell him that.

"The best part is that my nephew himself will be the one to sign your death warrant." He gestured at a metal square in the ceiling above her. "It's connected to the house's security system. Exactly sixty minutes after Hawk and whoever is here with him trip the system by breaching my property, you'll be dead."

With that ominous warning, he left her alone to mull over his words.

Even if by some miracle Hawk had come to Ireland for her it wouldn't matter. It would take him more than sixty minutes to find her down here and get her out of the hole before she was buried alive.

A sob built in her chest, and she no longer had the willpower to hold it back.

* * *

8:08 P.M.

HE'D THOUGHT they would have found her by now.

Hawk had already been dreaming about being Maddy's knight in shining armor. Coming riding in on a white horse to save her life, sweeping her up into his arms, showering kisses on her, and apologizing for how badly he'd messed up.

None of that had happened.

They were still at the house where he'd found Maddy's blood-streaked clothes. The half a dozen guards manning the perimeter had been secured and interrogated, although they had given nothing away saying they were merely hired to work security. They'd gone through all the secret passages that Maddy had mentioned when she'd spoken with his siblings after they found the connection between her and Sean.

They had found a whole grand total of nothing useful.

The passages were there, right where Maddy had said they were. They led from various rooms in the house to several basement levels and a number of outhouses, including a tunnel that ran all the way along for several miles to the ocean where a boat was standing by. It was obvious Sean had covered all his bases when it came to escaping. If they'd needed any more indications that he was involved in something illegal—which they hadn't—they had it. Nobody needed that many escape routes built into their house.

But in terms of finding the jackpot of evidence that would send Sean Oswald to prison for the rest of his life for weapons trafficking they had zero. More importantly, in terms of finding the jackpot of evidence that would lead them straight to wherever Maddy was being held they had zero.

His heart literally ached knowing she was hurting and

alone and he couldn't be there because he didn't know where there was. Knowing this entire mess was all his fault about killed him.

Like he had never been easygoing a day in his life, Hawk's control of his emotions snapped.

Fueled by a guilt he wasn't sure he could ever get over, he picked up a lamp on the nightstand in what had been Maddy's bedroom when she'd stayed at Sean's house and threw it across the room.

It hit the opposite wall with a *thunk* and bounced to the floor. The stained-glass lampshade shattered into a million pieces, raining colorful glass shards around the silver lampstand.

Instead of making a dint in his overwhelming emotions, letting them flow out of him in a healthy manner, he rounded on Falcon. "Why did you doubt her?" he screamed as he lunged for his older brother. "If you hadn't doubted her, I never would have."

Falcon didn't respond, and his brother's unflappable calm and refusal to ever be drawn into an argument was the straw that broke the proverbial camel's back.

Hawk swung a fist at Falcon's head and felt a molecule of relief from the crushing guilt when his fist connected with his brother's jaw.

His brother made no move to defend himself, but when Hawk pulled back his arm to swing again, Falcon side-stepped. "You only get one free hit, little brother, because I know you're hurting, but fighting with me isn't going to help us find Maddy, and it's certainly not going to make you feel better.

He wasn't so sure about that.

He had to do something.

He couldn't breathe, could barely function, and had no idea how he was going to raise his son on his own knowing that the reason Louie no longer had a mother was because his father had messed up in the worst way possible.

Maybe he needed his brother to hit him back.

Maddy was suffering physically, her blood-streaked clothes a testament to that. He needed to hurt too, needed to do something to even the score, to somehow balance out the pain he had all but shoved her headlong into.

When he swung at Falcon again, he was tackled from behind, shoved up against the wall, and held in place by several sets of hands.

Hawk didn't care.

He fought against them, desperate for physical pain to outweigh the mental and emotional pain currently smothering him.

"Stop it, man," Gage "Lefty" Haskins ordered. "This isn't helping her."

"He has her," Hawk raged. It wasn't fair, he would give anything for their places to be switched, for Maddy to be safe, and for him to be the one in his uncle's clutches.

"I know, man," Lefty said, and the tone of the man's voice gave him pause.

Hawk sagged against the wall, and sensing that he'd given up on his, force-his-brother-to-beat-him-to-a-pulp plan, the others released him. When he turned, he saw Lefty and Grover still standing between him and Falcon, obviously wanting to be a barrier between the brothers in case Hawk lost it again.

"How can my feelings for her be so strong when I've only known her such a short time?" he asked desperately. Sure, he'd met Maddy going on nine months prior, but they'd only shared one night together, one night he hadn't been able to get out of his head, but that wasn't enough to build the connection he felt for her. The few days they'd spent together had been amazing, and they'd spent hours talking, making out, and getting to know one another, but again surely that wasn't enough to fuel these feelings that consumed him.

"Sometimes it happens fast," Grover said with a shrug. "I felt an instant connection to Sierra the first time I saw her. I was disappointed when she never kept in contact like she said she would, but that connection didn't disappear. When I realized she was in trouble, I knew I would do whatever it took to get to her."

"Like get yourself kidnapped," Lefty muttered with an eye roll.

Grover shrugged again. "Hey, it worked, and that bond we shared only grew. I knew she was it for me, and yeah, our relationship developed fast, especially given she was dealing with being a POW, but that didn't—doesn't—make it any less real."

"I knew when I saved Kinley from protestors in Africa that there was something between us," Lefty added. "It sucked when I never heard from her again, and if we hadn't ended up meeting up a second time, I would have missed out on the best thing to ever happen to me. Even after we met that second time and she didn't keep in contact again, I thought I would have to get over her and move on, but I couldn't stop thinking about her. Knowing she was in danger was the worst, knowing I might not be there when she needed me was harder, and when she was kidnapped, and I didn't know where she was and if she was still alive … there aren't even words to describe that feeling. But Kins is strong, a fighter, she doesn't give up, and from what you've told us about Maddy she's a fighter too."

"We're looking at this all wrong, like Maddy taught us nothing," Falcon said, stepping closer, ignoring the dribble of blood at the corner of his mouth. "We keep trying to profile Sean, find out where he would go, where he would take her, what he thinks he has to gain in taunting us with her bloody clothes. We should be taking a leaf out of Maddy's book and profiling the victim, profiling Maddy. If our theory is correct, that Tiana Martinez was taking Maddy to Sean, then he knows about you and Louie, knows there's a connection there. That theory has to be correct because Maddy's clothes were left in his house. He wants you to come, he's waiting for you to come. This is about you, about our family, but it doesn't mean that wherever he took her doesn't have something to do with her."

Hawk looked helplessly around Maddy's old bedroom. If there were answers here, he didn't know where to start looking for them. "She hardly spent any time in this place as a kid, and she hadn't been back here in almost a decade. There's nothing of hers to profile."

"There's this," Lefty said, gesturing to a crack in the wall from where the lamp had hit. The walls of the castle were stone which gave the place a grand and medieval look, but it also made the house feel cold, there was nothing homey in the entire building. But in this one spot the stones appeared to be fake. Where they had cracked away, he could see something hidden behind them.

Brushing away the Delta operatives who were still standing between him and Falcon in case he lost it again, Hawk went to the broken bit of wall and pulled the stones away, revealing a small hiding space.

His gut churned.

"Sean was watching her," he said, his brain spinning in a million different ways, trying to comprehend what he saw and the ramifications. Channeling his inner Maddy, he kept the focus on her and not on Sean. "She never mentioned anything about him abusing her." Not that it necessarily meant that it hadn't happened. "But she said he made her uncomfortable, and it's clear he was watching her. Maybe she was just too young, then, only nine. Maybe he intended for her to come back and stay here after she graduated high school. She wouldn't have been a kid any longer." Something Maddy had said when she'd learned there was someone after his family tickled at the back of his brain. "Maddy looks a lot like mom," he said slowly.

"What do you mean?" Falcon's dark brows made a V. Hawk, and four of his siblings all took after their father. His Irish heritage, dark hair and blue eyes had touched all of them except Dove who was an albino and had the accompanying white hair and very pale eyes. But their mother had had lighter hair, a shade of golden brown similar to Maddy's, and her eyes had been hazel. Hawk remembered her jokingly complaining that none of her babies had inherited anything from her.

"Sean is our uncle, that means he spent at least some of his childhood on mom's family estate along with dad and the rest of his family, so he knew mom. Maddy wondered if whoever sent those two escaped felons to our farm was after more than just getting them out of the way or revenge. What if it was because he was angry that mom picked dad over him? Right around that time was when our grandparents were killed, meaning the fortune would go to our parents, and if they were out of the way, to us. What if all of us weren't supposed to die that day?"

"You think he wanted us alive?" Falcon asked, Grover and Lefty watching with interest as he talked out his theory.

"What if he intended to keep Dove? She was the youngest, the least likely to cause resistance, and the most likely to be able to be molded into whatever he wanted her to be. He'd only just started building his fortune, had just married Maddy's mom, so he had a case to get custody of her. And custody of Dove meant access to the family fortune. Only that never happened because Raven killed them and we all moved to the city, inheriting everything our grandparents had left to mom. Maddy wondered if mom and dad didn't run just because their families didn't approve of their relationship. What if they ran because Sean wanted mom *and* her money? He didn't just wake up one day and decide to become a criminal. He had to have shown violent tendencies even back then. What if mom and dad believed they were in danger from him and that's why they hid us all away?"

"That's a wild theory," Falcon said, looking doubtful.

"Is it ever," Lefty agreed with a whistle.

Hawk wasn't done yet. "Sean has made a lot of money, but it's nowhere close to what our family is worth. We know he orchestrated Cleo's abduction when she was little, but we didn't know why. What if he intended to buy her at that second auction, the one Raven and Max interrupted? He gets his hands on her and then takes the rest of us out, could be why he wanted Raven and Cleo brought to him. When that didn't work, he tried taking Hope, hoping we would go in after her because she'd been kind to Raven, and he knew we wouldn't leave her behind. That failed, so he tried going after Sparrow, and that failed too, so he moved on to Maddy. He's using her as bait, and he wants to destroy our family. But what if he wants one of the kids so he can get our money? It means he gets the best of both worlds. He removes all of us who are reminders that he didn't get his woman, *and* he gets the money. But to get the money he needs to take custody of one of our kids. As custodial parent, he's in charge of the entire fortune."

Ignoring the others, he strode to the window of Maddy's room. He knew he was onto something here. It fitted with what Maddy had suggested and explained a lot of what had happened to him and his family.

What it didn't do was tell him where Sean was right now.

Where Maddy was.

It was dark out but not so dark he couldn't see some of the surrounding countryside. The castle was, of course, built on a small hill, but while it was surrounded by woods you could still see it from a distance.

Sean liked to watch, the hidey-hole in Maddy's room was proof of that, but it wasn't the only way to watch someone. While this place provided plenty of escape routes should they be needed, it didn't appear that Sean kept his weapons stash here. This was his façade, the home he showed the world, where he lived with his wife, where he no doubt entertained friends, but it wasn't his real home.

Across the forest, laid out beneath the castle like a green carpet, there was another small hill, another similar, albeit smaller castle was visible.

A light shone from one of the windows.

With the right telescope, you'd be able to see from that building to this one. Perhaps even into this very room.

What better place to run your weapons trafficking empire from than one you could see from your home?

"There," he said, pointing at the light. "Maddy's there."

CHAPTER FIFTEEN

October 23rd

2:16 A.M.

MADDY LET OUT a pained breath and paused to stretch her cramping fingers, bringing them marginal relief from the somewhat pointless task of trying to make enough finger and toeholds to climb out of here.

Not that she was stopping.

Given enough time she might actually be able to do it too. The dirt was tightly packed, but it was still dirt and not concrete, meaning it was possible to work away small bits to make little holes. Problem was it took a really long time to make just one and she had to make enough to climb the ten-foot wall.

Sean hadn't been back which meant she hadn't had a

chance to try to talk to him, figure out how best to get herself out of this mess. It had been a mistake not to make a deal with him earlier when he had offered. There was no way in hell she would have gone through with it, but there might have been an opportunity to communicate with Hawk in some manner, and she was sure she would have been able to get a coded message to him.

Now that opportunity was gone.

She'd lost it because she couldn't get the image from her mind of Hawk's angry blue gaze shooting daggers at her as he'd hurled accusations at her. How could she live with herself if she became the very thing he'd accused her of being?

She couldn't.

Which was why she had refused to make a deal, choosing her self-respect and Hawk's if he had ever managed to find out her fate, over making the best and most logical decisions given her predicament.

That opportunity was now long gone, there was no going back, and she did not expect another to present itself. If she wanted to get out of here, she had to do it on her own.

It would just be helpful if her body was more cooperative. Not only did her hands keep cramping but her wrists stung like they were on fire as dirt continued to drift down into the open wounds. Her chest hurt with each breath she took, her head pounded, and her hip and ankle could only support her for short periods of time, and only if she was leaning against the wall of the hole, using it to take some of her weight. It hadn't been so bad when she'd been able to sit down to dig out little crevices in the dirt, but now that she was working around shoulder height it was taking a whole lot longer.

Maddy had no idea how she was going to climb up or even how she was going to keep working once she went above her head. She was pretty sure her body couldn't cope with balancing in the footholds she'd already made while she dug with her hands. But that was a bridge to cross when she came to it. At least working on an escape plan and not just sitting helplessly doing nothing was keeping her sane.

Sane until dirt began to rain down around her.

With a horrified gasp, Maddy looked up, shielding her eyes as dirt continued to fall.

The trip had been switched.

The chute above her opened.

Hawk had arrived, and her death sentence had been enacted.

Sean had told her that it would take an hour for her grave to completely fill, but the dirt was falling hard and fast, and her pulse immediately skyrocketed.

This was it.

Panic clawed at her, wasting precious seconds she would never get back.

Seconds that could mean the difference between life and death.

Was it possible for her to climb on the dirt as it came down and use it as a staircase to step her way up and out?

Doubt niggled at her. If it was that easy, there wouldn't be a row of grave markers beside the very hole that had been dug to be her grave.

Dirt was quickly filling the hole. It seemed like it was going to take a whole lot less than sixty minutes to fill. Maddy got down on her knees, ignoring the screaming pain in her injured leg as she shoved the dirt to the sides, trying to build a dirt stairway.

But as quickly as she moved the dirt, more took its place.

She tried to stay one step ahead of it, tried to keep it beneath her, but the dirt kept coming. It would slow for a bit then large amounts would suddenly dump down. It swirled in the air, getting in her eyes and making them sting and blur, getting up her nose and making her sneeze, clogging in her throat and making her cough.

Maddy had no idea how long she fought the losing battle. All she knew was that she could no longer move her legs. Dirt surrounded them from her feet to just above her knees. She didn't even know how it had happened. It seemed to be instantaneous. One second not there, the next she was trapped, but she knew it couldn’t have buried her that quickly.

Muddy tears streamed down her face as she began to frantically dig at the dirt piling up around her. Air sawed in and out of her lungs, her pulse raced, and the more she tried to calm herself down and not panic, the more in fact she began to panic.

She didn't want to be buried alive, didn't want to die, didn't want to be used as a pawn to destroy her own child’s family.

But it didn't matter what she wanted.

This was happening regardless.

Even though Hawk was on the premises somewhere it didn't mean he would find her in time or even be looking for her. Although things hadn't worked out between them and hadn't ended the way she’d hoped, Maddy couldn’t find it in her to regret those few special days they’d spent together caring for their son.

She would hold onto those memories as the dirt closed in around her head, stealing her ability to breathe.

The dirt around her was rising up to her waist now. It seemed no matter how much she shoved it aside more came down to replace it almost immediately.

Claustrophobia gripped her, and Maddy began to scream as she feverishly clawed at the dirt around her.

She had to get out.

Had to get out.

Had to get out.

There was no air left in the basement. She gasped, but all she could get in was the dirt falling through the air.

Logically she knew that wasn't true, soon it would be, but not yet. It was just her mind playing tricks on her, the horror of her situation sinking in, but try as she might, she couldn't calm down.

Which only made her situation worse because she wasted time panicking.

It was up to her shoulders now. Her arms were out at her side, still uselessly tossing the dirt away even as more took its place.

But she couldn't stop.

Wouldn't stop.

If she was doomed to this horrific death, she would go out knowing for certain that she had done all she could.

The dirt rose past her shoulders and up her neck. Maddy tilted her head back, wanting to delay the inevitable as long as possible.

"I'm sorry, Louie," she wept aloud. "I tried, baby. Please know that mommy tried, that she didn't want to leave you, that she never did anything to betray you. I love you more than I ever thought I could, and I ... I love your daddy too. It's stupid, he doesn't love me back, but it's true. I love him, and I love you so much, and I'm trying to get out of here, I'm trying ..."

Her desperation bled into sobbing as she shoved at the dirt with jerky, uncoordinated movements.

It covered her mouth, no matter how many times she flicked it away.

It filled her ears.

Then covered her nose, making its way to claim her eyes as well.

Covering her mouth with one hand, she wondered if she

could buy herself a few extra moments by creating a little pocket of air.

Her other hand continued to try to brush away the falling dirt, but her movements had grown sluggish.

"Maddy!"

Someone screamed her name.

She could have sworn that it was Hawk, but dirt covered most of her head now, and she couldn't really be sure.

It sounded like he swore, and then she was sure there was activity buzzing around her. She heard multiple voices, they all seemed to be chattering at once, but she couldn't make out what they were saying.

Tired.

She was tired now, exhaustion weighed as heavily upon her as the dirt, and the world started to shimmer away.

For a moment it looked glittering like a star, and she smiled.

Her daddy had loved the stars, and it made her love them too.

He'd been her guardian angel throughout her life, shining down upon her from the great expanse of the milky way. Now she would be Louie's guiding star, she'd watch over him, it wasn't the way she'd wanted it to turn out, but anytime her son missed her all he had to do was look up at the night sky, and he'd see her there, looking down over him.

1:01 A.M.

"MADDY!" Hawk screamed her name as he and the others came out of the tunnel into a room to find her trapped in a grave with dirt pouring from the ceiling on top of her.

One of her hands reached up toward him even as dirt covered her head, and he swore and carefully climbed down into the hole, careful to make sure he was behind where he'd seen her head, so he didn't add additional pressure to her already buried body and grabbed her hand gripping it tightly.

He wasn't losing her now when he was this close to saving her.

"We have to get her out," he said as he held her hand with one of his and with his other began fervently digging at the dirt around her face.

But dirt continued to rain down, quickly replacing what he managed to move.

"Have to stop the dirt getting on her," Grover said, already focused on the vent above her that the dirt was falling through.

Burying her alive.

The horror of what she was going through almost had him faltering, but somehow he managed to keep moving dirt, trying to get enough out of the way to free her mouth and nose so she could breathe. At least he knew her face had only just been buried—right in front of them—so if they could get her free quickly enough then she'd survive. But if they couldn't stop the dirt …

Hawk couldn't even allow himself to consider that possibility.

"We have to get her out," he said desperately. Falcon, Grover, and Lefty were with him. While the others had gone to approach the building they believed Sean was hiding in, he, his brother, and the two Delta operators had come through the tunnels. Hawk had been positive that if he was right and Sean did own the other castle on the hill, there would be tunnels connecting the two, and although it had taken him, Falcon, Grover, and Lefty a while to find it, once they had they'd moved quickly along the dark trails. The tunnel had ended in this very room, a torture and death chamber. The row of white crosses against the wall and the open grave Maddy was in made it clear what happened in this room.

But Maddy wasn't going to join the others in death.

"Lefty, empty my pack," Grover instructed his teammate, who immediately complied. Once the pack was empty, Grover held it under the chute, catching the dirt as it fell so it didn't land on Maddy.

Falcon had carefully climbed into the hole on the other side of Maddy, and between the two of them, they started quickly excavating the dirt from around her head. Hawk kept his hold on her hand, needing a connection to her, but her hand was limp in his hold. Limp but warm, she was still alive, and he intended to keep her that way.

"Maddy?" he called as soon as they had dirt cleaned off her face.

"She alive?" Lefty asked, leaning over them.

"She better be," he replied. Maddy had her hand cupped around her mouth and nose, creating a tiny pocket of air, probably the only thing that had kept her alive, buying them enough time to dig her out. Clearing away more dirt, he was able to get his fingers to her neck and immediately searched for a pulse. A sigh sagged out of him as relief rippled through his body. "She's alive," he murmured. "She's alive, she's alive."

"Pack is almost full," Grover called out, reminding him that Maddy might be alive, but she was far from safe yet.

"Lefty, get in here and help us dig her out," he ordered.

The Delta operator immediately lay flat on his stomach, his upper body leaning over the hole, not wanting to add his weight since they had no idea exactly where Maddy's body was beneath all the dirt and began to help him and Falcon shovel it off her.

"Pack's full. Give me a second and I'll empty it," Grover warned them, and although Hawk didn't look up, he heard the man moving, and dirt began to fall on them again. With three strong sets of hands digging, they were able to keep digging Maddy free, and it wasn't long before Grover dumped what he'd collected so far and moved back into position.

No one spoke. All of them focused on Maddy and getting her dug free and out of the hole. Uncovering her body took time, and as they freed her shoulders and worked their way down her torso, Hawk moved behind her to support her limp body.

"Whoa," Falcon exclaimed as the dirt beneath them suddenly began to shift as though draining away. Hawk quickly adjusted his hold on Maddy as the dirt moved.

"What's going on?" Grover demanded.

"Looks like the dirt burying her alive is being drained away," Lefty replied.

A moment later they were standing on solid ground, a metal grate beneath their feet. Hawk hoisted Maddy up into his arms, anxious to get her out of what had very nearly been her grave.

"Give her here," Lefty said, reaching down to take Maddy.

As hard as it was to let her go, even for a moment, Hawk knew there was no way he could climb up with Maddy in his arms. Well, he probably could if he had to, but it would be much quicker to pass her to Lefty then climb out himself.

Once Lefty had a grip on her and pulled her out of the ten-foot-deep hole, Falcon and Hawk used the corners to quickly climb out. As he did so Hawk noticed several crevices in the sides of the grave.

Maddy must have dug them. His strong girl had been working on her own escape plan, and probably would have made it too if the dirt hadn't started raining down on her.

Lefty had laid Maddy out and had his fingers on her slender throat, his cheek above her mouth. His brown eyes were grim when he looked over as Hawk dropped to his knees on Maddy's other side. "She's got a pulse, but she's not breathing."

Without hesitating he leaned over her, pinching her nose closed with one hand, his other tilting her head back and gripping her chin to open her mouth. Then he covered her lips with his own and breathed into her.

"Come on, sweetheart," he pleaded after he'd delivered another breath and paused to see if it would kickstart her lungs. "Don't give up on me, caramel." She didn't take a breath, so he leaned down again and puffed two more lungfuls of air into her. "Please, honey, breathe. Come back to me. I need you, Maddy, and so does Louie. Don't leave us." He wasn't ashamed to beg in front of his brother and the Deltas. He knew that if it were one of their women lying lifeless before them all three of them would be begging.

Maddy was his life. She had brought into his world things he hadn't even known he wanted but now knew he couldn't live without. He had been so sure that he was going to spend the rest of his life as an Army Ranger before retiring. No kids, no marriage, it all fell apart anyway, but Maddy had taught him something important. A relationship only fell apart if both parties weren't fighting to keep it together, and he was prepared to fight with everything he had to win her back.

All of a sudden Maddy's chest heaved as she dragged in a rough breath, and Hawk's vision swam as tears filled his eyes.

"There you go, caramel, just like that. Breathe for me, baby," he encouraged as she sucked in another breath and then another. Beneath the dirt and grime her cheeks were pale, and when her lashes began to flutter, he threw a quick glance at the others. "Water." He didn't even know who handed him a bottle, his attention focused on the beautiful woman beneath him, but when one was thrust into his hand, he poured water on her face and used his sleeve to wipe the dirt away from her eyes.

"Hawk?" Her voice was weak and scratchy, but she was speaking, and she was lucid, that was all he cared about in this moment.

"Right here, caramel." He shifted behind her, lifting her torso and resting it against his chest as his legs went out on either side of her. "Drink a little water." When he held the bottle to her lips, she greedily drank what he offered. Not sure how badly she was hurt or if she was dehydrated, he only let her drink a little before removing it, not wanting her to make herself sick.

"You're here." She sounded shocked by the fact, and he knew given how things had ended between them it was probably the last thing she expected.

"Of course I'm here. Anywhere you go, I go."

Her eyes opened slowly, and she tilted her head to look up at him. "Louie?"

"Is fine, perfectly safe and back at home with my sisters," he assured her.

"Sean wants him. I thought he wanted to kill you all, but I think he wants to keep Louie," she said.

"He definitely plans on keeping the baby," he agreed. "There's a nursery at his house, and your mom said he'd been talking a lot about adopting since they weren't able to have kids of their own." After realizing that money and revenge weren't all his uncle was after, they'd tracked down Maddy's mom and spoken with her. The woman had no clue who her husband really was but admitted he'd been talking a lot recently about a family, and that he had been disappointed when Maddy never returned after boarding school. His worst fears confirmed, Sean was obsessed with his stepdaughter, just like he had likely been obsessed with his brother's wife. "That's not all he wants though, honey," he said, tightening his hold on Maddy. "He also wants you."

"He tried to kill me," Maddy reminded him, shuddering as images of being buried alive no doubt ran through her mind.

"Scare you I think," Lefty said from beside them.

Maddy turned to look at the man. "What do you mean?"

"There's a grate at the bottom of the hole. The dirt started draining away before we dug you out. Even if we hadn't been here, it's likely you wouldn't have died," Lefty explained.

Maddy's brow furrowed, and she lifted a hand to rub at her temples as though her head ached, which it probably did. "I don't understand."

"That's Lefty, by the way," Hawk told her, "Falcon is here too, and the blond guy is Grover. They're both Delta Force."

"That doesn't explain anything," Maddy mumbled.

Hawk couldn't help but grin. Alive, in one piece, *and* trying to figure things out, his girl was back. "Sorry, honey. Your mom said you were with her the day she met Sean, and he showed no interest in her until he saw you. She told us that he was borderline obsessed with planning out your future, only he intended for you to return to Ireland after graduating. There was a hiding place in your bedroom, behind the wall opposite your bed, I'd bet every cent I own that he watched you while you were there, and this place is visible from your bedroom window. I think when we hooked up you made all his dreams come true. You're giving him an heir, you're giving him the keys to my family's fortune, and he thinks he can keep you for himself."

It was a lot to take in, and he watched as Maddy's hazel eyes grew round, then her mouth tightened into a straight line before fear bled into her face. "He wants me *and* Louie?"

"But he won't get either of you," he said firmly. No way was he letting anyone take what was his. "Grover and Lefty will get you out of here, while Falcon and I meet up with Eagle and the others and take out Sean."

Maddy shook her head. "He's here. He must know you're here too because the security system started the dirt falling when you breached it. He'll kill you, but if what you're saying is true, he won't kill me. You need to let me near him, I'll kill him."

It wasn't the determination in her voice that had him suddenly queasy or the fact that his girl was a bloodthirsty little thing. It was what she'd said about them setting off the security system and opening the chute above her grave, sealing what could have been her death.

Hawk released Maddy, turned, and threw up.

He'd caused this.

Again.

No matter what he did he caused her pain.

From the second he'd walked up to her that night in the bar she'd been in danger. She could have died in that hole, been buried alive. His head said she would be better off without him, definitely safer, but his heart was in love with her and couldn't imagine life without her.

Selfishly, he didn't think he could let her go. Reaching for her, he dragged her into his arms and crushed her to her chest, rocking her as tears fell down his cheeks. "I'm sorry, so sorry," he whispered against her hair.

Miracle of miracles, her arms came around him, and she ran a soothing hand up and down his back.

Hawk didn't know what the future held for them, if it was possible to fix things between them, but he did know that he didn't deserve the woman he held in his arms.

* * *

1:29 A.M.

. . .

IT WAS TIME.

Sean Murphy—or Oswald as he'd been born—lounged in his favorite armchair in his bedroom, staring out across the rocky cliffs outside the castle to the ocean below. Waves crashed against the stone cliffs, although he couldn't see them from his room, he had the window open and could hear them. The sound soothed him, and he often sat here and listened to them. A fire crackled in the hearth, warming him despite the icy chill wafting in through the window. This was his favorite place in the world.

His wife had no idea that he owned the property they could see from their home, but this was the place where he conducted his more secretive business, and the house where he had intended to raise an heir.

Only there was no heir.

His wife was unable to conceive because he was unable to produce sperm. Impotence robbing the ability to gain immortality. While no human lived forever the only way to create a lasting legacy was to produce an heir who would carry on your work, carry on your name, and create an immortality life refused to give.

Standing, he crossed to stare at the painting hanging above the fireplace.

Madeline Montgomery was supposed to be that heir. While he'd had no use for the grieving child, he'd known from the moment he laid eyes on her that she was the one. The eerie similarities between her and the only woman he'd ever wanted were too great to be denied, and once he laid eyes on the girl, he was determined to have her.

If she had ever touched the trust fund, she would have already been his. Unbeknownst to anyone but his most trusted lawyer the trust fund had a hidden clause. If she ever used the money for anything she was beholden to him and must return to Northern Ireland and remain with him in his home until she provided him an heir.

While the girl may never have touched the trust fund, and he had waited patiently for her to do so, she had in fact managed to provide him with the heir he craved. And one that would finally get his hands on the fortune that should have been his almost four decades ago. He might not have gotten the girl, but he was determined to wind up with everything this time.

All of it.

He wanted it all, and he wasn't going to be denied.

Sean had worked hard to build a business from the ground up, not an easy feat. But here in Northern Ireland, there was a certain need for weapons that he'd been able to take advantage of. Relocating to his family's homeland, Sean had started small, but it hadn't been hard to slowly grow his import-export business into one that trafficked weapons around the globe. He was proud of his accomplishments, and while he enjoyed the financial benefits it wasn't enough. Not if he didn't have anyone to pass it on to.

"Riley?" he called out.

His personal bodyguard opened the bedroom door and stepped through it. "Yes, sir?"

"Have someone bring up Madeline. I'm ready for her, and I'm sure she's more than ready to make a deal."

"Yes, sir." With a single nod, the man departed, and Sean stretched his back and readied himself for his stepdaughter's arrival. He wasn't a young man anymore, but he kept himself in good shape and had managed to keep his looks. A full head of hair, although it was no longer the silky jet black it had been in his youth. It was now streaked with gray, but he thought it gave him a distinguished look, and with his still smooth skin and twinkling blue eyes, women half his age and younger regularly flirted with him.

It was all in his attitude. Sean could be charming and charismatic when he wanted to be, and unless you betrayed him, he was fair and easy to both work with and get along with. Betray him as his brother had, and you found out what he was made of.

Tonight, he would finally get his revenge. While making Madeline his was not the same as claiming Georgette Hammond as his own, his stepdaughter was similar enough that he could pretend. And better than that, Hawk and any of the other Oswald siblings who had come after Madeline would be killed. The rest would soon fall, and once his nephews and nieces, their partners, and children were out of the way, Madeline's son would be the sole beneficiary of the Hammond fortune.

A fortune that should have been his when he had marked Georgette as his own.

To be betrayed by his own brother was something he could not tolerate.

John had swept Georgie out from underneath him. Wooed the girl and won her heart. Sean hadn't cared about her heart, only her bank account. That night in her bedroom, the night she turned eighteen and finally had access to her trust fund was supposed to cement the deal. He'd told her it was simple, either she acquiesced and gave herself to him, or he would kill John, and she could live the rest of her life knowing his death was on her shoulders. He had expected her to cave, but the following morning both she and John were gone.

It had taken him nearly two decades to finally locate them, but that night hadn't gone to plan either. Oldest son Eagle had already left the off-grid farm to join the military, and somehow the oldest girl had fought off two armed felons, thus saving her life and those of her siblings.

Again, the Hammond fortune had fallen through his fingers, and with the notoriety of the family at that time it hadn't been wise to make a move. So, he had waited and plotted, and bided his time. But no more, he wanted what was his, what Georgie had cheated him out of all those years ago, and he would have it.

The bedroom door opened again, and a dirt-streaked Madeline was led into the room. Riley wasn't there, but she was brought in by one of the men dressed in the same black fatigues that the rest of his security team wore. Assuming that Riley was off taking care of their other visitors, he nodded to the man.

"Bring her in, put her in the chair." He gestured to the one he had just vacated, and without a word, the younger man marched his stepdaughter across the room and shoved her into the chair.

Madeline was covered in dirt, her eyes red-rimmed and puffy, the white dress he'd put her in earlier was now brown, and her breathing sounded a little wheezy, no doubt because of the dirt she had inhaled. While her disheveled appearance was hardly what one could call attractive, the fact that she looked broken and defeated was more than enough to get his still active libido taking notice.

"Dismissed," he tossed over his shoulder to the guard, who he assumed left the room because he heard the door close, his attention fixed on the cowering woman. "It didn't have to be this way, Madeline, but I warned you. There are always consequences to your actions. Yours could have resulted in your death, but I was merciful. Your mother means a great deal to me, and I am willing to make you a deal if you are finally willing to stop acting stupid."

He waited to see her response, and when she finally lifted tear-drenched eyes to meet his, he saw a broken woman.

Perfect.

It was so much easier to mold a broken woman than it was to have to break them first. It was one of the things that had attracted him to Madeline's mother. Broken and grieving, he knew he could create the perfect socialite wife. And he had. Margaret was everything he needed. She was a wonderful hostess, she attended to his needs without being demanding, and so long as he showered her with gifts, and took her on vacations across the globe, she put up with him being away more than he was home.

His plans for Madeline were different. She would not be a part of his public life. She would remain here, locked away inside the castle, here to cater to his whims, and care for her son until he was old enough to fend for himself.

"What's the deal?" Madeline whispered, her voice hoarse and heavy with pain and despair.

"You remain here, your son will not be killed along with the rest of his family. You will get to raise him until he is old enough for me to form him into my heir, and you can live out your days here, having contact with him." As far as he was concerned it was a good deal and one that she was lucky to be offered.

"And if I say no?"

"Then you go back in your pit, and your son will never know who you are."

Her head dropped, and he saw her shoulders shudder. "O-okay."

Victory.

Sean closed the distance between them, grabbed a handful of her messy locks, and yanked until she was on her knees before him. "There is one more thing."

Tears dripped down her cheeks when he pulled her head back until she looked up at him. "What?"

He traced a finger along the slender curve of her neck before his hand curled around it, squeezing just enough that she gasped and lifted her hands to claw at his. "You will serve me in any way I demand."

"I will serve," she murmured. "If you don't hurt my son and let me be part of his life, I will do whatever you want."

Perfect.

It may have taken him forty years, but he was finally about to get everything he had ever wanted.

* * *

1:41 A.M.

MADDY SHIFTED her gaze from Sean to the floor, and then snuck a glance at the shadows by the door.

Lefty wasn't even noticeable if she hadn't been looking for him. She had no idea how he managed to do that, but she supposed it was something he had learned when he joined Delta Force. The only way Hawk would allow her to go anywhere near Sean was if someone went with her, stuck to her like glue, hence Lefty's presence here. For obvious reasons, Hawk couldn't be with her himself. Although that seemed to drive him crazy, she wasn't quite sure why. When someone had come to get her out of the hole in the basement, the guys had knocked the man out, and Lefty had taken his clothes and his place, escorting her up here.

Knowing she wasn't alone, that she had an elite warrior watching her back, was the only reason she hadn't fallen apart.

The guys were counting on her.

Lives depended on her.

It was a lot of pressure, especially given that she was hardly feeling her best. Panic clawed at her skin like a million spiders were crawling all over her. Her body was teetering at the edge of complete exhaustion. Pain had become her new best friend and one that she couldn't wait to ditch. But they weren't there yet. Sean was still alive, Hawk and his brothers were here in the home of someone who wanted them dead, their sisters, wives, and children at home weren't safe, and there were more of Sean's men than there were of the Oswalds'.

Maddy wasn't sure how they were all getting out of this alive, but she had to trust the experts. Hawk's friends seemed confident that they had this situation under control, so she had to believe in them.

Maybe she really would get home to her son.

"You can prove your loyalty now," Sean told her.

"How?" she asked without looking up. It was hard for her to play the subservient, broken victim—even though she had been victimized at her stepfather's hand—but she wasn't going to do anything to ruin the tentative plan they'd thrown together.

"I think it's time we seal the deal." The hand that circled her neck slipped lower until he had palmed one of her breasts.

Sensing rather than seeing Lefty tense, she shook her head hoping that Lefty would know it was aimed at him and not at Sean, who appeared to be preoccupied with her breasts. It was disgusting. Mostly because this was rape, even if she said yes and there was no SEAL standing guard, her assent would be purely to keep herself alive, not because she wanted to have sex with Sean. But it was also disgusting because not only was he old enough to be her father, he was sixty, she was twenty-seven, he *was* her father. Stepfather, but still he had been part of her life since she was just nine years old, and apparently been lusting over her ever since.

Because she knew Lefty wouldn't let it get that far, Maddy nodded. "Okay," she whispered, allowing desperation to bleed into her voice. She wanted Sean to continue to think that she was broken down, with no threat whatsoever.

While she wasn't the biggest threat in the room, the guys had given her a weapon, and as soon as he thought the ball was firmly in his court, she was going to make her move. Hawk had told her not to, that he was only giving her a weapon, so she wasn't vulnerable, and she knew that the Oswalds wanted to be the ones to take down their uncle given the hell he'd put them all through, but she wanted her pound of flesh too.

As Lefty watched over her and she played the role of number one direction, the others were taking out guards and closing in on Sean. He wouldn't even know it until it was too late and knowing that made her want to smile, but she tamped down on the urge. Nothing to tip him off, he still had home turf advantage even if his numbers advantage was dwindling without him even knowing it.

Sean still had a hold of her hair, and he used it to lever her to her feet. The sting in her scalp was nothing compared to the headache drumming relentlessly inside her skull, the tightness in her chest, the shooting pains in her left leg, or the burning in her damaged wrists. It was just a blip on the radar, and she was more focused on the bed he was dragging her toward.

When Sean pushed her onto the mattress her stomach cramped, and a cold sweat broke out across her skin. Even though she had fought to be part of the takedown she hadn't envisioned having to pretend to allow her stepfather to rape her. From the tent in his pants, he had only one thing on his brain. Quite possibly the same thing that had been on his mind since he had met her when she was nine years old.

His breath was hot against her skin as he moved in to attempt to kiss her, and while he'd released her hair, he'd reclaimed a hold on one of her breasts. He didn't notice when she slipped her hand between her back and the mattress, her fingers pushing the dress up enough that she could reach the knife hidden there.

As his lips approached hers, Maddy grabbed the knife and freed it. Without hesitation, she shoved it into Sean's side.

The second she did all hell broke loose.

Sean howled and slammed a fist into the side of her head as he realized she was the one to inflict the injury.

Lefty seemed to fly through the air like a ninja, tackling Sean to the ground.

Half a dozen men holding automatic weapons climbed through the windows.

The door was thrown open, and all three of the Oswald brothers stormed in looking like the heroes they were. Hawk might not be her hero, and she didn't think the way he'd hurled accusations and threats at her was okay, but she still believed he was a good guy.

Certainly the lesser of two evils in this situation.

"It's over, Sean," Eagle said, fire dancing in his blue eyes. Flanked on either side by Falcon and Hawk, all three brothers were a formidable force. One she was glad at least at the moment was on her side.

When Lefty dragged Sean to his feet, her stepfather was breathing hard, blood trickling from the side of his mouth. There was an almost maniacal glint to his eyes now. It was obvious he was outnumbered. None of his men had come running to his rescue, and yet he didn't look defeated, he looked almost cocky.

"It's never over till it's over," Sean countered.

Her stepfather's arrogance while surrounded by so many armed men made her anxious, and she shuffled back on the bed. Hawk noticed her movement and immediately broke away from his brothers to come to her.

"You okay?" he asked.

She nodded. She wasn't all right of course but what could she say? She was alive, she actually had a real chance of going home to her son, actually she was way better than okay.

"Always have to be the hero, just like your father," Sean sneered at Hawk.

"My father was a good man, unlike you," Hawk shot back.

"Your father stole what was mine. *I* claimed your mother, *I* was supposed to be the one she married, *I* was supposed to inherit her money, but your father swooped in and took her. The morning after he found us in bed together the two of them were gone."

"You raped her," Falcon growled.

"I took what was mine," Sean corrected.

"And now you're going to pay for everything you've done to our family," Eagle said, hatred for his uncle clear in his voice and his face.

"I don't think so." Sean grinned, pulling something from his pocket and holding it up. "On the contrary, I'm about to take half of you out."

Maddy had no idea what was going on, but it seemed like she was the only one because everything went crazy.

Hawk snatched her up, lunging out one of the windows with her.

They were falling.

At least that's what it felt like to her, but her brain eventually processed the fact that they weren't dropping through the air, they were in fact, climbing down a rope. Well, Hawk was climbing down one and holding her in his arms at the same time.

Voices shouted.

Gunshots fired.

Other people were dropping down ropes beside her and Hawk.

The ocean seemed to roar beneath them as they scaled the cliffs.

Then a huge explosion rocked the night, and they were falling for real.

So close.

Maddy had been so close to being rescued and getting home to Louie, being able to raise him, only to have it all come crashing down around her.

Literally.

When they hit the water, the cold stole her breath.

Things fell around her.

She couldn't see.

Couldn't figure out which way was up.

Looked like death would be coming for her tonight after all, only it would come at the hands of the water rather than the earth.

* * *

2:05 A.M.

WHEN THEY HIT THE WATER, Hawk lost his grip on Maddy.

He'd managed to use the momentum of the explosion to throw their bodies out and away from the rocks at the bottom of the cliff. But hitting the water from the height they'd been at when Sean set his castle alight felt like hitting concrete.

The momentary shock to his system was enough to cause it to spasm and his hold on her release.

While he and the others were wearing wetsuits under their fatigues, Maddy was wearing nothing but a dress Sean had put her in after taking her clothing. Hypothermia was as big a risk as drowning, and he immediately began searching for her. The water was rough, waves big and foamy as they crashed into the rocks. If he didn't find her soon, she could easily be picked up by one of those waves and tossed into the rocks, which would smash her body to pieces.

They hadn't talked about how good a swimmer she was, but even the best swimmers were at risk out here.

Hawk had lost his comms unit in the fall, so he had no way to check on his brothers, the Delta team, or Prey's Alpha team, but he prayed everyone else was okay. For now, he had to keep his focus on Maddy. Eagle, Falcon, and the others were all well trained, and he trusted they could get themselves safely to shore, but Maddy didn't have their same training, and she was injured, she needed him.

Diving beneath the water, he began to search for her. Not an easy thing to do at night in the remote oceans of Northern Ireland. Add to that the fact that the waves churned things up, bringing up sand and seaweed, sticks and rocks and other debris, and it was almost impossible to spot anything.

When his lungs were burning, begging him for oxygen, Hawk swam to the surface, dragged in a breath, and dove back down.

How long had passed since they went under?

It simultaneously felt like seconds and hours.

Surrounded by the inky darkness, in the end, it was pure luck that he found her. Something brushed against his leg, and he reached down, grabbed it, and swam back to the surface.

Relief hit him hard when their heads broke above the water, and he saw Maddy's long caramel-colored locks. She choked and spluttered as she sucked in air and looked around, dazed and confused.

There was no time to check her out, make sure she hadn't sustained any new injuries, he had to get them out of the water. Not an easy feat with the waves, and Maddy struggling against him, clearly disoriented.

It took everything he had to swim them both away from the cliff and toward the rocks where they could climb out of the water. It also took much longer than he would have liked, and the more time they spent in the water, the less Maddy fought against him.

Hypothermia.

He'd watched her be buried alive tonight, and now he was forced to watch her succumb to the cold, helpless to do anything to help her except continue swimming.

"Hawk!" a voice called from the dark, and they were suddenly lit by a powerful spotlight.

A zodiac was pulling up beside him, and when hands reached out to grab Maddy, Hawk helped push her up and out of the water, then allowed someone to help him scramble up and into the boat. Trigger had taken Maddy and was lying her down on the floor of the zodiac, and Kane "Brain" Temple and Porter "Oz" Reed were the ones who had grabbed his arms and hauled him out of the water.

"Everyone alive?" he asked as he crawled on his knees to Maddy's side.

"A few injuries, but everyone has checked in, you two were the last," Oz replied.

"Took me a while to find Maddy, she was fighting me at first." His worried eyes fixed on Maddy's pale face, her lips were tinted blue, and when he touched his fingertips to her neck he found her pulse sluggish. Grateful that his family and friends were all alive—although he had no idea how they all managed to make it out, the explosion Sean had set off must have been more for show than to do a whole lot of damage—right now he couldn't be anything but worried about Maddy. "We have to get her out of the wet clothes."

While Trigger pulled an emergency blanket from his pack, Hawk stripped off the soaked dress. Maddy's skin was ice cold to the touch, and they were still a long way from getting her somewhere safe where she could be evaluated and given the medical treatment she needed.

"Sean?" he asked the others as he pulled Maddy's limp body into his arms, the blanket tucked securely around her.

"No confirmation," Trigger replied.

Hawk swore. "We can't let him get away, my family will never be safe." His family which included the woman just starting to shake in his arms. There was no way he would allow Maddy to live in constant fear that her stepfather would come for her. No way was he allowing his son to grow up with this shadow hanging over his head. Sean had to be stopped.

"Bear just said his team spotted a boat heading for the shore, one man on board," Brain announced.

"Sean," Hawk said, this time his tone seething with a fury unlike anything else he had ever experienced. He had been angry with the men who killed his parents, angry when three-year-old Cleo had been kidnapped, when Falcon's team had been betrayed, when someone had gone after Raven, then Falcon, then Sparrow, but nothing compared to the rage inside him at the moment.

This rage was powered by his feelings for the beautiful woman he held close against his chest. She was his, there was a chance he might not be able to win her back, but that didn't matter, nothing and no one hurt her and got away with it.

"Ask him where the boat is," he told Brain.

"Bear, what's his location?" Brain asked. "Half a klick on our three o'clock."

"Go after them," he ordered.

Although the Deltas shot him hesitant glances, Oz began to steer the boat in the direction Sean was fleeing. This ended here and now. Tonight. Sean wasn't going to be alive when the sun rose.

"It's almost over, caramel, just hold on," he murmured to Maddy as he held her.

"Looks like he's getting off the boat, onto the rocks," Brain related what Bear was obviously telling him.

Trigger was driving the zodiac as fast as it would go, and it didn't take long for him to spot Sean's boat. When the boat pulled in beside it, he thrust Maddy into Oz's arms. "Don't let anything happen to her. If I don't make it, you get her to safety." Pausing only long enough to press a kiss to Maddy's too-cold forehead, he grabbed his weapon and climbed onto the rocks.

"You're not getting away, Sean," he called out, knowing the man was somewhere nearby. "You underestimated us. Haven't you learned by now that you're never going to win, never going to get what you want? Dad loved Mom, he didn't care about her money."

"Your mother's family was one of the richest in the world," his uncle yelled.

"But dad didn't see her as a meal ticket. You wanted to use her. She was too good for you," he said as he carefully made his way across the slick rocks. With the crashing waves, it was hard to pick up the sounds of footsteps, and this was Sean's home turf. He no doubt knew where he was going and how to get there, but Hawk was going in blind.

"She chose wrong and look what it got her. Madeline chose wrong as well, but it won't stop me, nothing can stop me."

"Hawk, watch out!"

Maddy's scream had him spinning just in time. Sean

appeared from behind a rock, firing at him. But Hawk, heeding Maddy's warning without question, fired at his uncle at the same time shots were also fired from the boat.

Sean's body spun at the force of the bullets hitting it, but Hawk didn't stop. He fired for his mom, then again, and again, for his father, for each of his siblings, his in-laws, nieces and nephews, for his son, and finally for the woman he loved.

The threat hanging over his family's head was finally eliminated once and for all, and the woman he feared he had lost forever had just saved his life. Hawk prayed it wasn't too late, that there was still hope for him and Maddy.

CHAPTER SIXTEEN

October 24th

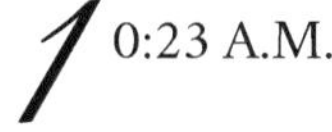0:23 A.M.

IT FELT SO good to be warm, dry, and mostly out of pain, and yet Maddy was antsy, wanting to get home to her sweet, little baby boy.

Most of yesterday was a blur. She had vague memories of a shadow approaching Hawk, screaming a warning, her fingers clutching at a weapon, and firing at the threat to her child's father. After that, things were mostly a blur. She didn't remember being brought on a helicopter to a hospital in Belfast, being checked out in the ER, or having tests and scans. Her memories started up again when she first woke in the hospital late afternoon.

Hawk had been here when she'd finally woken, but

between doctor visits, nurses coming in and out to check her vitals, and all the guys constantly hanging around trying to make her feel better and keep her mind off things the day had flown by. Not that she minded, she wasn't in any hurry to talk about her issues with Hawk. All she wanted was to see her baby. But their flight wasn't leaving until later today, so she still had another five hours to go until they left the hospital to head to the airport.

"Hey, Mads, how you doing?" Lefty asked as he breezed into her hospital room with a bouquet of flowers.

She couldn't help but laugh. "More flowers?" Her room looked like a florist had taken up residence. Every time one of the guys came to see her they brought another bouquet, she had close to five dozen now. The guys were great though, they'd told her how they'd met their wives, and boy were those some crazy stories. But it had kept her occupied, which she knew was the point, and turning her hospital room into a wildflower meadow certainly cheered her up, so she was very grateful to them.

"Can never have too many flowers," he told her, kissing her cheek before setting the bouquet into a vase. "You get to talk with your little boy?"

Maddy smiled. "Yeah, I spoke with Raven and Olivia, and I got to see Louie. He's totally fine, they're taking great care of him. He didn't even wake up," she added with an eye roll. "My son can sleep through anything. I think it's an Oswald blessing, at least for boys. Raven said Roman sleeps like a champ too, but Cleo didn't, and Luna doesn't. I'm glad Louie's so small that he'll never know about any of this, that he didn't miss me these last few days. I can't wait to see him though. I've missed him so much, for a while there I thought I would never see him again." As much as she couldn't wait to get home to Louie, at the back of her mind she kept worrying that Hawk would follow through on his threats to take their son away from her. Just because he knew she hadn't been working with Sean didn't mean he wouldn't get angry with her over something else in the future and use it against her.

"It won't be long now. A few hours and we'll be in the air." Lefty pulled up the chair beside her bed and gave her a quizzical look when she nodded distractedly. "What's going on?"

"I ..." it was on the tip of her tongue to tell him nothing. After all, she'd only met Lefty yesterday, but he'd risked his life to save hers, and she trusted him. Picking at the hem of the hospital blanket, she admitted, "I'm worried about how things will be with Hawk when we get back home."

Lefty's brown eyes crinkled. "I thought you and Hawk were a couple."

"It's complicated."

"Life always is. Tell me about it."

Since Lefty was being all attentive, and she kind of did want to talk to someone about it, she started talking. "When Hawk and I met it was supposed to be just one night, but I felt something between us, I thought he did too. When I found out I was pregnant I tried to find him, but I didn't know his name. I was so shocked when I walked into Prey, and he was there, and I had this dream that everything was going to be perfect. We'd fall in love, get married, raise our son together, have more kids, and grow old. A fairytale, you know? And then it all changed when Hawk said some things I'm having a hard time getting over."

Lefty looked thoughtful. "Well, it's up to you. If you can't move past it that's your choice. You don't have to put up with anything you don't want to, and certainly not a partner treating you disrespectfully. But can I tell you something?" When she nodded, he continued, "Whatever you felt that night, Hawk felt it too."

"He didn't." That she was sure of.

"He did."

"He didn't."

"Yeah, he did, Mads," Lefty said firmly. "Want to know how I know that he's crazy about you?"

Did she?

Was it worth it?

Even if Hawk was crazy about her, it didn't change the fact that she wasn't sure she trusted him anymore.

Still ... "Okay, tell me why you think he's crazy about me."

"I don't think it, I know it," he clarified. "He was out of his mind with worry when we didn't know where you were. And when we found you in that hole, the dirt covering your head, he looked gutted. I know that feeling, I've *felt* that feeling. When Kinley was taken, I felt like my heart had been ripped out. I didn't know how I would survive if we didn't find her in time. That's what I saw in Hawk." He took her hands. "He even beat up Falcon."

That surprised a chuckle out of her. "Beat up Falcon?"

"Well, he hit him, not sure you can beat Falcon up," Lefty joked.

She chuckled again before sobering. "Maybe he cares, but I'm not sure that's enough."

As though their conversation had conjured Hawk out of thin air, the door to her room swung open, and Hawk came breezing through. There were no flowers in his hand, but he did have a large envelope. He looked so good, strong, and safe, and yet every time she wanted to lean into him, let him take away her fear for just a little while, she remembered the look on his face when he told her he'd pay off a judge to get Louie.

"Whatever you choose to do is up to you, but remember what we talked about," Lefty said. He squeezed her hands, kissed her cheek, then slapped Hawk on the back on the way out of the room.

"How are you feeling?" Hawk asked as he took the chair Lefty had just vacated. His knuckles were white, gripping the envelope so tightly she expected the paper to rip, the only chink in his otherwise easy-going exterior.

"I'm okay." It was mostly true anyway, she had two cracked ribs, a hairline fracture in her left foot, and her hip was badly bruised. Her wrists were completely messed up, and the doctor had warned her there was a chance she might need skin grafts. But again, she was alive and going home to her son, she was lucky to have walked away from the ordeal alive.

Hawk reached for her hand, hesitated, and withdrew his hand, the façade dropped, and she saw the pain, regret, guilt, and fear in his eyes. "Maddy, I owe you a major apology. I was a jerk, no excuses, I never should have spoken to you that way. I'm so sorry."

She hadn't expected him to apologize so quickly, maybe Lefty was right, and he did really care about her. Maddy could understand that he and his family had been terrorized, and the timing of her showing up when she had could look suspicious, she supposed she could see things from his point of view. "Okay, I accept your apology."

He startled. "Really?"

"Yes." They had to co-parent Louie for a long time. It would be much easier to do if they cleared the air and there was no animosity between them.

"Thank you, I don't deserve that, but I appreciate it. Maddy, I know I don't deserve one, but I want a second chance. A chance to prove to you that I can be the man you deserve."

He was so earnest, and he seemed to be so sincere, but it wasn't that simple. "Hawk ..."

"You don't have to decide anything right now. I just wanted you to know that I'm not walking away from you. I'll do whatever I have to to earn your trust back. I don't care how long it takes or what I have to do, but nothing will ever be more important to me than proving I can be the man you and our son deserve."

"That's the thing, I'm not sure you can," she said truthfully.

"The day you disappeared I was coming to give you these. I want you to know that I regret what I said about Louie, always will, and I would never do anything to hurt you or our son." Hawk handed her the envelope, and she opened it.

Her mouth dropped open when she saw they were custody papers, granting both her and Hawk joint physical and legal custody of Louie. Tears blurred her eyes as her biggest fear faded away. Hawk had regretted his words enough to go to a lawyer and have papers drawn up. Indecision warred inside her. Was she making a mistake? Was she making too much out of it? It was obvious that Hawk felt bad about it, and he had taken a swing at his brother because he was so worried about her.

Maybe …

When she went to say as much Hawk stopped her, touching a finger to her lips. "Don't say anything now. You've been through hell and you're desperate to get home to Louie. I just want you to know that I can't give up on us." He stooped and whispered the softest of kisses to her lips before standing and leaving the room.

Maddy stared after him, touching her finger to her lip, she had a lot to think about, but finally the vice clamped around her chest was gone. Whatever happened between her and Hawk she wasn't going to lose her son. The relief of knowing that made it easier to see that maybe all hope wasn't lost, who knows, perhaps there was a chance for her and Hawk after all.

CHAPTER SEVENTEEN

October 25th

:32 P.M.

"FINALLY," Hawk muttered as there was a knock on his hotel room door. He'd told Maddy to stay at his place since the nursery was mostly finished and Louie had been bounced around enough in his very short little life. She'd been hesitant, but still weak and in pain and it hadn't taken much to convince her to stay. Besides, when she finally got Louie in her arms again, she'd been unable to put him down, so staying at his place meant she didn't have to waste time packing him up and going to a hotel. When he'd assured her he was going to go to a hotel for a few days it had sealed the deal.

Step one of winning back Maddy was now complete.

Only problem was he had no idea what step two should be.

Which was why he had brought in reinforcements.

"We brought pizza, brownies, and sodas," Eagle said as Hawk opened the door. "What exactly are you providing?"

"The room," he said with a shrug.

"We need an upgrade," Olivia said with a chuckle as she pushed Luna's stroller inside. "There aren't even enough chairs for everyone."

"You guys can sit on the bed," he told her. "Or the floor," he added with a wink.

"Lucky us," Raven said wryly as she set Roman's stroller beside his cousin's. "By the way, Cleo was totally bummed that she missed this brainstorming session."

"She can give me her input after school," he said. Actually, getting the teen's thoughts on his problem with Maddy wasn't a bad idea. Cleo was smart, and even though she'd spent ten years locked in a house forced to pose for child pornography photo shoots she was surprisingly smart and perceptive. She had a great natural ability to read and understand people.

"Trust me she'll be thrilled," Max said.

"Dovie!" he exclaimed when he caught sight of his little sister. "I didn't know you were back from London." He grabbed her and dragged her into his arms, hugging her hard. Between him being deployed most of the time and Dove living in London, they didn't get to see each other often. Although that would be changing, he had already decided he wasn't re-upping, he wanted to be around to raise his son and to be with Maddy.

"I came while you guys were in Ireland. With you going after Sean, Eagle thought I should come home and stay with everyone else. I missed you." She planted a kiss on his cheek and squeezed him hard before punching him lightly in the shoulder. “But stop calling me Dovie. I'm not five years old anymore.”

“Sorry, sweetie, you're always going to be the baby of the family,” he said, slinging an arm around Dove’s shoulders. “But if you would move back from England then we’d get to see each other a whole lot more.”

“It wouldn’t make any difference since you’re always deployed, hidden away somewhere in some war-torn country,” Dove countered.

“Not for much longer. I’m not renewing my contract,” he told his family.

“Really?” Dove’s unusually pale blue eyes lit up.

“Really.”

“Because of Maddy?” Hope asked from the hall. Falcon and his girlfriend, and Sparrow’s fiancé Ethan, hadn't yet made it through the door.

“Her and Louie.”

“So, you two made up?” Falcon asked as he guided Hope into the room. Ethan followed and closed the door behind him.

“No, that’s why you guys are here.” Everyone gathered slices of pizza and drinks and found places to sit around the hotel room. Once they were scattered across the bed, the floor, and the room’s two chairs, he jumped right down to business. “I need you guys to help me figure out a way to win Maddy back.”

“Win?” Falcon repeated. “She’s not a prize, and she doesn’t trust you right now for good reason.”

“Since when are you team Maddy?” he asked, irritated that all of a sudden Falcon was on Maddy’s side rather than his.

“Since she needs someone in her corner,” Falcon replied calmly.

“*I'm* in Maddy’s corner,” he shot back.

"Are you sure?" Falcon asked.

"I don't need to defend my decision to you. I already apologized to her, I told her there was no excuse for my behavior, and there is nothing I regret more than what I said to Maddy and how I treated her. I'd never treat her like that again. I love her," he admitted. Hawk had never been as sure of anything in his life as he was of his feelings for Maddy. "I felt guilty that I wasn't here to help when you were all fighting for your lives as Sean came after you and the people you love. Then I saw she had a connection to him and in my head everything just blew up. All that guilt came out and I panicked and self-sabotaged. It doesn't make what I said okay, and I'm ashamed of myself for what I did and said to her, but I love her, and I want to spend the rest of my life with her. You're right though, she doesn't trust me right now and I don't know how to earn her trust back."

"You really love her?" Raven asked.

"With everything I have. When I thought I'd lost her, it felt like my soul had been ripped out of my body and sent straight to hell. I want to spend my life with her, I know there's a chance it won't happen, that she'll never trust me again, but I have to try." It wasn't an option, his life looked bleak without Maddy in it.

Dove grinned and clapped her hands. "Hawk is in lu-uve," she sing-songed.

Ethan grinned at the littlest Oswald. "I wouldn't get too excited there, Dove, you know you're next."

Dove curled up her nose. "I have no intention of following in these lovebirds' footsteps anytime soon. I love being single, nothing to tie me down, and besides, it's so much more fun to play with my nieces and nephews and then hand them back off to their parents. There is no marriage in my future, at least not anytime soon."

"We'll see," Ethan said.

"Can we get back to my problem now?" Hawk said. His little sister would find love when the time was right, but his entire future was hanging in the balance right now.

"Well," Eagle said thoughtfully, "you have to do something genuine, not necessarily something that costs a lot of money."

"Agreed," Olivia said. "She told us what you said about Louie and paying off the judge to get custody." His sister-in-law shook her head like she couldn't believe he would say something so stupid. "So, if you make a grand gesture, it's just going to make you seem like a guy that throws his money around to try to get what he wants. She's not attracted to that guy."

"What *is* she attracted to then?" He'd never had trouble reading women before, probably because he'd never been serious about a woman before. All he usually cared about was getting them off and then getting off himself, but it wasn't like that with Maddy. Yeah, he couldn't wait to ravish her gorgeous body, but he also wanted to make her smile, feel special, feel safe, and be her soft place to fall.

"You," Hope said simply.

"She liked you before she knew you were rich," Raven added.

"She liked the guy who made her laugh, and talked to her, who got to know her, and who she couldn't stop thinking about," Olivia said.

"There you go, all you have to do is be that guy," Max said with a grin.

"You have to do something from your heart," Eagle said. "You should have seen how Olivia went all gooey when I made her one of those teddy bears that mom used to make for us when we were kids."

Olivia leaned over to kiss her husband's cheek. "That was the sweetest, and when he made one for Luna I melted.

Sometimes trust gets broken, but it can be repaired. Eagle and I had to rebuild trust after he locked me up because he thought I was a spy at Prey."

"And Raven and I had a lot of trust to rebuild after I left after Cleo was abducted," Max added.

"I made a huge mess of things with Sparrow because I wasn't sure I was ready to move on after losing my first wife," Ethan told him.

"I thought I wasn't good enough for Hope, and that meant I wasn't there for her when she needed me," Falcon volunteered. "I wasn't sure she'd forgive me for it."

"Because I love you," Hope said, leaning over to wrap her arm around his shoulders, leaning into him.

"If Maddy loves you too, she'll find a way to trust you again," Eagle said.

"What if she doesn't love me?" They hadn't discussed the L word before Maddy was abducted because it seemed way too soon.

"That's a risk you'll have to take," Raven said. "If you love her then you won't give up on her."

"I'm not giving up. I realized I made a mistake before she went missing and I had custody papers drawn up so she would know I would never take Louie away from her. I gave her the papers in Belfast." The relief on her face when she'd seen those papers had really hit home how badly he'd hurt her. He'd come so close to losing her time after time, and he was determined not to let her, and what they could have together, slip away.

"That's what you need to do, something else like that, something from your heart," Eagle said. "Not a grand gesture, not one that costs a lot of money. She doesn't need you to buy her a house, or fly her to Rome for dinner, or give her some extravagant piece of jewelry. She needs to see your heart, give her something that will mean something to her, or do something with her that will be special to her. Think about what you know about her and go with that, and most importantly, trust yourself. If she doesn't trust you right now, then you need to believe that whatever you decide to do is the right thing."

His family had given him a lot to think about, and already he had an idea brewing in his mind. Maddy had lost her family when she was young, been on her own for a long time, her mother trying to banish all memories of her dad and sister, and taking up with a new man had been a blow. She wasn't used to someone putting her first, caring about her, and making her feel important.

That was his job now.

CHAPTER EIGHTEEN

October 26th

1:44 A.M.

THE MORE HOURS that passed without anything going wrong, without any drama, the more Maddy began to relax.

While she wasn't really home, she was at least back in a safe place, and Hawk seemed to have lost the antagonistic attitude and been playing nice. She believed he was truly sorry for what he'd said, and she got that he'd lashed out because he felt betrayed and was afraid for his family's safety, their very lives. It didn't make it okay, but she'd meant it when she said she forgave him.

Now she needed to find out if she could trust him again.

She wanted to, she really did, but she was afraid of being burned again.

Time.

She needed more time.

Right now, just trying to process the horrors of the last few days was enough to keep her mentally and emotionally occupied, especially with a newborn to care for, but the problem was she needed someone.

Problem with *that* was that all her friends were back in California. After being the one to preach about how they needed to share Louie, she could hardly pack him up and go back to her house. Especially since Hawk had had papers drawn up. Even while he wasn't sure he could completely trust her, he'd gone with a gesture that meant more to her than he could ever know and proved that his words were a mistake and one he wouldn't repeat.

Yesterday when they'd hung out with Louie together things had been weird, and definitely awkward, but not unpleasant. While she had expected he might have made some grand gesture intended to prove that he was serious about earning her trust back he hadn't. They'd merely enjoyed their son, and the break from reliving the horrors of being buried alive had been nice enough she hadn't pushed for more.

Maddy didn't want to play games. She also didn't want to give Hawk false hope. A future with him was what she wanted, and yet she had to be sure that her heart believed in him again because Louie's happiness depended on it.

Her phone buzzed with a text, and she was surprised to see Falcon's name. Eagle had given her a phone when they'd first arrived back in the States. He'd said it was some sort of special, encrypted phone that was super secure, and that she didn't have to worry about paying the bill because it was added to the family's plan. In it he'd programmed everyone's numbers. Not just the Oswald siblings, but all the guys from

Prey's teams, the guys from the Delta team who had helped rescue her, and some guy named Tex who apparently knew everyone and was to be her go-to if she couldn't reach anyone else. He'd told her if she was ever in trouble, she was to reach out to one of them, and from the look on his face, it was clear he would be personally offended if she didn't.

Which was nice. Hawk's family seemed to have accepted her even though her future with Hawk was up in the air.

Even Falcon seemed to have welcomed her into the family. This wasn't the first time he'd texted her just to check in. She hadn't replied to the other texts because, well, he intimidated her still, but he was reaching out, and she had to do the same. If nothing else, these people would always be Louie's family, and she wanted to be on good terms with them. Actually, she wanted a whole lot more. She'd been so lonely after her dad and DeeDee died, she wanted to be part of a family again.

Responding to Falcon's text asking if she needed anything, she said she was running a little low on her chocolate supplies and she'd have to go shopping soon because Louie had grown a lot in the last almost two weeks and had pretty much maxed out his preemie size onesies and was ready to move into newborn. It felt weird asking anyone for anything, she was so used to taking care of herself, but it also felt nice to have someone care enough to check on her.

Falcon's response was almost immediate, and from it she had a feeling she'd soon be swimming in chocolate supplies and baby onesies.

There was a smile on her face when she heard the lift's ding alerting her that someone was about to enter the penthouse. Hawk was supposed to be here at noon to hang out with Louie, who was freshly fed and dressed ready for time with his daddy. She was going to make herself scarce, let father and son enjoy each other's company. It was weird living in Hawk's home, and she intended to find her own place soon, but for now it was nice to have that one thing taken off her mind.

"Hey, how're you doing?" Hawk asked as he walked into the living room.

"I'm good. How are you?" she returned politely.

The once over he gave her was probing enough that it made her self-conscious about the moon boot, and torn skin on her cheek, the loose-fitting clothes, and her hair which she had left to air dry after her shower this morning. Knowing she looked no better than her aching body felt, he on the other hand looked like he'd just stepped off the set of a film shoot.

"I'll get out of your hair, let you and Louie catch up," she said, intending to hurry past him, well, limp past him as fast as her throbbing hip would allow.

Hawk caught her forearm as she went to shuffle past him. His large hand formed a firm but gentle circle, and he tugged softly, turning her to face him. With his free hand, he pushed up the sleeve off her sweatshirt to reveal the bandages covering the road burn. A finger swept out to feather across the white gauze before he turned his attention to her wrists. Adjusting his grip until he cradled both of her hands in his, he swept his thumbs across those bandages. His touch was barely there, not enough to hurt, but enough to make her shiver, he was being so gentle, and there was genuine concern in his eyes.

When he lifted his gaze to her, his eyes seemed to caress her skin, and he lifted a hand to very gently palm her scraped cheek. "Does it hurt?"

"Not really," she replied breathily. It was hard to think of anything else when Hawk touched her like this.

"You have circles under your eyes. Did you sleep last night?"

Maddy hesitated, wanting to lie and say she'd slept fine, but the truth was she'd been afraid even though she'd known she was physically safe here. Nightmares didn't care about secure penthouses and taunted her every time she closed her eyes. Yet she found she couldn't lie. "I didn't sleep well," she admitted.

Instead of replying with some empty words about how time would heal her wounds, and that she should speak to a therapist, learn to move past the horrible things she had endured, he simply circled his arms around her and held her. One large hand urged her head to rest against his chest, and the warmth and sturdiness of the embrace snapped her shaky hold on her emotions.

Tears began to stream down her cheeks. She didn't even bother trying to hold them back because despite everything she *did* feel safe with Hawk.

There was no embarrassment as her tears morphed into sobs and the shock and horror of what she'd been through was finally allowed out. Memories of being trapped in the car's trunk, the pain as her body hit the ground when she jumped from the trunk, seeing Tiana Martinez murdered in front of her, and being buried alive, assaulted her all at once.

The fear, the hopelessness, they all poured out until she was shaking, her fingers curled into Hawk's shirt, clinging to him as his calm presence slowly chipped away at the wall between them.

When he scooped her up, her arms automatically wrapped around his neck. He sat on the couch with her on his lap, and she pressed her face into the crook of his neck and continued to weep. Hawk said nothing, just held her, his lips against the top of her head, one hand rubbing circles on her back. He was just *there,* and that was exactly what she needed.

"I had nightmares too," Hawk admitted when her tears eventually dried up. "You were buried alive, the dirt raining down on you just like it was that night, only I couldn't dig you free. Every time I woke up, I reached for you, but you weren't there, and every time I went back to sleep I had the same dream. I needed you, needed to see you, touch you, hold you." A sigh rippled through him, and he tightened his hold.

Maddy wasn't complaining. She needed this too. "I'm glad you're here." She felt him relax and it made her relax too. As much as she was enjoying this, he'd come to see Louie not her, so she reluctantly pulled away. "Thanks for that, but I don't want to eat into your time with Louie."

When she went to stand, he grabbed hold of her and kept her in his lap. "Stay. I came to see both of you, and this is exactly what I want, the three of us together."

She settled back down against him. "I want that too, and I'm trying to get past what happened."

Hawk kissed her temple. "I know you are, and I appreciate it so much. I don't deserve a second chance, but I'm so glad you're considering giving me one."

"I'm not considering it. I'm giving you a second chance," she said, done with overthinking it. Did she really want to push him away until he left and then spend the rest of her life regretting it?

The answer was simple.

A big, fat no.

"We should start over, pretend we just met, get to know each other some more, no pressure, but with the understanding that we have the same goals. I've missed being part of a family, I've been alone since my dad and sister died, and when I look at my future, I can see you there. So, let's start a fresh, clean slate," she said. You only lived once, she should have learned that lesson by now. Holding onto a grudge, one she believed Hawk was truly repentant for, seemed silly and a waste of time.

Before Hawk could respond, Louie snuffled in his sleep, making them both giggle. "Not a completely clean slate," Hawk chuckled as he reached over to rub the baby's belly.

"No, not a complete clean slate," she agreed. She would never take back her sweet, little son.

"I brought lunch, but I also got you something," Hawk said, reaching for a bag he'd set beside them on the couch.

"You don't have to buy me gifts, Hawk," she told him. She needed to know he trusted her so she could trust him, and that would just take time.

"This is for you and Louie," he said, pulling out an envelope. Since he'd already given her custody papers, she knew it wasn't that, but she had no idea what it could be.

Staying where she was because she wasn't ready to leave Hawk's lap yet, she opened the envelope and pulled out a laminated certificate. Maddy gasped when she read it, tears blurring her vision. "How on earth did you think of doing this?"

"You told me about how your dad loved the stars and how you know he's looking down at you. Now he is officially doing just that." There was a hint of uncertainty in Hawk's blue eyes, like he had tried to give her something that went beyond money, that would mean something to her, but he wasn't quite sure if he'd hit the right mark.

Wanting to reassure him, Maddy threw her arms around his neck and kissed him hard on the lips. "This is perfect. When I thought I wasn't going to come back to Louie, I thought about looking down on him, watching over him. This is just ... I just ... it's so perfect. A star named after my dad, I love it. I love *you*."

Hawk grinned, relief evident on his face. "I love you too, caramel."

She kissed him again only this time the kiss was warmer, softer, in it she felt everything else fade away. Happiness, belonging, love, it was all within her reach. Hawk wasn't perfect, she wasn't either, but he was perfect for her. Together their lives could be as close to perfection as you could get.

CHAPTER NINETEEN

October 27th

:37 P.M.

"YOU HAVE A LITTLE SOMETHING RIGHT HERE." Hawk touched the pad of his thumb to his tongue, then leaned over and wiped it across the smudge of spaghetti sauce at the corner of her mouth.

"Oh, I'm such a mess," Maddy said with a giggle as her tongue darted out to wet that spot, brushing against his thumb in the process.

The innocent gesture immediately sent all his blood plunging south to the one part of his body that had been vying for his attention ever since he walked into his penthouse at noon the day before. While he'd intended to leave after spending a little time with Louie and Maddy, she'd asked him to stay for dinner, then to spend the night, and then they'd spent the entire day together today.

Being this close to her and not being able to just touch her and kiss her whenever he wanted was definitely a form of torture. But Hawk was trying to take things slow, they were starting over, which meant they were building trust and a foundation before moving things to the next level.

Didn't mean he wasn't dying to run his fingers through her soft caramel locks and crush his mouth to hers. Touch her body and draw out those sweet little moans he still dreamed about.

But timing was everything, and he was leaving it in Maddy's hands to let him know when she was ready for more. Besides, he'd be leaving in a week, and then they'd have to spend the next year communicating via video calls and email until his current contract was up and he could come home to her for good. Maybe it was better to wait until then before he touched her again or he wasn't sure he'd be able to walk away, and he didn't want to end his military career by going AWOL.

When her tongue came out again, Hawk groaned. "Do you have to do that, sweetheart?"

"Do what?" Maddy asked. Then understanding dawned when she saw him shift uncomfortably. "Oh, that," she said with a grin and a giggle.

"Think that's funny, do you?" he teased, brushing his thumb across her bottom lip before curling his hand around the back of her neck and drawing her closer so he could kiss her. As he did, he let one of his hands drop and find its way between her legs, brushing his fingers back and forth across her center until he had her squirming. "Not so funny now, is it, caramel?"

"You will pay for that later." She mock glared at him and playfully punching his shoulder, making him laugh. A lifetime of moments like this was completely within his grasp, so long as he didn't do anything to screw it up again.

"You want to give Louie his bath now?" he asked, scooping up the sleeping infant.

"How do you shift gears so easily?" Maddy asked, following him down to the master bath. Her cheeks were flushed a healthy shade of pink, her eyes twinkling despite the shadows still lurking there—shadows he wanted to banish but knew it would take time—and even with her injuries and the pain he knew she was still in, she looked fresh, and happy, and alive.

Because of him?

Did he have the ability to shine light into her world?

He hoped he did but feared he didn't.

Catching her hand as he turned on the light, he brought it to the bulge in his pants. "Seem like I've shifted gears, caramel?"

"Uh … no," she said, her eyes round with desire as she stared at said bulge. When her tongue darted out again to slide along her bottom lip, he let out a pained groan.

"What did I say about that?"

"Oh." She gave a delighted giggle. "I forgot. It's your fault anyway, you know. You shouldn't look so sexy if you don't want me to drool over you."

Shooting her his sexiest smirk, he balanced Louie in the crook of one elbow and pulled Maddy close with the other. "Sexy, huh?" he whispered against her ear. "You think I m sexy?"

She shivered in his hold. "You know I do," she said breathily, tilting her head to give him better access.

Hawk touched his lips to the slender column of her neck, sucking lightly before moving back and blowing on the damp skin, making her shiver again. "I do now."

Louie chose that moment to coo softly as he woke, drawing their attention back to their son.

"Right, baby bath," Maddy said, stepping back, but her gaze was heated and lingered on his bulge before deliberately looking away. She grabbed the baby's bath and set it on the vanity. "The doctor said that we don't have to worry about using soap, although he did recommend a great one for babies, so I ordered some. I put your address as the delivery one, I hope that was okay."

Turning on the tap, he put a hand under the water to test it as it heated. "Maddy, what did I say about this place?"

"That it's mine too and I should consider it a home."

"Right. I'm leaving in a week. I have another year left before I'm out, I want you to stay here, and hopefully by the time my contract is up we're ready to take our relationship to the next level."

"You mean us living together?"

He meant marriage, but he nodded. "Sure."

Maddy rolled her eyes and nudged him, holding the baby bath under the faucet to fill it up. "Yeah, sure."

Kissing her temple, he laid Louie down and began removing his clothes. "I want to spend the rest of my life with you, Maddy. I haven't made that a secret, but no pressure. We get there when we get there. Although I do have a joint venture, I hope you'll be interested in."

"What is it?"

"Well, you need a new job since you're staying here, and I'll need a job when I get out. I want to work at Prey, but I wasn't sure what I'd do, then I thought of something we could do together. Sparrow and Ethan are starting Prey Search and Rescue because they're both pilots and Sparrow was saved by a search and rescue team last February, so I thought maybe we could capitalize on your skill set. I talked to Eagle, and he thought us heading up a serial killer hunting branch of Prey. We'd consult across the country helping law enforcement with serial killer cases, you'll get to do what you're good at, and I'll be the brawn."

"You'd be my boss?"

"No, we'd be a team, hopefully adding a few more men—or women—once we have the division up and running."

"I like the idea a lot," she said as she turned off the faucet and set the bath back on the vanity. "I like the idea of working with you too, but what am I going to do for the next year?"

"Take care of this little guy," he replied.

Maddy rested her head against his shoulder. "We make beautiful babies, don't we," she said, reaching out to touch the soft, fuzzy hair on Louie's head.

"The most beautiful," he agreed.

"I wouldn't be averse to the idea of giving Louie a little brother or sister one day."

Hallelujah. They were totally on the same page even if Maddy was being a little more hesitant to admit it. "I want a whole gaggle of kids."

"A gaggle, huh? I guess that would be okay." She stood on tiptoe to kiss his cheek. "You want to pop him in?"

"Nope, you do the honors.."

Picking up the baby, Maddy confirmed the water temperature with her elbow, then gently lowered their son into the water. Louie's eyes grew wide, and he scrunched up his little face for a moment as though he was about to scream, but then he relaxed and began to wriggle his little body.

"Look at that!" Maddy squealed. "He loves it! I'm so glad. I was a total water baby as a kid, we had a pool, and I spent every day of the summer swimming in it. I hated when we had to go back to school because I could only swim for an hour or two once my homework was done."

"We used to have a pond my brothers and sisters and I

would swim in when we finished our chores." They'd spent many a happy summer evening swimming, playing, and splashing with each other.

"We need a place with a pool or maybe even a pond if we went with a bigger property out of the city. Or we could move near the beach," Maddy said as she used one hand as a cup to gather water and drizzle it on Louie's tummy while supporting him with her other hand.

Unable to wipe the smile off his face at her talk of what kind of place they'd end up living in, Hawk simply stood and watched as the woman who would one day be his wife, washed his son.

"What?" Maddy asked when she caught him staring.

"Just happy, enjoying watching you two."

She smiled at him and then lifted Louie up. "Can you get the towel?"

"Sure thing."

They dried Louie off, put on a fresh diaper, and then zipped him into his pajamas. Laying him down in the bassinet beside the bed they both stood and watched him. He was really going to miss moments like this when he left. Hawk knew it wasn't forever, and a year in the scheme of things wasn't that long, but he'd only just gotten Maddy and Louie, and leaving them again so soon sucked.

Not reaching for her was hard, but he shoved his hands in his pockets and restrained himself. Maddy wanted to rebuild trust, and he didn't want to ruin that by mauling her like he was a teenager who couldn't control himself.

Turned out it didn't matter.

Maddy faced him, stepped closer, and fisted his shirt, kissing him like she was every bit as hungry for him as he was for her. "I want you."

"I want you too, babe. Are you sure?"

"Totally sure. My body feels like it's on fire and you're the only thing that can put it out. I need to feel you, I know we can't have sex yet, but I need … something … you … I just need you." She shifted against him, brushing against his bulge, and the control he'd been clinging to snapped.

"You'll always have me," he assured her as he lifted her up. "I think it's time mommy and daddy took their own bath."

Hawk carried her into the bathroom, turned on the faucet in his huge soaking tub, added bubble bath, then leaving the tub to fill, he turned to Maddy. She was only wearing leggings and a sweatshirt, no makeup, and her hair in a messy bun, but she was without a doubt the most gorgeous creature he had ever seen.

Apparently, they were both eager to do this because clothes flew off at warp speed, and then their hands were on each other's bodies, exploring as though this were all brand new again. In a way it was, they'd made love that one night nine months ago, and then fooled around a little after Louie was born, but they still had a lot to learn about each other. Finding exactly how Maddy liked to be touched was top of his to-do list.

"Red again," he drawled when he saw her discarded panties and bra. At Maddy's confused look he continued, "You were wearing a sexy, red lacy bra and panties set last February."

Maddy blushed. "I can't believe you remember that."

"Caramel, I don't just remember, I've looked at that bra almost every day for nine very long months."

Her mouth dropped open in surprise. "I thought I left it behind at the hotel."

"I may have pilfered it," he said with a grin.

"Oh, that's …" she trailed off.

"Stalkerish? Creepy?" he supplied.

"No," she giggled. "I think it's kind of sweet, kind of sexy. Red is my favorite color. I have lots of red bras and panties."

He groaned, the comment shooting blood straight to his groin. "Next time you wear them I'm removing them with my teeth and eating you till you scream."

She shivered. "Can't wait."

The tub filled, Hawk turned off the taps, lifted Maddy into his arms, and stepped into the water. It was just hot enough to cause steam although he suspected he and Maddy would be making more steam of their own.

As soon as he sat, Maddy between his knees, she reached for him, but he nudged her hands away. "Not yet, I want to woo you a little."

"Not necessary, consider me well and truly wooed."

He laughed at her impatience and reached for a bottle of shampoo. "Not yet but you will be." Settling her against his chest, he poured some shampoo into his palm and began to massage it into her scalp. He'd have to rebandage her wounds when they were done because her bandages were soaked, but it was worth it to have these moments with her. "Lie down," he instructed when he was done, helping her stretch out until she was floating on her back. This time he moved between her legs and slid a finger along her opening.

"Mmm," Maddy moaned.

"You tell me if anything hurts, okay?"

"That definitely doesn't hurt," she said as her hips moved, seeking more contact.

Moving closer, Hawk wrapped her legs around his hips and settled his length against her center. He couldn't penetrate her yet, but that didn't mean he couldn't soak up the feel of her. Rubbing himself against her, one of his hands palmed one of her breasts, squeezing before teasing her nipple. His other hand found her little bundle of nerves and began to rub circles on it with his thumb.

"More," Maddy breathed.

"So impatient," he teased, slowing his pace to drag things out as long as he could.

"Hawk," she whined. "Hurry up."

He chuckled, increasing his pace a little.

"Hmmff," she muttered and reached for his length, grasping it firmly and squeezing hard enough to make him groan.

"You don't play fair." He huffed.

"No?" She arched a brow, a smug smile on her lips. "You complaining about this." With expert fingers she traced him, applying just enough pressure to drive him wild without letting him come.

"No, caramel, I'm not complaining. Come here." Gripping her hips, he sat her back up and pulled her close so she was straddling his thighs, his length between them, snug against her center, her breasts right near his lips. Because he couldn't resist, he reached out and took one nipple into his mouth.

"Perfect," she murmured, throwing her head back.

Close to bursting, when Maddy began to rock, rubbing him against her heat, he found her hard little bud again and this time worked it faster, harder, bringing her closer to the edge. He held off his own release, wanting to come at the same time she did.

He felt her entire body tighten, and then a moment later she came. Only then did he let himself let go. His orgasm fired through him with a strength he had never experienced before. Hawk held onto Maddy and continued to touch her until she finally sagged against him.

"Perfect," she murmured again, tucking her face against his neck, her lips touching light kisses to his skin.

Hawk couldn't agree more. The woman he held in his arms as aftershocks of pleasure continued to ripple through him was the most perfect thing he had ever seen. And she was his. Not only that but she had given him the most perfect little baby boy.

"Perfect," he agreed.

Dove Oswald is convinced she doesn't want a man in her life, until a sexy bodyguard from her past shows back up in the sixth book in the action packed and emotionally charged Prey Security series!

Click here for the next in the series, Protecting Dove. Available NOW!

ALSO BY JANE BLYTHE

Prey Security Series

PROTECTING EAGLE

PROTECTING RAVEN

PROTECTING FALCON

PROTECTING SPARROW

PROTECTING HAWK

PROTECTING DOVE

Saving SEALs Series

SAVING RYDER

SAVING ERIC

SAVING OWEN

SAVING LOGAN

SAVING GRAYSON

SAVING CHARLIE

Candella Sisters' Heroes Series

LITTLE DOLLS

LITTLE HEARTS

LITTLE BALLERINA

Broken Gems Series

CRACKED SAPPHIRE

CRUSHED RUBY

FRACTURED DIAMOND

SHATTERED AMETHYST

SPLINTERED EMERALD

SALVAGING MARIGOLD

River's End Rescues Series

COCKY SAVIOR

SOME REGRETS ARE FOREVER

PROTECT

SOME LIES WILL HAUNT YOU

SOME QUESTIONS HAVE NO ANSWERS

SOME TRUTH CAN BE DISTORTED

SOME TRUST CAN BE REBUILT

SOME MISTAKES ARE UNFORGIVABLE

Detective Parker Bell Series

A SECRET TO THE GRAVE

WINTER WONDERLAND

DEAD OR ALIVE

LITTLE GIRL LOST

FORGOTTEN

Count to Ten Series

ONE

TWO

THREE

FOUR

FIVE

SIX

BURNING SECRETS

SEVEN

EIGHT

NINE

TEN

Christmas Romantic Suspense Series

CHRISTMAS HOSTAGE

CHRISTMAS CAPTIVE

CHRISTMAS VICTIM

YULETIDE PROTECTOR

Conquering Fear Series

(Co-written with Amanda Siegrist)

DROWNING IN YOU

OUT OF THE DARKNESS

ABOUT THE AUTHOR

Jane Blythe is a USA Today bestselling author of romantic suspense and military romance full of sweet, smart, sexy heroes and strong heroines! When she's not weaving hard to unravel mysteries she loves to read, bake, go to the beach, build snowmen, and watch Disney movies. She has two adorable Dalmatians, is obsessed with Christmas, owns 200+ teddy bears, and loves to travel!

To connect and keep up to date please visit any of the following

Email – mailto:janeblytheauthor@gmail.com
Facebook – http://www.facebook.com/janeblytheauthor
Instagram – http://www.instagram.com/jane_blythe_author
Reader Group – http://www.facebook.com/groups/janeskillersweethearts
Twitter – http://www.twitter.com/jblytheauthor
Website – http://www.janeblythe.com.au

There are many more books in this fan fiction world than listed here, for an up-to-date list go to www.AcesPress.com

You can also visit our Amazon page at: http://www.amazon.com/author/operationalpha

Special Forces: Operation Alpha World

Christie Adams: Charity's Heart
Linzi Baxter: Unlocking Dreams
Misha Blake: Flash
Anna Blakely: Rescuing Gracelynn
Julia Bright: Saving Lorelei
Cara Carnes: Protecting Mari
Kendra Mei Chailyn: Beast
Melissa Kay Clarke: Rescuing Annabeth
Samantha A. Cole: Handling Haven
Lorelei Confer: Protecting Sara
KaLyn Cooper: Spring Unveiled
Janie Crouch: Storm
Jordan Dane: Redemption for Avery
Tarina Deaton: Found in the Lost
Riley Edwards: Protecting Olivia
Dorothy Ewels: Knight's Queen
Lila Ferrari: Protecting Joy
Nicole Flockton: Protecting Maria
Hope Ford: Rescuing Karina
Amy Gamet: Guarded by the SEAL
Michele Gwynn: Rescuing Emma
Desiree Holt: Protecting Maddie
Jesse Jacobson: Protecting Honor
Rayne Lewis: Justice for Mary
Callie Love & Ann Omasta: Hawaii Hottie
JM Madden: Rescuing Olivia

A.M. Mahler: Griffin
Ellie Masters: Sybil's Protector
Trish McCallan: Hero Under Fire
Rachel McNeely: The SEAL's Surprise Baby
KD Michaels: Saving Laura
Olivia Michaels: Protecting Harper
Annie Miller: Securing Willow
Keira Montclair: Wolf and the Wild Scots
MJ Nightingale: Protecting Beauty
Melinda Owens: Betraying Katie
Victoria Paige: Reclaiming Izabel
Danielle Pays: Defending Sarina
Lainey Reese: Protecting New York
KeKe Renée: Protecting Bria
TL Reeve and Michele Ryan: Extracting Mateo
Deanna L. Rowley: Saving Veronica
Angela Rush: Charlotte
Rose Smith: Saving Satin
Lynne St. James: SEAL's Spitfire
Sarah Stone: Shielding Grace
Jen Talty: Burning Desire
Reina Torres, Rescuing Hi'ilani
LJ Vickery: Circus Comes to Town
R. C. Wynne: Shadows Renewed

Delta Team Three Series

Lori Ryan: Nori's Delta
Becca Jameson: Destiny's Delta
Lynne St James, Gwen's Delta
Elle James: Ivy's Delta
Riley Edwards: Hope's Delta

Police and Fire: Operation Alpha World

Freya Barker: Burning for Autumn

B.P. Beth: Scott
Jane Blythe: Salvaging Marigold
Julia Bright, Justice for Amber
Hadley Finn: Exton
Emily Gray: Shelter for Allegra
Alexa Gregory: Backdraft
Deanndra Hall: Shelter for Sharla
Jenna Harte: Dead But Not Forgotten
India Kells: Shadow Killer
Reina Torres: Justice for Sloane
Aubree Valentine, Justice for Danielle
Maddie Wade: Finding English
Laine Vess: Justice for Lauren

Tarpley VFD Series

Silver James, Fighting for Elena
Deanndra Hall, Fighting for Carly
Haven Rose, Fighting for Calliope
MJ Nightingale, Fighting for Jemma
TL Reeve, Fighting for Brittney
Nicole Flockton, Fighting for Nadia

As you know, this book included at least one character from Susan Stoker's books. To check out more, see below.

SEAL Team Hawaii Series

Finding Elodie
Finding Lexie
Finding Kenna
Finding Monica
Finding Carly
Finding Ashlyn (Feb 2023)
Finding Jodelle (July 2023)

Eagle Point Search & Rescue

Searching for Lilly
Searching for Elsie
Searching for Bristol
Searching for Caryn (April 2023)
Searching for Finley (Sept 2023)
Searching for Heather (TBA)
Searching for Khloe (TBA)

The Refuge Series

Deserving Alaska (Aug 2022)
Deserving Henley (Jan 2023)
Deserving Reese (May 2023)
Deserving Cora (TBA)
Deserving Lara (TBA)
Deserving Maisy (TBA)
Deserving Ryleigh (TBA)

Delta Team Two Series

Shielding Gillian
Shielding Kinley

Shielding Aspen
Shielding Jayme (novella)
Shielding Riley
Shielding Devyn
Shielding Ember
Shielding Sierra

SEAL of Protection: Legacy Series

Securing Caite (FREE!)
Securing Brenae (novella)
Securing Sidney
Securing Piper
Securing Zoey
Securing Avery
Securing Kalee
Securing Jane

Delta Force Heroes Series

Rescuing Rayne (FREE!)
Rescuing Aimee (novella)
Rescuing Emily
Rescuing Harley
Marrying Emily (novella)
Rescuing Kassie
Rescuing Bryn
Rescuing Casey
Rescuing Sadie (novella)
Rescuing Wendy
Rescuing Mary
Rescuing Macie (novella)
Rescuing Annie

Badge of Honor: Texas Heroes Series

Justice for Mackenzie (FREE!)

Justice for Mickie
Justice for Corrie
Justice for Laine (novella)
Shelter for Elizabeth
Justice for Boone
Shelter for Adeline
Shelter for Sophie
Justice for Erin
Justice for Milena
Shelter for Blythe
Justice for Hope
Shelter for Quinn
Shelter for Koren
Shelter for Penelope

SEAL of Protection Series

Protecting Caroline (FREE!)
Protecting Alabama
Protecting Fiona
Marrying Caroline (novella)
Protecting Summer
Protecting Cheyenne
Protecting Jessyka
Protecting Julie (novella)
Protecting Melody
Protecting the Future
Protecting Kiera (novella)
Protecting Alabama's Kids (novella)
Protecting Dakota

New York Times, USA Today and *Wall Street Journal* Bestselling Author Susan Stoker has a heart as big as the state of Tennessee where she lives, but this all American girl has also spent the last fourteen years living in Missouri, California,

Colorado, Indiana, and Texas. She's married to a retired Army man who now gets to follow *her* around the country.

www.stokeraces.com
www.AcesPress.com
susan@stokeraces.com

Made in the USA
Monee, IL
22 November 2022